PENGUIN BOOKS

THE CURATIVE

Charlotte Randall's first novel, *Dead Sea Fruit*, won the South-East Asian/ South Pacific section of the Commonwealth Writers' Prize for Best First Book. Randall has a background in psychological research and is now a full-time writer. Born and raised in Dunedin, New Zealand, she now lives in Wellington with her husband and two children.

For Freddie

THE CURATIVE

Charlotte Randall

PENGUIN BOOKS

PENGUIN BOOKS
Penguin Books (NZ) Ltd, cnr Airborne and Rosedale Roads, Albany,
Auckland 1310, New Zealand
Penguin Books Ltd, 27 Wrights Lane, London W8 5TZ, England
Penguin Putnam Inc, 375 Hudson Street, New York, NY 10014, United States
Penguin Books Australia Ltd, 487 Maroondah Highway, Ringwood,
Australia 3134
Penguin Books Canada Ltd, 10 Alcorn Avenue, Toronto, Ontario,
Canada M4V 3B2
Penguin Books (South Africa) Pty Ltd, 5 Watkins Street, Denver Ext 4, 2094,
South Africa
Penguin Books India (P) Ltd, 11, Community Centre, Panchsheel Park,
New Delhi 110 017, India

Penguin Books Ltd, Registered Offices: Harmondsworth, Middlesex, England

First published by Penguin Books (NZ) Ltd, 2000

3 5 7 9 10 8 6 4 2

Designed by Mary Egan
Typeset by Egan-Reid Ltd
Printed in Australia by Australian Print Group, Maryborough

The assistance of Creative New Zealand towards the production of this book is
gratefully acknowledged by the Publisher.

ACKNOWLEDGEMENTS

I am deeply indebted to *Three Hundred Years of Psychiatry 1535–1860* by Richard Hunter and Ida Macalpine, without which this novel could not have been written, and which still affords me much pleasure and amusement. I am equally indebted to *Masters of Bedlam: The transformation of the mad doctoring trade* by Andrew Scull, Charlotte McKenzie and Nicholas Hervey, which provided necessary detail concerning the 1815 enquiry and was the initial inspiration for this book. Information about Captain James Cook came from *The Dictionary of New Zealand Biography, Volume One, 1769–1869* (ed. W.H. Oliver), although his private thoughts are my own invention; and details of treatments according to the exploded theory of revulsion came from *English Madness 1580 to 1890* by Vieda Skultons.

Many thanks to my editor Jane Parkin, my publisher Geoff Walker and to Creative New Zealand for financial assistance. Very special thanks to my agent Michael Gifkins for his constructive criticism, and his unflagging interest and support.

When John Haslam was appointed apothecary to Bethlem Hospital in 1795 there were heated disagreements amongst mad-doctors about how lunatics should be managed. There were those who declared the insane were unmanageable without recourse to chains and straitjackets; others claimed that kindness and gentleness would sufficiently calm the lunatic so that he might more easily be cured. Haslam himself publicly claimed to have adopted this latter approach of 'moral treatment', yet an inspection of the dilapidated buildings in 1814 revealed lunatics in leg-irons, others lying naked on straw due to incontinence, and a number of lucid men and women who had been kept in chains for more than a decade.

THE MIDDLE

Mysterium tremendum

THERE ISN'T MUCH I can do here. I am hamstrung. Yes. A little joke at my own expense. I could go out of my mind; *they* think I already have. But no, I know my own name, though there are plenty here who don't. Of course, there's no one to listen to me say my name, no one to check it, realise that it isn't just a moan amongst the moaning. They merely look after me in the accepted way: feed me, hose me down. My name is William Lonsdale and I am about fifty-five years old. But I don't know precisely how I got here – which just goes to show how serious a temporary fugue can be.

Now fugue is a lovely word. I admit I prefer the musical definition: the thought of a soul abroad in the world lost to his family and his memory – well, frankly it's frightening. I myself spent some time in such a way and it was pure terror. It's the clamour of the people and the passion of the weather that tears at the unhoused soul.

But here is the hose. Cold or warm today? There is a pleasing moment when it could be either. In fact . . . arrghhh . . . it's always cold.

Now for the food. The food is abominable. It is soft and all mixed together, unrecognisable. Pabulum. That's another of my favourite words. Not that it strictly means the food I've just described. Again I prefer another meaning: insipid intellectual fare. At least that's what it meant when I last had a chance to check meanings. There's no chance of that now – I have to rely on what I remember, on what I believe to be true. This of course makes me a thoroughly unreliable narrator. However, since there is no one sane to tell my story to this hardly matters. I tell it all to myself – a monologue, an unpunctuated drone between washings and feedings. For myself alone I make it elegant. My only pleasure.

To get back to pabulum. There are things I want to say about it. I remember once, such a long time ago, in the days when I would hold forth in a rose garden wearing breeches and a powdered wig, some wit saying that narrative is pabulum. At the time I adopted a certain posture – feet in ballet position four, and arms rather invitational, as if asking someone to waltz – and said, in that tone the self-assured use to haul back the admiration of the audience after it has gone sniffing in another direction, 'But how can you have a story without a story?'

Alas, now I know. In fact, the story where none exists or can exist is a fascination for me. And more: it is essential, the only way I can now exist for myself.

~

And so I hang here on the wall, like a painting, as useless as a painting; and since I don't have the luxury of going out of my mind, I can only go into it. Some time ago I began a little mental game. I began to search for the perfect word that would sum up my situation. Needless to say, neither fugue nor pabulum is the word I'm looking for. I want a word that includes the present but also the past, that expresses something of the way the past is always part of the present; and the word must also – yes – contain a sense of the ineffable. Perhaps I could say to the other moaning fools: Guess the word before I say it, even before I know it, and . . . what? The straw will turn to gold? The water to wine, the pabulum to strawberries and asparagus? But that makes it sound like some kind of Rumpelstiltskin game, instead of a mystery; and anyway, there's only one other man in this cell with me and he never speaks.

The mystery is the word. I am going to pursue it, relentlessly. Hunt it down. The word will explain everything, just as finding the criminal always does. When I find the word, my lips will tremble a little as they prepare to utter it, my skin will break out in a light perspiration. My heart will beat faster with excitement and I will strain agitatedly against my chains . . .

I've no doubt that the word will be slightly arcane. I mean, who says pabulum and fugue these days? Well, I do. And I say floccinaucinihilipilification. It makes me chuckle. I'm saying it now to the poor filthy wretch down on the straw beside me. I call him Horatio. Now he *is* mad. I'm sure of it. Never once has he uttered a coherent sentence, never once displayed a recognisable emotion. However, he was already here when I came, and who knows what he was like before I witnessed him? Perhaps he arrived in an embroidered waistcoat and slipped into madness only as it rotted. Perhaps he once spoke foreign languages, or could name stars, and took up moaning only to fit in, to do as the English do. It sends shivers up my spine to ponder on the extent of his deterioration.

Still, we all deteriorate. It's not just a condition of the inmates, but rather of the world. That keeper who's been here longer than I have – well, he was a fine strapping fellow once, and now look at him. I've noticed he forgets the names of things, gives long addled descriptions instead, and his helpers get angry and mutter and shake their heads. And I suppose, in truth, the way I feel about the wretch on the floor is the way the keepers feel about me. But someone must remember my fine clothes, the clean mono-grammed handkerchiefs. Someone must have wondered, bent an ear to my utterances, looked into my eyes for reason's flicker. Unfortunately, at the time, reason may have been flickering rather too unpredictably – which isn't reason, is it?

So of course they stopped looking or listening, and if I came out with a sentence such as, Floccinaucinihilipilification – the action or habit of estimating as worthless, I'm sure nobody would bat an eyelid.

~⌒

And so I hang here on the wall, like the crucifixion, useless as the crucifixion. Strange, but if I had to describe the exact nature of the way I felt about the world before I came here, I would have to use the word *loose*. That should make you laugh, Horatio. But it's the truth. Looseness was not always a pleasant feeling. Sometimes the world seemed too large, too unknowable, ungraspable. I felt that my attachment to it was of the nature of a pining lover to someone utterly puissant and indifferent. Consequently my attachment would sometimes go slack and I rattled in a world of objects, not knowing what to do with myself, what I should work for, hope for.

It's easy to fool yourself that other people enjoy a sense of direction and purpose; that it's only you who are detached and baffled, somehow lonely. But in here, with so much time to think about it, I have come to the conclusion that it is human nature to be thus. Social relations, it is frequently asserted, are the answer to problems of bafflement and loneliness; but our relationships are fitful, and others whom we have wooed with charm and wine and a good table go off us, or we off them, and cease to visit or communicate, unless compelled into each other's company – as we are, Horatio.

Will we cease to be everything to one another, Horatio?

For me, social relations were not the balm they should have been. Indeed, I grew more and more uneasy at the social table, ate more and more, drank more and more, became too glorious, and grew plump rather than serene. Increasingly, my serenity was to be found in a rather narrow range of activities: street-acting, making money, amusing my children with games, and seduction. So I became obsessed with these things, withdrew from other activities unless thoroughly pressed, and began to leave behind the running sore of friendship, as I had fidelity's unscratched itch.

When I think about these obsessions – the ones I had immediately before my fugue – I start to ponder on interests more generally. I think about self. A self is defined by his interests, surely. My interests changed over the course of my life, and yet, while I was in the grip of any particular one, it seemed impossible that I not obey its dictates. Thus I was driven hither and yon when I believed I was only being driven forward, driven home. One day – I was quite old by this time – I asked myself how it was that I got these particular interests. Having them suddenly seemed so arbitrary. How was it that one man had a driving passion for chess while another stood by and yawned? Why would another man drive himself to drink and poverty just to write verse? When I looked at it, each human being was being driven by a gale that had blown up inexplicably – and no one thought to get out of it! To take shelter, enjoy a backwater.

But of course the becalmed were not calm. They were the most anxious of all. 'How can I be happy if I am not propelled?' they wailed. 'I am not fulfilling myself.' And I too would have felt like this were I not a man with serious business interests and a passion for the theatre – of which, dare I mention it, I was once a respected critic. (Or should I say I was this sort of person between the ages of twenty-five and forty. Before that I had different driving interests. And after. Yet I absurdly believed myself to be a man of consistency.)

Well, one day I decided I would change my interests. Why not? They were arbitrary, and to tell you the truth, theatre had become a thorn in my flesh. Take it out, I admonished myself. And so I took up archery. Just like that. With no previous or current desire. I gave my season ticket to the theatre to my best friend. I bought a bow, quiver, arrows, suitable apparel. I went down to the archery field and paid my gold coin and wrote my name in the ancient book, and I was an archer. A bad one.

But as the arrows flew I interrogated myself about pleasure. Is this less pleasurable than a bad play? No, I concluded. Is it less pleasurable than a good one? Yes – but I haven't had to see the bad ones to find the good one. Is it, I persisted, as another arrow fell miles from the target, is it less pleasurable to do archery than to see a string of bad plays and the occasional good one? No, I answered.

All things considered, though, there was a certain sameness, a flatness about it. I found I wasn't particularly excited when the arrow got near the target, whereas I could always get up a real froth about a rotten play. Is it possible to do something, then, and not care about it – something you are not compelled to do by anybody or anything? It is. But . . .

Ah, here is the keeper with the hose and pabulum. I will have to return to these thoughts later. As he goes past I say loudly and clearly, 'Floccinaucinihilipilification – the action or habit of estimating as worthless.'

'This one's reciting again,' the keeper says to his helper. 'Here, have a drink on me,' he adds, and turns the hose straight into my face.

~

At night I can't sleep. Not enough action in the day. I try to remember things. Places, people, events. I remember things I once read. I remember someone saying that a human being has to hold himself back from the world. That he must not dissolve himself in its merenesses. How I have longed to dissolve myself in the merenesses of the world! In the moonlight, I cry out to this man, whoever he was: Look at me – is this how we should live? Chained to a wall, reliant on the simulacrum of living that passes through our minds? Should I be here chasing words, rather than out in a dappled wood chasing a soncy in a brightly coloured skirt? That man would reply, To dissolve yourself is to lose yourself. But who is it that I have found here?, I would shout. My best self?

He had it all wrong. Dissolution – that's the answer. Dissolution in the merenesses. A man can be dissolute in the theatre certainly; some feel it to be compulsory. The archery field, on the other hand, is a little more difficult. To dissolve, one has to let go of oneself, forget oneself. A man cannot dissolve whilst carrying on a relentless self-interrogation. In the end this is how our interests rule us: like mad dogs, they are quietened only by being exercised. And so, by and by, I put away my archer's kit, sought a refund of my gold coin, had my name eradicated from the illustrious book, and took up acting in the public squares.

And what a fine thing it was. I could forget being the critical eye in the crowd, the non-participator who always knows how it should be done. I didn't care if no one came to watch or if the crowd jeered and threw apples got by the moth. I could forget being the one who counted heads to verify worth in the proceed-ings. I proceeded. That was the worth. It was like discovering a secret, a joke – that the most agonised are the watchers, not the doers, who always have the joy of dissolving; the watchers are nailed to their criticism, crucified by standing back.

At night I also remember women. My judgement was always poor in this respect. I remember women I couldn't live without. Then I was living without them. I never wanted the right ones, only the ones who riveted me. And why did they? Who ever knows? A look, a gesture, an insinuation and I'd die for her. For how many hours of my mature life did I walk round with my corset nearly bursting with lust and longing and melancholy? Oh, I was a very greedy man, you have no idea. Sometimes I would ask myself, If a man had spent some of his life starving, would that justify gluttony whenever food became available? The trouble was, I'd never starved, just imagined it. And that was enough for me.

I was a man who liked variety. Of course, the world is so arranged that variety is forbidden, but I didn't let that stop me. Even when I married. Especially when I married. I don't mean to suggest that I was a cold libertine; on the contrary, it was my intense emotions that propelled me. They were fickle, in the end. This is the irony of it all. Did I feel guilt? No, I did not. I could not have been moral without my passions. It was knowing that passion is not enduring that kept me happily married for thirty years. My commitment to my wife was a true moral commitment: arduous, tedious, patient, made in the full knowledge that all infatuation finally turns sensible and expires. And so I kept my passions where they belonged – out by the lake in the fleet forgiving moonlight.

Which makes it all sound so tidy. Oh, but sometimes the mess underneath was appalling. Usually with the foreign-born, those you slide past in mutual incomprehension – but sliding so slowly, like mud on its torpid flow, sticking you to the other in a coagulant embrace. There were two I recall especially – different as night and day, except in the one respect that we couldn't understand each other. But who wants understanding? You want mystery.

Now look at me. I am indeed starving now. My own hands are never free. I have longed to be the type who could ask a keeper to lend a hand. I am not; and certainly the keepers of that persuasion prefer the etiolated boys. In the moonlight I let my head loll and I moan my pain like a cow in travail . . .

Enough of this! Do you think this horrible noise in your ears will help, even if it's your own mouth it's coming out of? Many a man has been driven mad by the racket of his own lament. How much easier it is to suffer the lamentations of others – your own cries always sound louder, more insistent, more agonised, like the cries of your own child.

I shut my mouth obediently. Imprisonment has turned me into a man split in two: the chained beast who wails, and the trainer who admonishes, warns, punishes; who occasionally also dispenses a quick pat on the back – Well done, you kept your mouth shut, showed a bit of dignity. And so I hang on the wall in the moonlight, and my own silence calms me. I feel my eyelids drooping and I fade into that shadowy world where sometimes I am a madman chained up in Bedlam and sometimes I am a free man out to slay Napoleon.

~

I startle awake. Porlock has come in. He comes straight over to me and lifts my eyelids as one does a dead man. I leave my eyes open or he will do it again. I can smell the alcohol on his breath. Not that alcohol is Porlock's main problem: he's the once-strapping keeper who's been here longer than I have and who now forgets things. Perhaps he has forgotten that we are all stark staring mad, because he has taken to moonlight talks with me. That is to say, he talks and I listen.

'Oh, woe is me,' he begins this particular night.

I sigh. Woe is pretty regular with Porlock. It's usually because of money.

'My creditors gather round. Last night it was the tailor, and the night before the oil merchant. I don't know where it will end.'

Invariably it ends with Porlock forgetting what he started with. By the time the sun comes up, Porlock has roamed somewhat incoherently over ten or twenty topics and I have dozed fitfully, coming to full wakefulness only when he enthusiastically gets onto his favourite topics: food and corruption in the hospital's administration.

'A pork chop it was, grilled almost black along the fat and the white meat sizzling, exactly as I like it, with a turnip and some ale, and then the apples done in a sweet pie . . . I told that what's-his-name we can't go on having these rich hospital visitors, I don't care who they pay, or what they come to laugh at. You can see some of them don't find it all that funny in the end. There'll be talk.'

I wonder who the paying guests ogle – certainly no one has come to entertain themselves with either Horatio or me. And does this mean that the institution has fallen on hard times or simply under the control of a deviant entrepreneur? I would venture a question along these lines, but in response to my questioning in the past Porlock has come up and stared straight into my face, and looking back into his eyes I have seen the madness of fragmented memory. His pork chop was perhaps last night – or last year. The apple pie was likely part of a different meal. As for the paying visitors, they could be anybody: doctors' wives meeting their husbands before an annual dinner; benefactors or trustees checking if monies are well spent. Or nobody: figments of Porlock's memory wandering in from some long-ago ball, over-dressed apparitions stumbling onto the wrong stage.

Porlock groans, stands up, and goes out grumbling. He will go home to sleep now and then come back again in the late evening. I don't know whether I hope he will talk to me again tonight or not. I cannot trust a word he says. Sometimes I want proof: I want to say, Well, bring me something, a lace handkerchief, the tip of an imported cigar, anything to prove that these divine beings do indeed waft through our wretched halls. For it excites me to think that there might be someone to whom I could appeal, someone who might see that I am not like all the rest . . .

But I must have dropped off: here are the day keepers with the hose and buckets. Today they change Horatio's straw. They roll him off, sweep away the offensive matter, swab the flagstones, distribute the new material and roll him back on. Throughout all this, Horatio utters not a sound and does not alter his body posture: he remains huddled up like an expelled foetus. The keepers turn to me. They loosen my chains enough so that I can squat, and they place the bucket beneath my haunches. My ragged tunic provides no hindrance. One keeper carries off the steaming offering and the other tightens my chains. I avoid his eyes. Even after all this time I am ashamed.

The first keeper comes back in with the pabulum – a thin gruel which he feeds to me impatiently with a too-large spoon. I have to gulp it or choke. Horatio doesn't get any if the keepers are rushed – three days out of five – because of the trouble he causes them: he has to be propped against the wall and then kept from slipping sideways. And all the while he turns his head this way and that, in complete opposition to the spoon, and his tongue pokes out so that the stuff is more outside him than inside. After all this, the keepers leave and we have the day to ourselves. We can do what we like. The whole day is ours to make of it what we will.

∼

I am glum. The day stretches out like a dark tunnel. But it's not true that I have nothing to do. I must work.

My work is to get myself along each day's tunnel and greet the moonlight sane. Like any worker, some days I am reluctant. The effort seems too much. I'd prefer to go back to bed. And if my bed were a sanctuary of fine and soft materials upon which I could stretch right out, I would indeed be the world's worst sloth. But since my bed is indistinguishable from any of my other furniture, and my sleeping posture is identical to my working one, I quickly adapt to the inevitable – which is the wisest thing any of us can do, even if we might perversely refuse to do it.

I begin each day with memory exercises. Each morning I select a member of my extended family, or one of my long-ago friends – a business or theatre acquaintance from the days before I gave friendship up – and try to recall everything I can about him. It is not sufficient merely to recall physical characteristics and pre-dominant personality traits. No. I must recall the most subtle detail, must summon the person up as if he stood before me, must light him so carefully and delicately that indeed I know him better now than I did then. I must turn him round and round in this exquisite and penetrating light, and understand him completely for the first time.

Today I have chosen my favourite son, my third son, Thomas. Thomas is an extrovert. That is to say, Thomas is a gift to the world. You think this is going too far? I don't think so. An extrovert realises that something is required of him in social relations; that merely being there, being human, being oneself, is not sufficient to oil the social wheel. An extrovert goes beyond himself, reaches out – and closes the aching gap that the merely human stubbornly pretend not to notice. And why are they so committed to this pretence? Because they want to be loved for themselves and not for their party tricks. If only there were something to love!

Alas, there is not one of us who cannot benefit from a little social artifice. We are not gilding the lily. We are creating a spell, an enchantment, around human-in-the-raw – something far less attractive in its natural state than the lily, rest assured. Something far meatier, ranker and prone to quicker degradation.

Thomas was never a loud, insensitive, thigh-slapping extrovert. These anyway are not the true extroverts, but frightened boys covering up their fear with coarseness and noise. True extroverts realise that the world is watching and behave so as to bring pleasure to the world's eyes. Well, that's how I view it, and who here can argue? 'Horatio, what is a true extrovert, can you tell me?' See, no answer. I am unassailably right, here in my little kingdom-of-one.

I myself was an extrovert for a time when I was young. I gave it up. I developed a rather nasty little interest in watching social mingle become social mangle. I could have oiled the wheel, but chose not to. Thomas, I'm glad to say, has not such a perverse turn of character. Perhaps there is still time.

I am sure Thomas must wonder where it is I have gone. It is painful for me to think of him suspecting that I have simply run away. My detention in this establishment must be unknown to him – indeed to all my children. I cannot imagine they would have tolerated my admission for an instant, much less forsaken me once here. No. To imagine any of them, but especially Thomas, capable of such cruelty is to quite undo my knowledge of them.

~

In the afternoons – the keeper brings soup and the bucket at noon – I usually play my word game. Lately I have not advanced very far. I am stuck on *flocci* as if there never was a better word for the whole of creation. So the afternoons are now quagmires of boredom, thick and stagnant pools of frustration.

'It's the boredom that's most intolerable after the hunger and cold, don't you think, Horatio? I find it's a feeling that is actually physical, as if the body itself is going mad from too little exertion, too little change. I remember boredom in my previous life – a feeling of dissatisfaction from having sat too long in my study over a book or suchlike – but the miracle was, you could just stand up and put on a coat and go striding out! Did you ever dream that you could lose such a simple freedom, the freedom of walking down a street, one leg in front of the other, arms swinging?

'Now I know what true boredom is. And I'm ashamed that life was ever not quite exciting enough. That was the real secret of my many seductions, you know. Securing trouble. Eliciting chaos. Did I care if I might find myself duelling with an enraged husband? I did not. I liked the thought of a pink dawn, a gold waistcoat, the red blood of the husband trickling into the bright green grass. God made a big mistake when he gave mankind colour vision, Horatio – it constantly diverts him from morality.'

I fall silent. It is painful for me to recall these things. I was so spoilt I never dreamed life could be that much worse.

'It is an error ever to think that an ordinary and free life has reached its lowest ebb, Horatio. If it is not riddled with incarceration, poverty, sickness or death, I can assure you there is plenty of available space through which to fall.'

And I close my eyes and see myself falling from the multi-coloured joys of duels into this dark oubliette.

∽

I wake up. Boredom must have sent me to sleep. I am relieved to see the evening keeper with his buckets and crusts, am eager for the stiff bread made from plaster of paris and for his mean concrete conversation. Then, by and by, it is night again.

In the moonlight, they all come back to me again, the myriad beautiful women, my constant wife. I haven't forgotten the tone of my feeling for any one of them. As if each feeling could be accompanied by an instrument: a piccolo, a harp, a cello, a clarinet – or, for my wife, the whole orchestra. There was but one for whom I cannot name the tone. Music of the spheres? For her I reserved my most outrageous behaviour.

'Would you like to hear the story, Horatio? Surely you cannot be asleep down there in your stinking straw? I will take your silence as assent.

'Well, I was rich. And she was in need of money. Not for any particular reason – just that blind endless need that many people have. She was not hungry. She was not ill-clothed. She rode horses. I don't mean out of necessity or occasionally. I mean obsessively, for pleasure. I myself have never been much of a horseman – I far prefer the carriage. We therefore had little in common.

'I went to her and offered her money in return for a favour. She frowned, and said, "What is it?" I told her that this would be revealed in due course. She laughed scornfully and said, "So I am to take your money without knowing what I will be committing myself to? What if I don't like the favour when the time comes?" "Then you may refuse to do it," I replied. "And give the money back," she said a little sneeringly. "No, you may keep the money," I told her. Of course she looked surprised. "I'd be a fool to refuse then, wouldn't I?" "You would indeed," I answered and I think I bowed graciously. "And I am sure you are no fool."

'I backed away, saying that I would send my valet round with the first payment. She took out her fan and fluttered it as if she were hot. Greed, fascination and embarrassment were fighting it out in her lovely face. On the way home I smiled and stroked my victory. An hour ago she was a lady I had no right to talk to. I bought that right. That is all. Now whenever I see her I can smile and doff my hat. I can ignore her if I choose. Or I can make some small comment, something witty and endearing. How churlish she will feel not to permit me so little! Thus we are bound. It is too late for her to refuse the favour. For it is done.

'Well, almost. There *was* another small part. I will come to that later.

'As the sum grew over the months, she became both anxious and deferent. Anxious perhaps that the money might stop, deferent because of the terrible inequality of the bargain. Perhaps she hoped to show me she was not so venal that she could not be pleasant, agreeable. And so gradually, stealthily, a genuine warmth sprang up between us. Before, she had been rather arrogant and irritable, particularly in the early mortgaged days. She had been dismissive of me – because she was fit and wild and daring, and I was a little too old and plump, too *poudré*. Of course it was all on the outside: I have always been a man ready to take considerable risks to get what I desire. I would never ride a horse for her – that would be embarrassing. But I would ride life. Yes, that's what I planned to do once my money had given me entree. I had no doubt that we were made for each other . . . in that space under the unfettered moon.

'Let me tell you, Horatio, it wasn't simple and it wasn't brief. But I did not intend it to be so. You get to an age where you desire complexity. In fact, I believe life to be a process of increasing complication no matter how hard an individual seeks to render everything simple. The simplicity-renderers are merely those who ignore most of the salient facts. After greenest youth, simplicity becomes ever duller, especially in relation to our carnal adventures. After all, there is nothing sexually simpler than wedlock; and what is simpler than this? You might be thinking by now that I wished only to seduce the lady. That my goal would be sexual. That is not correct. But like her, you will have to wait until the time is right. This is a matter where prematurity ruins everything. The goal is utterly risible to all but the enchanted.

'There were occasions when we found ourselves together, when

she did not talk to me nor I to her. This was sometimes dis-
concerting and sometimes thrilling. But always the bond was
there. Other people must have thought we did not know each
other, or perhaps did not like each other. Not so. For myself I did
not want to overplay my hand, did not want to be left without
aces at the crucial time. For her – well, sometimes I admit I did
wonder at her indifference. But she never refused a payment, and
this alone was the sign that, no matter what the surface said, the
game went on. The cynical might laugh and say, The game was
never on; what did she have to lose by taking your money, knowing
it need have no influence on her future actions?

'However, this is to misunderstand the essential nature of knowing another human being. Unless our minds are gone, we cannot
unknow someone. We can be rude and not speak to someone we
know, or we can be polite and greet them, but both of these
responses constitute relationship. So, no matter what she had
decided, or felt, our relationship continued. And taking my money
was relationship in an even more potent form. This is not to say I
had no abiding interest in the outcome, or that I did not wish for
an outcome in which she honoured the final small part of the
favour; just that as long as there was a relationship, there was a
card table. There was something onto which I could play out the
hand, arrange for the flutter of the aces. And so I was happy.

'Horatio? Do you hear me? Just moan – yes, just like that – if
you think it's a fine story. I will tell you more – but later. The need
to sleep is finally coming over me. I must confess, however, I am
very jealous of all your lying down.'

～

I wake up. The sky outside the grimy little window is grey. It is a
long while since there has been rain, and the snow is late this year.
In other words, there is no point in looking out of the window:
one of my few amusements has been suspended. The day keepers
bustle in with the buckets and breakfast. Once I used to believe

that there was a reason for their constant hurry – a new admission, a round of inspections by the physician. Now I know it is just so they can get back to the fireplace and their card games. Off they go, and I again stare glumly down the long tunnel of the day. I know I must do my memory exercises, but I am bored. Perhaps it is because I sense that I am about to select my oldest son as a subject.

George always bored me slightly. As a small child he was fond of collections and catalogues. If we went to the forest, he would collect leaves and sort them by shape or colour or size and then write up the results in a book which I would then have to approve. He carried this habit into adulthood, except that it was his income he sorted and monitored, and it was his mother he took his ledgers to, and she admired them genuinely. 'William,' she'd say, after the lad had gone solemnly away as if it were the Bible he was carrying, 'can't you see the wisdom of such bookkeeping? The boy already knows the rents he gets, and the profits from his harvests.' 'Good for him,' I'd reply. 'Does he know anything else?'

His mother would turn away and I'd feel a little guilty: it is not kind – or wise – to tell a child's faults to his mother. Or father, for that matter. Whenever a tutor complained about Thomas, I was always instantly enraged. No matter how hard I tried to be reasonable, I always suspected it was the tutor's lack of insight or intelligence that made him find fault with my favourite. Even now I feel a little guilty at my partiality.

Of course George had some good points. He was ever the gentleman: polite, upright, firmly spoken. He would always take care of his mother, accompanying her to the theatre and dressmaker and church. In fact, he *always* went to church, even if his mother was having a little headache in a darkened room with cachou cakes for company.

By the time I have again reviewed my objections to church-going it is noon. The keepers come in with the buckets and lunch. After their visit, I cannot face another single second of boredom.

My word game will have to wait until I can get excited about it once more. Instead I will continue with the story I have been telling Horatio.

I clear my throat loudly in preparation. 'Horatio, are you listening? Or engaged in a postprandial snooze? Never mind. The story must continue. Now, where was I? Oh yes, I had just told you that I was happy. Because I had arranged a table for the flutter of the aces. And what were my aces? you might well ask. Well, as I told you previously, I was rich. I believe I still am. Not that wealth is of any use in here. The horse-riding lady – shall I call her Juliet? – was in my debt. But debt does not inspire gratitude, much less any of the finer feelings I was hoping for. I had to have something else to offer her whenever she spoke to me, or self-interest and resentment would have curdled her heart. And so, if wealth was my ace of spades, wit was my ace of clubs.

'I am going a little pink in the cheeks telling you this: it is difficult for a man trained in modesty to declare himself witty. But even if I am not witty in the general round, I can assure you I made a very special effort for her. I spent hours racking my brain for quips and anecdotes. Timed with a watch my *bons mots*. Stood in front of the mirror and endlessly practised my delivery. Plagiarised what others said. In the end, it came naturally, so much had I sharpened my mind, my observation. And even if wit is learned, are we not to claim it as our own as we would other learned capabilities?

'In short, I made her laugh. Not a deep vulgar belly-laugh but the laugh of pleasure. I'd make her laugh like that and then I'd walk away. Oh it is like dessert, this game: very rich, very sweet, but best not to overdo it. Never did I make her labour through a treacle-load. I'd walk away and points of light would dance about my shoulders. Now *that* feeling was vanity, Horatio.

'And so, after a time, her eyes would brighten when I came into a drawing room and she would find a way to seek me out. Those days when she would sometimes not speak to me were gone.

'I must admit to a certain sadness at their passing: when you are an old rogue like I was – am – you always cherish those acute moments when success is not necessarily assured. To desire, to gamble – perhaps to lose? This is the time of greatest poignancy. The time of a delicious pain that is not yet a mortal blow. So she would seek me out and flutter her fan and flirt. "I am still waiting," she would say. "Waiting to hear my sentence." "Oh, indeed," I'd reply, feigning disinterest. "I am starting to believe that you have forgotten what your valet does," she once continued. "What does my valet do?" I asked insinuatingly, and she blushed. It was my first light and veiled sexual reference, and I slipped it in, thinking: From now on, the tone between us will begin to change; I will talk sex with this lady and she will listen.

'But Horatio, what is the matter? I have not heard you groan like that before. It is as if you are in pain. Real physical pain. Not simply that ordinary psychic pain with which we are all afflicted. Should I shout for a keeper? Should I?'

～

That evening Porlock alone brings the meal, a gristly stew. As he is feeding me I say, 'Release my arms and I will feed myself.'

'What?' he growls, and squints into my face. He is so close I can smell his stinking breath, can see which of his rotten teeth are missing.

I repeat my request.

He cackles. 'Do you think I'm a lunatic too? As soon as I free you, you'll go into a frenzy. I've seen it all before.' He hands me the bucket and does the required loosening of chains. Not freedom, merely a lengthening of the leash. 'None of you are to be trusted, that's what what's-his-name says. Keep eyes in the back of your what's-it.'

'Oh? And where exactly is your what's-it?' I ask, reflecting that Porlock is tonight in an even worse state of forgetfulness than usual. But Porlock has already turned away grumbling to himself.

'What's wrong with *him*?' he demands, indicating Horatio.

'I hear he's mad.'

'There's blood coming out of his what-d'you-call-it.'

'Blood? Out of where?'

'Mouth. Out of his mouth.' Porlock sighs heavily.

'You'll have to get someone,' I tell him severely.

'Who? Who can I get? Tonight they've all gone to the ball.'

I can't believe what I'm hearing. I would shake the old bugger if my hands were free.

'It's the benefactors' winter ball,' he carries on, stressing the season as if there might also be such a thing in summer, autumn, spring. He is quite precise about it too, as if someone has stood over him, yelling *benefactors' winter ball* into his uncomprehending idiot face. He sits down on a straw bale near the door and takes out a flask and drinks. A dribble runs down his chin. 'It's cold in here,' he complains, and huddles in his jacket.

'Why didn't *you* go to the ball?' I ask. 'Why are you playing Cinderella?'

'There's a bit extra tonight. That's what I've been promised. I need the extra. The coalman's coming tomorrow night . . . or is it the night after? Anyway, he'll want his money, make no mistake. And the missus wants a new . . . something, I don't know. A hat, was it? I'll tell you both something now: there isn't much difference between thee and me. Nope, not that much difference at all. You're prisoners of madness, and me, I'm a prisoner of money.' Porlock swigs from his flask. 'Actually, debt,' he corrects himself. And then these moments of lucidity pass into an incoherent ramble about specifics, sums small and large owed here and there, each new, hardly audible enumeration accompanied by groaning and a twisting of the head.

Contrary to my expectation and his usual habit, Porlock leaves quite soon, complaining that it is too cold to remain. I close my eyes in relief and then open them again. I am not at all sleepy. I look out at the moon. I begin again to sift my vocabulary for the mysterious word. I reason that part of the trouble I am having finding it is that I have failed to define it properly. What do I mean, I ask myself sternly, when I say that I want a word that will sum my situation up? In fact, I do not mean exactly that. What I want is a word that will sum up . . . well, life. My life. A word that can accept, enclose, the freedom I used to enjoy with the imprisonment that I now endure. That can make some sense of the latter, so that I might become resigned, then detached. That will locate my own freedom even in the chains.

The word I am chasing tonight is fluttery, iridescent, ocellated. A butterfly of a word. A word that hints at beauty, brevity, fragility. Surely these are the qualities that must be considered in an attempt to sum up a life? I imagine myself in my own library – oh what a place, I spent a fortune on it – taking down a large and heavy book. The word I am seeking is pressed somewhere inside its tissue-thin pages; but by opening the book I have at once released it, and it flutters ahead of me, just out of reach. From being enchanted a moment ago, I am now frustrated. My tongue reaches for the word, my mouth attempts to shape it. But no, the word eludes me, just when I have decided it is surely the one I want. It is *exactly* like life: it is like the past (ineffable), like the future (unknowable) and like the present (completely frustrating).

I am trying to relax a little when the word chatoyant pops into my mind. 'Chatoyant!' I exclaim out loud. 'A lovely word, isn't it, Horatio? *Cha – toy – ant*. It means of iridescent, undulating lustre. But it sounds more like a satin sheet than a butterfly, don't you think? Is life like a satin sheet? Of iridescent, undulating lustre – but basically flat and cold? Ha, I am teasing you. No matter how lovely chatoyant is, it won't help me. A word that describes life in terms of bed sheets is a word fit only for a Frenchman . . .'

Porlock suddenly rushes back in. He claims to have lost his flask. It is quite obvious to me that the flask is not in this cell, there being only a couple of straw bales here, besides Horatio and myself. But Porlock hunts for it around the bales, appears to forget, and hunts again. I look at him without sympathy. I wish he would leave me to the moonlight, to the words I am chasing like moon-flies through silver and shadow corridors.

I close my eyes and see myself running with a net. It is so soothing, this graceful moonlit vision, I find some brief respite from Porlock's tiresome dementia, Horatio's terrifying blood.

~

I wake up. Porlock has vanished like a bad dream. It is morning. It is raining. The early-winter dry spell has broken. I've always liked the rain. A delicious shiver ripples up my spine. Now the rain is thundering onto the roof like a galloping herd. In here, it is the rain and wind that cause all the drama. The sun, when it is out, can be seen through the small window, but its warmth hardly penetrates. True, it makes interesting patterns on the flagstones, but proper enjoyment of the sun involves the feeling of it on the skin and the effect of it upon your spirits; in here it is hard to feel anything other than a strong sense of deprivation. With the wind and rain, however, you can enjoy it as others do, as a feeling of safety-yet-excitement.

The keepers come in with the buckets and gruel.

'How was the ball?' I inquire politely (after the buckets have been removed, the gruel gobbled).

'You what?'

'The ball. Last night. How was it?'

'Hey, this one thinks we've been to a ball. Did you go to a ball, Thumbscrew?'

'Don't recall that I did, Strappado.'

'Me neither. Perhaps we're losing our marbles.'

'Perhaps we weren't invited.'

'Now there's a thought. Balls at the lunatic asylum and the keepers not invited. What's the world coming to?'

They go out together, laughing and slapping each other's shoulders. I think, Porlock, I'll wring your scrawny neck. The last thing I need is to say things that might confirm my insanity. Not that such confirmation is needed. To be here is to be insane. It's a stunningly simple diagnostic system – aided and abetted by the classification system: throw them all in together. Any behaviour that might indicate sanity is always simultaneously exhibited by some wretch who is quite clearly deranged.

I look at Horatio. At least they fed him. And when they cleaned him up, there was no more blood. Perhaps he only bit his tongue. I feel a little less anxious for him.

'Horatio, I believe it is Sunday,' I announce. 'A day for changes in one's routines. Therefore, I will carry on with my story now rather than making you wait till the afternoon.'

I clear my throat. 'As you can no doubt hear, it is pouring. Let your mind roam. Can you not imagine the water cascading off the roof, other roofs, eaves, shop awnings? Can you not see yourself standing under some shelter watching the torrent? Perhaps you put your hand to your collar to tighten it. You wrap your cape around yourself more securely. You wait. Passing carriages throw up water, and the galloping horses steam. The wet world appears to be divided up into the rushers and the waiters; into those who must get out of it as quickly as possible and those who are prepared to endure it. And the endurers can be further divided into those who are simply stubborn and those who obtain some real enjoyment from all the liquid commotion.

'I myself am standing in front of a coffee shop. I have been in there partaking of coffee and cakes – coffee and cakes, Horatio! – with some of my female relatives, and now we have dispersed in our separate directions. But the sudden cloudburst has detained me. I stand there pretending to be somewhat aggrieved with this interruption to my progress, but secretly I am exultant. I enjoy the rain for its own sake; for that special shiver it brings to the skin; for the feeling that the world is full of secrets, hidden intimacies, in a thousand marvellous, melancholy rooms. But also, my Juliet's house is nearby – of course, it is the reason I selected this particular coffee shop – and I can stand here for who knows how long without appearing lovesick or suspicious. As it happens, she does not chance by. No matter. The anticipation is glorious.

'You may think, Horatio, that in the course of my tale this is rather a non-instalment. Doesn't quite advance our cause. But you are mistaken. For in that small period of joy, I have decided to raise the stakes. I have decided that when I next send the valet to Juliet, he will take double the usual sum. What will she do when she opens the purse?

'I stand in the rain and try to imagine. She will realise immediately that it is a sign – a sign that events are thickening towards their conclusion. Her heart, surely, will be beating harder, her head will whirl. She ought not to accept it! That will be her first conclusion. Then she will gradually come to realise there is no real difference between this sum and the sums she has previously accepted. Or is there? She will be confused. Where on the slippery slope should she apply, or have applied, the brakes? Well, Horatio, what do you think? At the very beginning? But why not relieve a fool of the burden of his money? Why not indeed. Best make sure he is a real fool first.

'Well, my silent friend, he *was* a real fool. Just as he was beginning to think he would have everything his own way, just as he was about to play his ace of diamonds – and I won't tell you now what this consisted of – something happened to make him sick at heart. I'll return to the first person if you don't mind.

'Sometimes, when talking to Juliet, I had been slightly vain about my acting. In fact, I used my acting to imply that I looked down a little on the equestrian, that there was some lack in a person who so emphatically embraced the physical life. I remember with shame the sort of gently swelling pride that my own talk inspired in me, and I certainly made myself out to be better than I was. It was my security against her own tremendous skill: I have this, I'd say to myself, and thus I can relax, compete.

'Then one day – I'll never forget the moment – somebody made a reference to a very famous actress, a woman I'd only heard the name of, never met; and she, my Juliet, blushed and said, "Oh, I don't use that name any more." My whole body immediately turned to stone. I excused myself as soon as possible and could hardly breathe on the way home. Every time I recalled the way I'd talked, I squirmed with embarrassment. I acted in the streets, Horatio! And she – she had been one of the most famous stage actresses of her day. While she was young of course, and before she married – but still! It became impossible for me to look down on her. She was a fine horsewoman *and* a famous actress.

'I went home and crawled into my shell. My good wife kept putting her hand to my forehead and asking, "William, are you sickening with something?"

'Yes, I thought to reply (but dared not), I am sickening with myself. She, Juliet, had outclassed me, and having done so had made my attraction to her painful. It's one thing to trick yourself into thinking you are gambling for a bauble; it's quite another to discover you have actually been gambling for a jewel.'

I stop. I can't go on. I listen to the rain. Above its noise, I become aware of other noises. A fracas seems to have broken out somewhere down the corridor. I can hear running, and the loud voices of Thumbscrew and Strappado. I smell smoke. It comes in the half-open door, first as a light coil, as off a cigar, and then thicker and blacker, as if someone has boiled a pot dry or set fire to a blanket.

I try to stay calm. Of course the keepers will put the fire out, and even if they don't, they will surely free us so we can flee. I look at Horatio. I will have to drag him out with me on his pile of straw. I start to cough. The thick smoke is catching in my throat. I start to doubt whether any keeper would even think about us while trying to save his own skin or theoretical soul. Already in my mind's eye the cowardly keepers are running screaming from the burning building, leaving the inmates to incinerate.

I close my eyes so as not to see the flames licking round the door . . . and then suddenly Thumbscrew dashes into the cell, beating back the smoke with a large wet cloth. 'It's out now,' he tells us, before rushing off again. Joyfully, I look down at Horatio, hoping to see some sign of happiness in his slumped body. Instead I see a little pool of blood right beside his mouth.

~

We don't get any lunch on the day of the fire. And by the time Porlock comes in in the late afternoon I am dying for the bucket. I relieve myself copiously while he looks on in disgust. 'What are you – a bloody horse?' he asks.

He carries it off, and I smile with relief and malice. I call after him, 'I may be mad but at least I don't have to empty pisspots.'

When he returns, he comes up to me and stares into my eyes. 'You'd probably drink it,' he says, and starts his awful cackle.

'How did the fire start?'

'Slut down the hall got hold of some matches. Set fire to her what's-it, thing you sleep on.'

'Mattress. Usually.'

'There'll be hell to pay. Where'd she get the bloody matches, eh? Out of the pocket of the trousers of the keeper who's sticking one up her. That's where.'

'How do you know?'

'Look, there's women and there's men, and wherever there's the two of them together . . .' Porlock shoves his right index finger through a circle made with his left index finger and thumb.

'Do you do it?'

'Used to,' he says, scratching himself. 'Fucking thing won't stand up for me now.'

I laugh loudly, but Porlock has already wandered off to find the evening pabulum. He has put it down somewhere and lost it. The food – a thin soup – is stone cold by the time he returns with it and starts to feed me.

To turn my attention from it, I ask him what he had for his last meal. His little eyes grow bright. 'Chicken. Stuffed and roasted. Had to kill off one of the old birds that'd stopped laying. And with it, a sauce I can't recollect the name of. Onions. Then preserved rhubarb. Or was it plums?'

Rhubarb! How long has it been since I've tasted it, experienced that very peculiar coating of the teeth? How unjust the world is. Sex and food available to a man who can't get it up and can't remember the names of sauces and fruit.

Porlock goes over to feed Horatio.

'There's more blood,' I point out. 'You'll have to do something.'

'I do not,' he snarls. 'What's one less of you to me?'

'We're your work, your livelihood.'

'I get my pay if I turn up. Don't get any deductions for corpses.'

'Well, he isn't a corpse yet. You could help him. You *should* help him.'

Porlock shakes his head incredulously. 'Look at him. Better off dead if you ask me. What good is he to anyone?'

'He's some good to me, and I could be some good to you,' I reply, feeling as if I am bluffing. I stumble on. 'I am a very rich man. I . . .'

'You, rich? What're you doing in here then, you ignorant fool?'

I pause. 'It's true I am not sure how I got here, but . . .'

'I know how you got here,' Porlock interrupts. 'Dragged by two constables, kicking, screaming, filthy. Found you down by the what-d'you-call-it. Place a ship leaves from. Trying to board it. Saying you were a sailor. But not in those clothes, they said, push off.'

I am stunned. Never before has Porlock volunteered any information about my arrival.

'So I had good clothes on?' I ask quickly before his mind strays. 'Even though they were dirty?'

'Excellent clothes,' Porlock replies.

'Someone must have paid for them. Even if I were not rich myself, I must have had a benefactor . . .'

The word benefactor appears to have an effect on Porlock similar to a prod on cattle.

'There's many benefactors who visit here,' he says, frowning. 'Is one of them yours?'

'I don't know. Is one of them mine?'

I watch Porlock's wizened face working in time with his brain. I wait patiently for whatever calculation he might arrive at.

'I can't look in the books,' he finally says. 'Wouldn't be right.' But there is doubt in his voice, as if he is waiting only to be convinced.

'Yes, you can.'

'It's not as easy as you think to get into the offices without someone seeing.'

'You've tried it, have you?'

Porlock looks outraged, then shamefaced. 'I did look at the books once or twice. To get some information about yourself.'

'And what did you find out?'

'Not much. That you're here. Which I already knew. A letter from the court.'

'Well, that's certainly worth hearing. Why didn't you tell me before? A letter from the court can only mean a trial.'

Porlock shrugs. His lack of interest is obvious.

'Porlock, go and get the letter.'

'No! I'll lose my job if I get caught. D'you think I'm going to risk my job for you?'

'Of course not, perish the thought.'

I look at him. Where did the memory of my arrival and the existence of the letter suddenly spring from? Or has he invented both?

'Listen to that rain,' Porlock says, straightening up from the squatting position in which he has been feeding Horatio. 'All this rain after a drought,' he mutters darkly. He fears all rapid changes in the weather, sticking steadfastly to the old-fashioned super-stition that such changes dangerously mix together pure and tainted air. But I do not wish to endure another tirade about pollution.

'Tell me about the winter ball,' I say to change the subject, and to keep him here, keep him talking, while I work out how to persuade him to get the letter.

'Ball?'

'Yes, the one you told me of the other day.'

'What d'you think this is – a palace? And you're the King, I suppose. Like all the bloody rest of them. King of the dung heap, Bedlam!'

I stare at him. His little marble eyes are swivelling unsynchronised in their sockets. If I were a keeper, he'd be first against the wall, first for the treatment. I'd give him the spinning chair, the anal leech, the sudden douche. And I wouldn't care if it bloody killed him. But there's still Horatio to consider.

'I will get my benefactor to pay you a good sum if you get the apothecary to Horatio,' I state loudly, clearly, convincingly, as if I am standing up in court.

'You? Pay me?' he snorts, before shuffling towards the door. 'The ones with money aren't chained up. That's what what's-his-name says. The physician. A gentleman wouldn't like it. That's what he says.' And off he goes, clearly concluding that it is the absence of restraint that maketh the gentleman.

~~⌒

I decide to refuse my food until someone calls the apothecary to me. In the beginning, the keepers are pleased that there is one less lunatic to feed. But then, after three days, Porlock starts to worry that some punishment might befall him if I starve to death in his care.

'I'm going to have to fetch the apothecary,' he warns me.

'No, anything but that,' I plead weakly.

'It's no use being sorry now. I've made up my mind.'

'Couldn't you unmake it?'

'What d'you think I am – a lunatic too?'

And off he stomps, leaving me to smile victoriously, even though my stomach rumbles and groans mercilessly.

I have to wait some considerable time. No one, especially a medical man, would drop everything, anything, at Porlock's bidding. Eventually, however, the redoubtable shadow of Mr Haslam the apothecary looms in the doorway, and the owner follows closely upon its tenebrous heels.

'The keeper tells me you've been refusing your food,' he says from the door.

'That's right.'

He advances into the cell and stands in front of me. We look at each other. He is not an old man, but his body is fleshy in the way of old men. He takes up his usual overbearing and aggressive posture.

'And do you have any reason for this refusal?'

'Certainly. First, the food is abominable. Secondly, my cell-mate is sick and I want someone to help him. Thirdly, I wish to read the letter concerning my trial.'

Mr Haslam is taken completely by surprise. As I intended.

'There is no letter about your trial.'

'Do you expect me to accept that the court sent me here with no documentation?'

'Well, such things are easily misplaced . . .'

'That may be so. But my letter was not misplaced.'

Mr Haslam comes up to me and stares into my face. 'And how would you know that?'

'I believe that when a man is wrongly imprisoned, as I am, his jailers would want to keep evidence of the court's directive. To exonerate themselves.'

Mr Haslam smiles. 'I don't think we will ever be called on to do that.'

'I see you are determined to deny there was a letter. But you do not deny there was a trial?'

Mr Haslam's eyes glitter splendidly.

'I'm afraid I don't care whether you eat your food or not,' he then announces. 'You can starve yourself to death if you have the courage. There's nothing I can do to stop you.'

'You can force-feed me.'

'Is that what you want? To gag and choke and get your front teeth knocked out? A word of advice, Mr Lonsdale: don't *you* attempt to force me. You will find me a formidable opponent.'

Since I appear to be making no progress, I decide to try to flatter him. 'I hear you've improved upon the spouting-boat for forcing liquids and medicines into lunatics against their will. They say you've invented a special key to hold open the patients' mouths. I've heard it said that no one has lost any front teeth since you started using it.'

Mr Haslam looks rather pleased, 'Well, what of it?'

'It indicates you are a man of invention, therefore a clever man. It indicates you care about the way things are done, that you want them done properly. For these reasons I believe you are sure to have kept all correspondence from the courts. But, being a busy man, I conclude you have simply forgotten that you had such a letter concerning me.'

'Is that so?'

'I am certain of it.'

'Lunatics are certain of many false things. That is why they are lunatics.'

'I beg you to review your files again. I'm sure . . .'

'That won't be necessary, I know exactly what is in my books.' He spins on his heels and stalks towards the door.

'Before you go . . .'

He turns. 'Well?'

'Shouldn't you examine Horatio? He's very ill.'

'He looks fine to me,' the apothecary says, and walks out the door.

Otium cum dignitate

I LOOK TOWARDS the little window. It is dark. The moon is full. There is a stilled, solid quality to the air. At night in the full moonlight I am sometimes brave enough to think about how many others there might be like me who lost themselves, lost the plot, for hardly more than a moment, and who now dwell permanently in this cimmerian institution. My heart does not thud for the truly insane, since who knows where their minds take them? My heart beats in fear for the lucid, who must themselves direct their minds away from the present moment; how often do they fail, as I do, and have to endure hours, days, nights of the most soul-destroying boredom, punctuated only by short interludes of insult, ill-treatment and shallow sleep?

Porlock staggers into the cell. He throws himself onto the bale of straw.

'What, no flask?' I say to him.

He ignores me and I watch him struggling to sit up. I see he is so drunk his flask would be redundant. And my plan to persuade him to get the court's letter will have to wait. Suddenly I'm irritated with his useless company.

'It's nice of you to keep coming to see me like this but . . .'

'What?'

'I'm afraid I've left behind the running sore of friendship.'

Porlock attempts to glower but instead turns idiotically cross-eyed.

'Actually, I use the term loosely, to describe all those people you gather in the course of your life, people you would prefer remained ungathered, but who nevertheless attach themselves to you by frequent contact rather than affinity. Porlock, are you listening to me?'

I notice he has fallen flat on his back.

'You know the kind of thing I mean,' I carry on relentlessly. 'Someone at an enforced gathering sidles up to you and makes a comment; you comment back, as politeness demands. The next time you see him, you must say hello. Several times later, you must converse about the weather, your family, your recent fortunes. Before you know it, and having already decided he is a clod, you must meet him for a drink. And it is all downhill from there. You must meet his ugly daughters and badly behaved sons; you must listen to his stupid wife and his own uninformed opinions. All the while, you revile yourself for suffering this unpleasantness yet feel guilty for accepting his hospitality – a hospitality you never wanted, but which nevertheless commits you to a reciprocity that fills you with rage. And so it goes on, already too late from the first politeness to call a halt to the injury, which then threatens to weep for evermore.'

Porlock struggles to his feet and comes over to me unsteadily. When he is standing in front of me, when his alcoholic breath could scorch my face, I continue tonelessly, 'So you see, at some point I decided to steel myself against the initial assault. If anyone made a small gesture towards me, I would take care to be cool while I assessed the gesturer. Such an assessment was not always easy. Nervous or shy people often do themselves a disservice when they present themselves to another for the first time; confident people often go the other way. And whoever lets their real opinions show on the first few encounters anyway? In the end, it's opinions that drive you mad in friendship. How can you talk to someone who disagrees with everything you say?'

'What the fuck are you on about, lunatic?'

'I'm talking about us. You and me. We're not made for each other. I'd prefer you to leave me alone at night.'

'Oh, would you? Well, you don't get preferences.'

'Oddly, you'll find the stress is on the first syllable in that word.'

Porlock turns aside to spit – I'm glad he thought to turn – and then wanders back to the straw. Perhaps I can drive him away by hectoring him.

'It is because of what I've just told you that the apothecary once alleged I have no interest in reciprocity,' I bellow. 'That my perfect companion could only ever be someone like Horatio, someone who never contradicts me, never answers back. I admit I have always preferred his response to the rattle of empty vessels. Or to the kind of conversation mad-doctors and their ilk employ, which is always an attempt at verbal subjugation. Porlock, can you hear me? I am too uppity for the mad-doctors. And why shouldn't I be uppity, I ask you; when was my assent sought or given for the way the social world would be laid out? What if I don't happen to like the kinds of characteristics that are generally admired? What if I notice that thrift often turns to meanness, intelligence to arrogance, enterprise to greed, and power to Napoleon?'

Porlock, again sprawled face-down across the bale, farts loudly, conclusively.

～

I wake up. Porlock has gone. Thumbscrew comes in with the bucket. I do the necessary. He puts the bucket by the door and goes over to Horatio. 'He's still sick,' I tell him. The keeper merely grunts and goes out. Then I do not see anyone at all until Porlock comes in with the bucket and lunch. Goes out with the bucket. Comes back and feeds me. Props Horatio against the wall and tries to feed him. As usual he is too uncooperative and the sustenance too liquid.

'So, what's new in the world, Porlock?'

'Don't talk to me, I've got a headache.'

'Come on, what am I going to think about all day?'

'Well, I don't know about the world,' he begins sourly, 'but I hear there's a famous new lunatic here. A Mr Hadfield.'

'Oh? Didn't you tell me about him once before?'

'Tried to kill what's-his-name. King George.'

'Are you sure the King didn't imagine it?'

'It was in a public theatre,' Porlock says, warming to his topic. 'Tried to shoot his majesty with a pistol.'

'Well, it's good they didn't rely on the King's account.'

'It wasn't the first time either. A woman tried to stab him with a kitchen knife. She's in here too. Or used to be. I can't recollect.'

'They could start a club.'

'There was a what-d'you-call-it, thing with a judge.'

'A trial.'

'That's right, a trial. They decided he was a lunatic. Stands to reason.'

'Well, I don't know about that. You've got to be careful declaring the madness is in the act rather than the person.' But I'm pleased that Porlock's thoughts have wandered unbidden back to the subject of trials.

'It was in his person, all right. Said the world was about to end and he had to sacrifice himself for its salvation. Another bloody Jesus. Brings us to about a hundred and thirty of them. Still, makes a difference from effing kings, I suppose.'

'So he's saving the world from the inside, eh?'

Porlock narrows his eyes at me but makes no reply.

I laugh. I discover I am in quite a good mood today. Don't ask me why. Nothing has improved. Mood is our enemy.

'I'll tell you a funny story, Porlock. It's a true one. There was once an earl – his name escapes me now, something to do with ferrets, I think – who murdered a servant. He pleaded insanity, but – here's the amusing part – he had to defend himself. That was the way they did it in 1760. So he had to be sane enough to prove he was mad. Of course he was hanged.'

'What's funny about that?'

'Absurd then. It was absurd.'

'You're absurd.'

'That's true. But my problem is the opposite one. I'm trying to prove I'm sane, which in this establishment can only be taken as a sure sign of madness.'

'Your problem is the way you turn everything inside out and upside down. And I don't get the connection between this Earl of Ferrets and Mr Hadfield. Mr Hadfield was defended by the Lord Chancellor. Not by himself.'

'Ah, so he wasn't more clever or mad than the Earl. The law has become slightly less absurd. But the punishments have become even sillier. Why hang a sane man and imprison a lunatic? The first doesn't know he's dead and the second doesn't know he's alive. The punishments aren't equal to their levels of appreciation.'

'Whereas yours fits you perfectly,' Porlock says sarcastically. He lets Horatio sag back to the floor, picks up the food bucket and prepares to go out.

'Before you go. . .'

'What is it now?'

'You don't have to bring me the court's letter. You could just go in there and read it, tell me what it says.'

'You're not on about that again, are you?' Porlock sighs heavily and presses his scrawny hand melodramatically against his forehead.

'What do you expect?' I shout. 'I've been tied up like this for years and . . .'

But Porlock has already stomped out the door.

～

I accept food again to build up my strength. When the diet is so poor, it doesn't seem wise to starve oneself without respite. But when I am back to my old self – tolerably hungry and tolerably weak – I again begin to refuse food. The apothecary duly appears in the open doorway of the cell.

'I hear we have a famous new regicide in our company now,' I say to him as he stares at me in silence. 'Hadfield,' I add, trying to provoke a response.

'You've been taking too much notice of that cretinous keeper again,' Mr Haslam comments dryly. 'Hadfield's been here for years.'

'I thought I'd already heard of him.'

'Anyway, are you refusing your food again because you thought someone tried to kill the King?'

'Not at all. I'm only interested in the fact that *he* got a trial whereas I apparently did not.'

Mr Haslam crosses the cell and stands before me.

'What makes you think that?'

'Did I have a trial?'

'Of course you had a trial.'

'I don't remember it.'

The apothecary smirks. 'That's hardly surprising, given the state you were in.'

'And what state was that?'

'Loud, violent and incoherent would sum it up, I think.'

'And what was this trial seeking to establish?'

'Your fitness to conduct your own affairs, of course.'

'Was it a fair trial?'

Mr Haslam laughs. 'It was a farce.'

'A farce?'

'Well, obviously you weren't fit to conduct your own affairs. You could hardly conduct your own *toilette*. You were filthy, disgusting.'

'You find this funny?'

'Look, you weren't tried, you were exhibited. You were quite capable of doing all the damage yourself.'

'What was the point then?'

'Your money, of course. Your money couldn't be left to its own devices, could it? Either you were fit to take proper care of it or you had to be relieved of it. And so you were. Responsibility for your financial affairs passed to your eldest son.'

'And I was bundled off?'

Mr Haslam doesn't deign to reply.

'Who brought this suit?'

'The Justices of the Peace. On the grounds that you were a vagrant and a danger to yourself and possibly others.'

'And the trial established all this?'

'The trial established your unfitness to manage your own affairs owing to obvious insanity.'

'In what way obvious? Is it insane to be dirty? Insane to be in a rage?'

'You couldn't answer the jury's questions,' Mr Haslam replies smugly. 'Except polysyllabically. Then they thought you were making fun of them.'

'The jury asked questions of me directly? Is that permitted?'

'The Chief Justice ordered it.'

'And were the questions sensible?'

'Of course not. They were singularly stupid. How many pots are there in a hogshead, and so forth. You couldn't answer. Then one of them asked how much profit your farms made in such-and-such a year. And you said, "Sufficient to discombobulate the yokels that habitually rook me." And when other members of the jury persisted, you said, "How the fucking hell should I know?" A lady fainted.'

'Am I to know all my accounts backwards? My farms function as a virtual charity – that's what I meant.'

'You were unlucky, then, that you are – or were – rich enough to disregard such things. The jury all knew how every last penny of *theirs* came and went.'

'So now I'm guilty of being rich?'

'In the end you were – *are* – guilty of being arrogant.'

'Ignoring, just for the moment, the way you so vertiginously alter your tenses, when did the common arrogance of the rich turn into uncommon madness?'

But Mr Haslam just shakes his head as if I am stupid. 'Let's just say that at your trial there were other interested parties.'

Then he walks over to the door. 'You'd better start eating again,' he warns me before he leaves, 'because I won't be returning. There are too many curable lunatics in need of my expertise.'

I wake up. It is so cold I expect to find that snow has fallen inside instead of out. Porlock is asleep on the straw, his uncapped flask lying empty beside him. The morning keeper kicks him awake. Porlock grabs his flask and lid, and crawls out of the cell like a whipped dog. The keeper, a truculent old half-cripple with one good kicking leg, performs the usual services in a perfunctory manner and leaves me to the endless morning. A long time has passed since the apothecary informed me of the existence of other interested parties at my trial. I cannot imagine who these people were, and eventually conclude that I have learnt very little. I return glumly to my usual routine.

Today, I will put my wife and youngest daughter under the magnifier. Although I regularly perform my memory exercises, I have not often selected my wife as a subject. The few times I have done so, I have invariably found a reason to discontinue in a notably short time. Today I will look at her unflinchingly – I hope.

She – her name is Mary Grace – was only sixteen when I married her, a shy serious girl from a good enough country family – not that I had need of her income or her connections. It was a gentle marriage from the beginning, not one born of passionate attraction. It remained kind and decent through the years, through the births of our six children, through my wife's growth in self-confidence, through the development of mutual polite boredom. I enjoyed family life: my children, and their activities, and the noise and innocence of family gatherings. Marital boredom seemed to me the price one had to pay for the stability that a happy family life requires. And anyway, I soon found outside entertainments, first the theatre and then the actresses.

I pride myself on the fact that, until the end, my wife knew nothing about the latter. And I, too, was always careful to mind my own business in her direction, never questioned her closely about her outings, nor monitored their frequency nor the time of her return. She sometimes went on holidays alone, and I never once surreptitiously checked her arrangements as many a husband might, nor turned up at the location by surprise. In short, I avoided all those things that I myself dreaded; and if she had a little dalliance over the years, I am none the wiser.

Does this mean I never loved my wife? No, it does not. Marriage is a long row to hoe, so why should we object to small breaks for refreshment? In the beginning I loved her because she was new and pretty and I had sex with her; in the middle I loved her because she was the mother of my children; in the end I loved her because she was inevitable, as much a part of myself as my own skin. If anyone wants to say that what I have described is not love, then it is better that he or she never marries, since what I have just described constitutes love in a good marriage, and the only alternative is the steady growth of disaffection in a bad one. No doubt such a detractor would claim that real love is passionate and unreasonable and volatile, and that is often true, but it cannot stay that way or it will be burnt out in a year. And as I have said before, marriages must go on and on and on.

So it is better if one starts as one means to continue.

Of course we had our arguments; we were not really people of a similar point of view. She always felt the need to go to church, and would never admit that this was a social obligation rather than a religious one; that is to say, in my opinion, she confused the desire to be *seen* at church with the true spiritual need to be there. Hence her headaches, the timing of which was always influenced by who would be present or absent on any particular Sunday.

And she didn't have the best sense of humour in the world. My jokes and ironies she called *carrying on*. I was always carrying on, in her estimation. Well, so I was. But that is my nature, and how could I be expected to change it? Never mind – I found company that liked nothing better than for me to carry on, company which sought entertainment above all else; and isn't that the best thing to do with those qualities that your spouse dislikes – take them for an outing?

Nevertheless, my wife and I, however divergent in other ways, did share an interest in collecting. That was something we had in common, apart from our children. She liked to collect interesting recipes, both traditional and current, from the countries we visited, although her main motive was to impress our friends at dinner parties, which is perhaps not the same as an interest in collecting *per se*. Still, it was amusing for us to discuss our acquisitions together, and to plan our joint holidays according to what we wished to acquire.

I stop thinking about my wife for a moment while my mind roams fondly over my collections. After I have mentally delved again and again into the large trunk that contains them, have brought out one document after another and turned it over lovingly in my hands, I find myself seriously diverted from the exercise of recalling her. Instead, I fall into a long and pleasant reverie concerning my expeditions and purchases.

A noise startles me. Perhaps another tile falling from the roof, or brickwork somewhere collapsing. I chastise myself for failing to complete the morning's work. Earlier I'd decided also to recall my youngest daughter, Artemis. Yes, by the sixth child, my wife and I have got through all the Georges and Thomases and Elizabeths and Catherines, and my wife, running out of ideas, allows me to choose the child's name. She adamantly vetoes

Calliope and Polyhymnia, goes sour over Harmony and Melody, and says she will vomit if she has to call out Iphigenia. So Artemis it is. ('Don't worry, Mary, it's just like Diana.' 'Well, why not call her Diana then, William?' 'But don't you see, Mary, that misses the whole point.' 'What *is* the whole point William?')

Artemis, like all youngest children perhaps, is spoilt. She likes music and painting and nothing else except sweetmeats and dresses and dashing about screaming. My picture of her is of a very loud ringleted child flying down corridors or garden paths in billowing pink or lemon confections with little beribboned baskets of sugar-fruit. But she plays the violin beautifully, and paints very pretty watercolours on the riverbank, and is always very affectionate to her Papa. And such a gorgeous child too, all pink and gold and pouty.

Alas, now that I come to think of it, I dare say she is not a child any longer. She must be quite grown up. Will she have become like her Bible-carrying older sisters, always walking slowly, talking quietly, and daintily under-eating? I doubt it, for the simple fact that they are both slightly plain, and plainness always demands decorum or it is despised. It is only extreme prettiness that can get away with outrageousness, can indulge itself in public, can be as flirtatious and fickle as it pleases. She will be driving her mother to distraction of course, but it warms her father's heart to think of her sweet butterfly freedom.

But perhaps she has already found a husband. I wonder what such a man would be like. All buttoned-up like George, but reliable and heir to a great fortune? Or someone like Thomas, sweet and sensitive, but a trifle more unpredictable, with a smaller inheritance and a good social life? Perhaps like Henry, my second son, about whom it's difficult to say anything in particular, and about whom I've said very little at all.

Let me rectify that omission immediately. Henry is extremely handsome. Handsomeness has done for him what it often does: gradually obscured every other quality and defect, and finally done away with the need, or desire, for a fully developed character. As a child he was anxious, that I do recall – until he caught sight of himself in a mirror one day and was instantly transformed into an oozlum bird, satisfied to spend the rest of his days secreting oil from his preen-gland and lubricating his fine feathers.

The keeper interrupts me with the bucket and lunch. He impatiently feeds me the thin and cold soup, and goes out again without bothering with Horatio.

'Ignorant prick,' I shout.

Horatio groans. I look at him in alarm but he is lying quite still. Perhaps he was only adding his own emphasis to my hurled insult.

In the afternoon I try to sleep, but I am forced by the cold to spend the hours in a stubborn wakefulness. I stare at the walls.

I spend many of my waking hours staring at the walls. They are blackened from the early days when the fires were always lit. That was before scientists discovered that heat is debilitating, that the loss of elasticity or somesuch in one's internal air causes weakness, even prostration, and swelling of the fingers; before they discovered that dangerous miasmas result from our own fetid perspirations, and thus they sought to chill us with a gelid atmosphere; before they discovered that this was all wrong, and air was not an element laden with the poisonous substances given off by bodies, animal and vegetable, but a mixture of gases and phlogiston. But still the fires remained unlit, because a certain equilibrium was necessary to slow down our own putrefaction – a process that had been discovered to proceed apace even in living bodies, and such equilibrium was deemed best achieved in cool temperatures.

The walls have been re-blackened with the soot of fumigants, used fanatically after the removal of corpses, and then greased up by the residues of heated aromatics, prescribed to stem the lunatics' own putrid exhalations.

Porlock fears that he will catch a disease from the miasmas in the walls, alleges that the putrefied odours from gangrene and scurvy and insanity still lurk within the crumbling matter that composes them, waiting only until a man is weak enough to be overwhelmed. He also fears cracks and fissures in the floor which, he says, allow the escape of miasmas from the earth. I have compounded his terrors by telling him that the souls of the mistreated also escape, and return, thirsty for revenge, to where they were so miserably imprisoned. When he is especially drunk, I can have him ducking and diving like a lunatic to avoid the life-threatening passage of noxious blasts and murderous ghouls.

But when I am alone, and I stretch out a finger to wipe the wall – one finger is all I can manage – and it comes back black and greasy, it is not the history of therapeutic temperature that oppresses me. It is the thought of all the bodies that have hung here year after year; all the people who have died with their arms in chains and their feet in excrement.

~∽

I look down at Horatio. He is on the floor in such a way that I can't see his mouth. The fact that I can't tell if he's bleeding doesn't make me any the less anxious on his behalf. 'Will I carry on with my story to cheer you up?' I ask him.

'Would it surprise you to know that getting Juliet to honour the favour took nearly two years? Perhaps you thought I was interested only in quick results? It was after the first year that I discovered the information which so upset me. About her having been a well-known actress, I mean. But it was something I could not have known without taking an increased interest in her affairs. So you see, by the time I found out, it was already too late to cancel my affections, and I had to incorporate this painful information into my view of her – or do without: pack up, go home, find another table on which to play.

'I got off my bed, ordered some new waistcoats and breeches – golds and scarlets and yellows, updated my aromatics and ointments, and decided to make do with whatever talents and persuasions I had to hand.

"'What, are you well again, William?" my wife exclaimed as I strode through the house.

"'Never felt better," I asserted.

"'I was going to fetch the mad-doctor to you," she said. "To cure your melancholy."

"'It wasn't curable in that way," I retorted and went out into the fine spring air – yes, it was spring – full of robustness and confidence.

'I ordered my carriage and went straight to Juliet's house, carrying the money my valet usually took. She looked surprised, alarmed even, but I opened the purse wide and let her gaze upon the gold. She then looked up at me and I could see that she understood.

'Now was the time she should have shut the door. Opening it, in some coarser people's view, was as good as opening her legs.

'She bade me enter and sent the maid to the cook for refreshments. I handed her the money with a lingering look and she took it, blushing. I do not want to make her sound like a silly naive girl, though. The blush was not due to naiveté – rather to knowledge. Clearly she expected me now to seduce her.

'Instead I drank my tea, talked politely, then left.

'Well, you might say, how perverse. Not at all. I could go to the whorehouse if it were only flesh that I desired. I could go to my wife if it were only companionship. I could go to the theatre for scintillating conversation and displays of naked wit. But I was attempting to purchase something far more valuable.

'As I walked home – I'd sent my carriage on – I rejoiced in the fact that we could now be alone together in private. This is always the thing that makes the difference; we cannot loosen ourselves from social constraints in a public drawing room, no matter how much adroit fan-fluttering goes on. And so we began our walks and afternoon teas and, once I had bought a small townhouse, our dinners and evenings and other arrangements.

'The careful and subtle arrangement of these entertainments was my ace of diamonds. Why? Because an unthoughtful man can move too fast, causing a woman to feel forced; or, worse, he can move too slow, leaving her time to think that what is coming might not be inevitable – and woe betide the sluggard who gives the lady time to rediscover her morals!

'Amidst the presentation of delights, I did not give her time to do so. And so we came, by and by, to a light kiss on the cheek and thence to a brush on the lips, and later still to a concentrated bout of French kissing. Do you know what French kissing is, Horatio? Why do we label everything unmistakably lascivious French . . . well, sometimes Italian? Do the English not do these things? One only has to say that a lady is French for everyone to assume she is a prostitute. But I digress. Later we moved on to other kissing – the Italian kind. I hope you can guess my meaning. And there we stayed for a time while I prepared the ace of hearts . . .'

I stop. Horatio is writhing. He looks like wild cats tied up in a sack. But no sound at all comes from his mouth.

'Keeper,' I start and keep shouting. 'A man here requires the doctor!'

Nobody comes.

Eventually I am hoarse, and soon after Horatio lies still again. He lies so still I fear he is dead. But when the evening keeper comes and snatches him up by his hair, he emits a loud bellow and fights the negligent spoon with unusual ferocity.

⁓

I am wide awake. It is night and it is snowing. Why that should be a relief, I've no idea. Perhaps because it gives me something to watch and wonder at. I always loved the way snow muffled the world. The first thick snowfall of the winter was always for me a magical event, a perfect white blanket under which man and all the noise of his works and sins was silenced. Later, of course, it gets dirty and mushy and a plain nuisance. But in here, I am confined to the sight of the flakes drifting past the small window: no blanket, no mush.

When I was considered curable, I could sit by the stove in the long gallery and warm myself. And we used to get our frozen feet inspected for sores and then wrapped. The price we all paid was the enforced treatment. But to be always cold, numb-cold, is intolerable. It is worse than the boredom and the loneliness and the carnal frustration together. I fear it even in the summer. I fear it as much as hunger, that unseasonal year-round torment we never get a day's respite from. On the other hand – and perhaps this too contributes to my current sense of relief – the sooner the worst starts, the sooner it stops.

Tonight, I've got to end my fixation on *flocci*. That's what I've come to call it now. But I myself don't habitually estimate the world, life, as worthless, even if others do, and the word has become an obstacle. If only I had access to a reference book! I could logically work my way towards an expression of worth – at least away from worthlessness. All I can do, however, is grab each word as it buzzes into my mind and examine it for its temporary worthiness. Ah, here comes a good one – it was my thinking of buzzing that brought it flitting in. It is a word that buzzes: sprezzatura.

'Do you know what sprezzatura is, Horatio? No? I will tell you. It is studied carelessness or nonchalance, an ease of manner, in speech, art or literature. For myself, I have only to think about the word and it makes me want to stand up straighter, smile more, develop a greater ironic eloquence purely for its own sake, at least for my own enjoyment. Doesn't sprezzatura make you think of a man in harmony with the world? He is attractive because of his confidence: there is never a fly in his ointment, though the rest of us spend all our lives trying to scrape a little ointment off the fly.

'Yes certainly, *flocci* is laid to rest by sprezzatura. I know this might make you feel a little uncomfortable, Horatio, since you are not in a position to effect easy and nonchalant speech. Never mind. I will cast my verbal net wide so that it embraces you as well; you will be protected from being deemed worthless by my own sprezzatura.'

I am about to give an example of the kinds of things I might say when Porlock wanders in.

'What are you doing here? There's no moon.'

'What's the moon got to do with it?' he asks, and belches loudly. He throws himself down on the straw bale and takes out his flask. 'I'm glad the snow's come. It'll freeze the emanations.'

'What emanations? Stercus? Is that what you're on about again?'

'Shit. That's what I'm talking about. All that faecal matter under the foundations.'

'Shit, stercus, same thing. Give me a sip,' I add, before he once more begins to list the poisonous miasmas circulating about us.

'Waste good spirits on a lunatic? You're out of your mind.'

'Very droll.'

'What d'you want a drink for anyway? You're intoxicated enough with madness.'

'I've been bored all day. Utterly. And now I'm freezing.'

Porlock doesn't answer.

'You could treat me better, you know. You *should* treat me better.'

'Why should I? Lunatics don't know one sensation from another.'

'You don't believe anybody could be wrongly imprisoned here, do you?'

'It's not up to me. Thank Christ.'

'Before the Vagrancy Act of 1744 . . .'

'Eh?'

'Don't you know any of the history of your own enterprise?'

'This isn't my enterprise. If it was up to me you'd all be put on the ship of fools. Sent off to that place on the other side of the world. You know, down there on the bottom. They say you could dig a tunnel through.'

'The Antipodes.'

'That's them.'

'Under the current circumstances, that could only be a mercy. But let's stick to the point. The 1744 Vagrancy Act decreed that two or more Justices of the Peace had to be present when handing vagrants over to the constables or the church wardens. Why was that act passed, do you think? Because even at the turn of the century our famous Defoe was writing about the abuses that asylums could be put to. The incarceration of rich relatives or unwanted wives . . .'

'Defoe may be famous to you but I couldn't pick him from a rat's arse.'

'Other, less esoteric publications have also gone on at length about it. The *Gentleman's Magazine*, for example.'

'Do you seriously suppose I'd spend my money on stercus like that? So I can learn which colour waistcoat to wear this season: canary-yellow or claret?'

'It has published serious accounts of persons unlawfully detained in institutions such as this.'

'Good on it,' Porlock replies with considerable sarcasm.

'What I'd like to know is, were there two Justices of the Peace present when I was handed over?'

'Who knows? Who cares?' he replies.

'You *know* I've been wrongly imprisoned here and I have children who would want to find me. Bring me a hospital visitor so that I may talk to him, and you can be assured my family will reward you.'

Porlock goes over to the straw bale, sits and takes out his flask. 'It's getting colder all the time in here,' he grumbles between swallows.

'Didn't you hear me?'

'I heard you.'

'Well?'

'I'll think about it.'

I feel a little encouraged. But I am not sure what tack to take next.

'At least you have a coat and proper shoes,' I say conversationally, if also a little bitterly. 'What do I have? A single rag summer and winter. I'm nearly dead from the cold. Look, my feet are blue and my hands have sores.'

'Piffle. You brutes are insensible to reason. Why should the temperature matter?'

'Then why do they try to drown our mad thoughts with cold water?'

But Porlock is not interested in the far reaches of medical science. He swigs from his flask and begins his monologue about food and debt. I close my eyes. If I could, I would stop my ears. I fear it is no use trying to seduce Porlock with money. He is certainly a greedy man, and also in dire straits, if his own assertions can be trusted, but he is too shickered by drink to appreciate my offer.

And really, with a whole palace full of kings, of England, or Bedlam or Heaven, what interest should he have in my particular bribe? Why take a gamble on me when the place is full of the rich and famous, all of them ready to give the whole world in exchange for simple favours?

Porlock gets up and moves towards the door.

'When are you going to get the apothecary for Horatio?' I call, fearing he has forgotten.

'That's not his name. Who told you that was his name?'

'What is his name?'

Porlock screws up his eyes. 'No, it won't come to me.'

'Anyway, I think he's now very ill.'

'Bah. There's lots like him. It's just his form of madness.'

'Bleeding and coughing fits are not madness.'

'They are if you're trying to eat up your own tongue.'

'What?' I am incredulous.

Porlock begins to shout. 'Yes, that's what they do. They try to take a bite off their own tongue and when they can't they try to swallow it whole. Mr Haslam told me.'

'He was having you on, you ignorant fool.'

'He certainly was not. They're doing it all over the place.'

'It's a physical sickness that's all over the place. An infection, a disease. In the lungs, judging by all the coughing.'

'How would you know?'

'Get the apothecary. He will verify it.'

Porlock shakes his head. 'What about my supper, eh? I've got a good piece of sausage with my bread tonight. Do you think I don't have to eat? That I can wait on madmen hand and foot without eating?'

I sigh. 'How could I forget.'

Porlock goes out of the cell, muttering under his breath.

~

I am awakened by a blast of cold water from the hose. The half-cripple is standing in front of me, cackling maniacally. Cold water streams off my body and forms a large puddle on the floor.

'Do you want your breakfast, lunatic?'

'What is it?'

'Dog's water.'

I open my mouth and the keeper starts spooning in the gruel with his habitual lack of pacing. Then he goes over to Horatio while my tongue seeks out the last vestiges of solid matter from between my teeth. What do I care if it's a dog hair?

'You'll have to mop this puddle up,' I complain. 'I can't stand in it all day.'

'It's all right. It'll probably freeze. I'll bring an icepick with the lunch.'

He goes out again and I am left standing in the puddle of cold water. I am despondent. I have failed to persuade Porlock to fetch the apothecary for Horatio. I have failed to persuade Porlock to bring a hospital visitor to our cell. And now my feet will freeze solid and turn to pulp in the thaw.

'Horatio, how about a story to warm and cheer us up? A further instalment concerning my sex life is what I had in mind, if that suits you. Yes? No? As usual, I will take your silence as assent. Now, where were we? Ah yes, French kissing. I think I told you that later we moved on to Italian kissing, but let us slow the story down a little and concentrate on the circumstances that immediately preceded a first leisurely and thorough French kiss.

'We'd eventually got around to talking about acting, Juliet and I. I would say it was this that signalled an interesting moment in the development of our relationship. It was the first time she showed any serious interest in me. She had always been interested in my money; she had learnt to be interested in my carefully manufactured wit. And she listened when I talked on that lower – or is it more sublime – level, that level on which men and women who are secretly attracted to each other talk. Yes, yes, it was a trifle unbalanced at this exact time, with my attraction to her being rather stronger than hers to me – but she couldn't quite stop herself being flattered and fascinated by it, and that is always an excellent sign.

'She knew *of* me, of course; she'd known of me since she came, married, to my town. I had been no small fry in the theatre world of the area; I could certainly make and break careers. She told me that my critical pieces had always amused her, that she had long wished to make my acquaintance.

'"Ha," I said, "And I have wasted so much money on you."

'She laughed. "You were too fast. When you offered me the money, I didn't know it was *you*. All I saw was a . . ." She trailed off and blushed.

'"All you saw was a . . .?" I prompted her.

She fluttered her fan and looked around to avoid my gaze.

'"All you saw was a little old fat man with his tongue hanging out?"

'She fluttered her fan agitatedly and went red.

'"It's all right," I reassured her. "We special people are hard to recognise in a crowd."

'She laughed and relaxed. "That's what I like about you, William – no one can leave a dent on you."

'"You could," I said.

'Of course, by this time I was no longer a theatre critic. Yet her interest in my former critical career was genuine and focused. It was not that empty yet envious admiration which, in the past, I had so come to loathe: Yes, yes, loved your piece and how much do you usually earn churning out this stuff? She wanted to discuss my opinions of particular plays, of particular performances and interpretations. She offered her own opinions which were, I thought, insightful and shrewd.

'Then we talked about her own acting career, now in the even more distant past. I have to admit I was jealous of it. Not jealous of her successes – God knows, I never wanted to be an actor myself. Even when I took to the streets all I'd wanted to do was lose myself: I ran to and embraced failure as a friend who might drag me under. No, I was jealous of all those eyes on her, all those thoughts being thought about her, all those feelings felt. As if each look, each idea, each heartbeat stole something away from her, ultimately away from me. It is sordid to admit that when the stage-light that lit her shone down the years and finally reached me, all I could see was theft: theft of my Juliet's youth and beauty by a thousand nameless others who had no right to look upon her.

'This is the extent of our rapaciousness, Horatio, when we say *mine* with our whole being. We try even to plunder the past, to walk round the stalls with a basket, saying, "You have seen her. Here, pluck out your eyes. Pluck out your eyes and give them to me, so that I can destroy the fact that you have looked at her and seen something which has been denied me." Do you believe a human being could really be like this, Horatio? I was. And alas, it is enough for there to be one of us for there to be many others.'

I stop. I feel a little depressed. I miss her. Even reduced to this degradation, I would like to see her. Not for her pity nor her help, nor even for a break from my numbing routine. For herself alone

I would like to see her – for her pride and courage, for the folds of fabric over those thighs that grasp the horse. . .

'Horatio, I'm afraid I must have a little rest. The story has got me a little excited.'

I concentrate on banal and bloodless thoughts till my excitement abates. Then I begin again.

'I'm going to tell you about the process, Horatio. The process I am referring to is very specific. I experienced it for the first time when I was young – about twenty. The first time I fell in love. I won't bore you with the details of that particular fiasco – young love is all the same: arrogant in the belief of its own uniqueness, utterly boring in its conformity. Sufficient to say here that the process was not new to me by the time I met Juliet. But, although I had frequently experienced it, I hadn't attached much importance to it. It was only when I met Juliet that I realised its deep significance. Now, you will soon accuse me of speaking in riddles, so I will try to make myself as plain as possible.

'Think of the summer, Horatio. What comes immediately into your mind? Warmer weather of course. Perhaps long evenings. Strawberries. As soon as I say strawberries, I see a pool. A pool with a central fountain and water lilies. As soon as I say pool, I see Juliet. And then, through a mysterious series of linkages, when I say strawberries, I see Juliet. Long evenings – Juliet; summer – Juliet. And it works the other way too: I say Juliet and the summer flares. This, then, is the process to which I am referring. I won't try to describe it any further. It is in fact a simple and widely recognised state: gradually seeing the beloved everywhere in the things of the world; and seeing the world in the beloved. Really, it is the very description of infatuation.

'Spring precedes summer, does it not? What comes to mind then when I say spring? Ah, the approach of summer. Juliet approaches – the central fountain and the water lilies, the strawberries, the long evenings, summer itself; but now all of this is linked to the word spring. And when I say Juliet, I see trees in blossom, sudden downpours, delicate continental cakes.

'Why the cakes? Well, in the spring I was in the habit of taking an afternoon walk in a fashionable district near a continental cakeshop. And the association between spring and cakes became even stronger once Juliet and I started taking that same walk together. One afternoon when we were out walking we passed the shop just as my Juliet said the word *fellatio*. We had been discussing whether oral sex *really* constitutes adultery (we decided it did not), and the word fell from her lips just as a small, overly ostentatious but splendid little mouthful of delight came into view.

'Cake, downpours, blossoming trees, spring, summer, warmer weather, longer evenings, strawberries, pools with fountains and water lilies: all of them lead to Juliet and all are evoked by her name. This process of linkages is the essence of love Horatio, and that is why to lose love is to feel as if one has been torn out of the world.

'And what about the fellatio? you shrewdly ask. You have left it out. Not at all – we went home and got onto that right away.'

Mare pacifico

I STARE AT THE gibbous moon. I am glum. Frozen. Wide awake. For many nights I have failed to advance beyond sprezzatura.

'There is nothing after sprezzatura, Horatio. In the end, my sprezzatura will fail you as it does me. The world does not doff its hat at a fine sentence, much less a fine word; it exists only to silence us. You don't believe me? Tell me, then, a word you can hurl at it? You are dumb? I will have to tell you the only one: impassable. After sprezzatura, there is only the impassable world.'

I'm silent for a moment or two while I ponder on the implications of what I have just said. I will have to stay on the right side of sprezzatura or my word game will have to stop. And what do I have but these words – my own unique insanity, as my tormentors would have it.

I am a ghost in chains, an effigy made of words. I am no longer a real man, only a device, a disembodied voice, an extended instance of prosopopoeia.

'Ah, well there's a word, eh Horatio? Prosopopoeia – it just popped into my head. What a little beauty. Shall I tell you exactly what it is since you do not have recourse to a dictionary? Prosopopoeia is when an absent or imagined person is represented as speaking or acting; when an inanimate or abstract thing is personified or given human characteristics; when a person or thing is represented as the embodiment of a quality. There we are – pretty good for a ghost in a dungeon, don't you think?

'What do you imagine the adjective is? I'd go for prosopopoeic, though truth to tell, I've never heard it mentioned. So, shall I say to the apothecary, if I ever see him again: Disappear, for you are only prosopopoeic, merely the embodiment of eighteenth century rational, secular ideals; and shall I say to Porlock: Vanish, because you are only the voice of a thousand, a million, whining workers, certain that money is happiness . . .'

I wake up. The morning keepers have arrived.

'Hey lunatic, do you need a bucket?' Thumbscrew asks.

'Be off with you, gomerels, for you are only prosopopoeic . . .'

'Only what?' Strappado says.

'Sounds downright disgusting,' Thumbscrew puts in.

'You are the tedious embodiment of the crowd's need to be entertained, the sugar syrup in the oleum cephalicum.'

'That last word has a phallus in it, doesn't it, Strappado?'

'It certainly does.'

'All popular entertainment has a phallus in it, gomerels.'

'Really? Do phalluses entertain you, Thumbscrew?'

'Not if I can help it.'

'Me neither. I think the lunatic should be careful what he's alleging. Some of us aren't as modern as others. Some of us think that queer buggers should still be buried alive. Just because *he* likes a prick in his entertainment.'

'Why don't you give me my food and go away?'

'We've got to sort out your pissabed friend first. The physician's coming today.'

'Then tell the physician when he comes that a man in here is sick.'

'I don't see any men. Do you, Thumbscrew?'

'Nope. I only see an old sack and a lunatic that keeps on talking to it.'

They go out with Horatio's used straw and my bucket, laughing and slapping each other. I wait for them to return with the pabulum. I wait in vain.

Porlock comes in much later with a large bowl of gruel. He asserts that it is the lunch, but I know it is the breakfast, turned cold and lumpy while forgotten by the keepers in some corner. However, their forgetfulness has satisfactorily done away with the morning and my tedious memory exercises.

'Tell me, what is going on out there?' I ask, hoping to hear of some apocalyptic event that will reorder the world. Porlock is a gold-mine of solid nugget and glister.

'There's lots of talk about some system that came in late last year,' he informs me. 'England won't trade with anyone who trades with them on the side of Napoleon. Or something.'

'Oh? What year was last year?'

'1806, you fool.'

'And what else?'

'The apothecary says the cook has been turned into a sandwich.'

'What? You've got something wrong there, gomerel.'

'No, I haven't. Mr Haslam said so, I heard him distinctly. The cook called James.'

I laugh with derision. 'James Cook was killed on the Sandwich Islands – that's what he must have said. But it was in 1779, nearly thirty years ago.'

'Well, those islands contained cannibals,' Porlock remarks. 'He got eaten.'

'Why does the apothecary talk to you about Captain Cook?'

'Not to me, you fool. He talks to that assistant of his. I'm just standing by in case of trouble. Well, I can't close my ears, can I?'

'I'm surprised you'd care to listen.'

'I didn't until Mr Haslam started talking about the map.'

'What map?'

'An original one, he says. Italian. Of somewhere godforsaken in the Pacific Ocean.'

'Where in the Pacific Ocean?' I ask suspiciously.

Porlock struggles to remember. He shakes his head. 'Now it's been included in some book, I heard Mr Haslam say. An Italian book. Something *geographico*. Those macaroni words – I can't ever remember them.'

I fall quiet. A memory is coming back to me like a ship approaching through the fog.

'I think that was my map,' I say.

'What? You've got a good imagination, you have. Mr Haslam said it's worth a lot of money. In the right places.'

'I told you I was a rich man.'

'Well, just acting like I believe you, which I don't, where would you get a map like that? And what were you running about with it for?'

'I don't know what I was running about with it for. I'm in darkness about that particular period of my life. I can tell you though, in better times one of my hobbies was map-collecting. I spent a fair sum on it, though not much energy. I collected the lazy way – with gold.'

'But it wasn't only money, was it? This sort of map – Mr Haslam said you'd have to know the right people.'

'I did know the right people. Once.'

'Well, why would you waste your money on things like that then?'

'The reason I am rich and you are poor is that I can always recognise an investment and you can only recognise a bargain.'

'Is that so?'

'But an investment entails risk, whereas a bargain only greed. Which is why you fail to take up my offer and rescue me. I am an investment and not a bargain. But I am an excellent risk and you should take it.'

'You think I'm going to take advice from a lunatic?'

'You heard yourself, the map was worth a lot.'

'I heard about the map. I didn't hear you owned it.'

'Well I did.'

'Well, you don't now.'

'That is a moot point.'

'I don't know what a point of that sort is, but I've heard someone say possession is nine-tenths of the law. So maybe you still own it by a tenth. If you ever did.'

'There must be a record, surely, of what people had in their possession when they came into your care?'

'What the *paupers* had, I can tell you right off: rags and lice. And what the criminals had: pistols and kitchen knives.'

'You already said yourself that I was wearing good clothes when I arrived.'

'Did I?'

'You know, you should stop all your drinking. Your memory is going. You might end up here, nailed to the same wall.'

'What's drink got to do with it?' Porlock growls. 'It's age and worry that's doing my memory in. That's what it is. And I can't stand here talking to you all day, I've got the rest to feed.'

Porlock picks up the utensils and bucket and goes out.

~

When he has gone, I find myself dwelling bitterly on the map. I am sure it was mine, an original, in Italian, of the navigations of La Nuova Zelanda by Captain Cook. A long story concerning authenticity was, as usual, attached to it by the merchants' agent. As usual, I took the story with a grain of salt. I bought the map because I liked it. I liked the names *Eaheinomauwe* and *Poenammoo* all mixed up with *Li Poveri Cavalieri* and *Capo Addio*, and those English capes, Kidnappers, Turnagain and Runaway – a narrative in themselves. I liked the fine handwriting and the beautiful yellow paper. Of course, being a sensible man, I sent it on for examination by a reputable firm: an investment, they cried – *and* a bargain.

'Horatio, what did you think of our conversation? I can tell you I'm quite riled up about it. It's one thing to lose your mind – quite another to lose your prized possessions. It's beyond Porlock's comprehension why anyone would want such a thing. But how many new countries are there to be discovered in a finite world? Already James Cook has shown that the fabled southern continent, *Terra Australis*, reputedly joined to Africa, does not exist. That there is only the great southern ice shelf. Does Porlock think this is something that's found out every day? Does he think the coastline of a new country is charted every week? He is a very ignorant man. An ignorant fool who loves only money because it can be so easily applied to the appetites above and below the belt.

'They stole my map, Horatio. I'm sure of it. Perhaps – who knows? – I am here because of someone's wish to have it. What better way to rob a man than to imprison him in a lunatic asylum? Were the true owner later to get to court, his allegations would at once be denounced as the ravings of a madman. Oh, very clever.'

My bitterness silences me. And then I am restless and agitated all morning and cannot settle to my work. Each time I try to discipline myself, rage causes me to tremble. The gruel and the bucket and the hose come and go in the approximate middle of the day, and then the afternoon settles malevolently upon the cell.

'Horatio, would you like to hear more about my map, since the afternoon is so cold and long? Let's begin at the beginning. It is true that I didn't go all over the place *chasing* maps. But I did use the purchase of a map as a good excuse to get away on my own. "I have to go to The Kingdom of the Two Sicilies" – or Paris, or Prague – I'd announce every so often to my family. "They're holding a map over there for me to look at." I would make arrangements to see a few collectors; but I would also arrange to see a tailor or two, a parfumier, a perruquier, a shoemaker, a silversmith, a sculptor, a woman. I'd come back loaded up with suits, perfumes, wigs, boots, jewellery, sculptures and satisfaction. Sometimes I'd even come back with a map.

'I continued this practice even when I was purchasing Juliet. Why not? Had I made any promises to her? Certainly not. Why are we always promising, Horatio? Why are we always swearing to give things up, to sacrifice our enjoyments? We cannot believe that good things will simply be bestowed upon us, that is why. We have to beg and plead, offer an exchange. We still make blood sacrifices, Horatio. Sublimated, contorted, dishonest ones. But where was I? Oh yes – going off to purchase maps.

'Do you want to hear about the trip I took to secure the map that has been stolen from me? Of course you do. I had to go to Naples. What was the situation in Naples at the time? Naples was enjoying a lull before the storm that has since blown up. Napoleon's brother had not yet been placed upon the throne; the kingdom had not yet been overswept by expanding French happiness.

'Anyway, there I am. The climate is pleasant, not yet too hot, and the bay is beautiful. I am busy with two objectives – my map, and my wife has begged me to bring her some recipes. Not the take-two-pig-trotters type, but the first-clean-one-hundred-pheasants kind, or whatever the Neapolitan equivalent is. As I said, she likes to show off at dinner parties. This second objective is easy: the women I frequent, whores of the higher type who sit in expensive salons drinking wine and conversing about art, are pleased to offer me recipes for their frivolous concoctions. Even whores have to eat. And they provide them at no extra charge.

'Sometimes I ponder on the contradictions involved in what is paid for and what is free. I pay for an essentially useless map of a foreign country and get the secrets of ice cream for nothing! Many worried men sweating in dark suits pore over my map with special magnifiers to ascertain its authenticity, while the whores are so sure about their ice-cream recipe they just hand it over and change the topic. I'll tell you what it is, Horatio: the map is important because already, in their hearts, the men have coveted the new land, have already parcelled it out. But ice cream? The stuff will slip down inside you as smoothly as a cool dream, or it will melt in a trice in the hot sun, and either way it is gone.

'I take leave of the belladonna whores, carrying my swag of recipes for chocolate ice cream and my instructions concerning the correct price that should be paid for ice that has to be dragged in blocks down from the mountains, and I get on to the more tedious part of the trip: authentication of the map. "Yes, yes," the men with the magnifiers cry when I identify myself at the merchants' office, "a Neapolitan must certainly have been on the ship, as our agent said . . . Or at least had access to Cook's charts," they add in the same breath.

'Another Englishman walks in, just as the merchants are unctuously mentioning price.

'"As you can see, the gentleman I told you about is here," the alarmed head merchant says to him, and indicates me.

'The Englishman looks annoyed.

'"I said: Only if he didn't come. But he has. So the merchandise is his."

'I look closely at my competitor for the map. He is heavily bewhiskered, and clearly hot and irascible.

'"We have some other things you might be interested in," the merchant ventures.

'"I very much doubt it," the bad-tempered gentleman replies.

'"What is your interest in that country?" I inquire.

'"None at all. I am producing a book."

'"You do not wish to go to the South Seas?"

'The irascible gentleman looks at me as if he finds me annoying.

'"Why should I wish that?"

'I shrug. "Adventure?"

'"I am not a boy. I do not need adventures."

'"Well, you see, I do. And the map is mine."

'"You'd do better with a ticket. Are you going to sail the boat yourself?"

'"A map is a trigger for the imagination."

'"Is that so?" smirks my competitor. "Is your adventure going to take place merely in your head?"

"'There's nothing mere about the inside of a head, sir. Our whole life takes place there. Still, we'll see how things turn out. English melancholy doesn't suit me at the present time."

"'Oh? What would suit you instead?"

"'Something a little more continental."

'The gentleman ignores me and turns to the merchant. "I'll give you double what this man offers."

'I laugh. "Do not compete with me on price, sir. I am a man unaccustomed to limits."

'Oh Horatio, am I a man unaccustomed to limits now? How our boasts rise again to haunt us!

'The gentleman turns back to me. "I wonder, then, if you would be so good as to exchange addresses? Then, if you should desire to sell the map at a later date, you will be able to contact me."

"'Certainly. But why should *you* require my address?"

"'I should like to write and persuade you."

'I gave him my address, Horatio. Was that my fatal mistake? Was the book that this man wanted to publish the same one referred to by Porlock? Am I now to harbour suspicions concerning a relationship between this gentleman and the physician or apothecary? Or perhaps between this gentleman and the events that led to my wandering about the docks hoping to board a ship to the Antipodes?'

~~

Porlock enters the cell with a candle.

'Listen,' he says, holding up the candle as if I needed light to hear.

'What? What is it?'

'The thaw.'

'The what?'

Porlock does not answer but continues to hold the candle aloft. I listen carefully and hear water. Not rain, but a subterranean easing, an oozing. The spring thaw always terrifies Porlock. He imagines that cloacal spectres escape from their graves of ice and haunt the flowing warmer water.

'Go away,' I tell him.

'You'll see,' he hisses. 'You'll all be sick in a trice.'

He goes out, and hours later, in the depths of the night, I hear the rain start. It begins tentatively, but soon builds to a dull roar. It flings itself into the grate and against the window. I am wide awake and restless.

'Listen to the pouring rain, Horatio. Imagine being out in it. Doesn't the thought excite you – out in the dark in a wild storm? Or during the day, imagine it drenching the spring trees. The magnolias. I love magnolias. Perhaps you are not familiar with them? In spring, they are completely naked apart from large cream and pink globe-like flowers which cover the branches profusely. It always rains when the magnolia flowers are out. I used to take my carriage to an avenue of magnolias and sit looking out at them while the rain cascaded off the roof. I like that particular melancholy. The poetic kind. An exquisite sadness and a spring-fresh desire. You could put music to it, a symphony, something long and complicated, in a minor key. Something very nearly tragic, yet uplifting. Do you think I am peculiar? In fact, I am. I have a taste for moodiness, and grandeur, and the racing losing heart.

'Perhaps not so peculiar. That taste was just becoming shared by the world in general when I was snatched in here. Hadn't you noticed, before our confinement – assuming yours to correspond roughly to my own – a certain mood overtaking us all? A veritable spring-rain and magnolia swoon? A passion for the lawless, genius poet capable of expressing all losses, all desires? Such a man was on the horizon, I can assure you. For whatever it is that the public hankers after, whatever mood it is they believe they have lost, or been stripped of, the poet will arrive to supply it. The steam engine comes to rule the world and suddenly the public taste is for the free man on horseback!'

I stop to listen to the heavy rain. 'Remember the process I told you about, Horatio? Summer, spring, trees in blossom, sudden downpours, delicate continental cakes? In this weather, I find it impossible to tell you any other story than Juliet's. But I warn you, so that you may prepare yourself: this will be the final instalment, and it will be brief. Luckily, you already know that my tale has an unhappy ending.

'Fellatio. That was the last thing I said. Well, this particular practice went on for quite a while as I prepared the ace of hearts. Are you still with me in this carnal card game? Spades: money; clubs: wit; diamonds: perfectly paced seduction; hearts – well, what do *you* think? Let me set the scene. Summer and most of autumn have passed while I prepare the ace of hearts. Quite a long while, yes, but she is struggling hard against my aces. She is a married woman after all, and I am a married man. However, only when the last ace has been played will I be able to extract the final small portion of the favour.

'The ace of hearts is finally played – by her – on a park bench one day in the last month of autumn. I had had it in my own hand at the beginning, but all my contrivances had been towards smuggling it into her own hand to play. And so she did. Perhaps I should have played it myself, but there is always the possibility that you will lose when revealing the ace of hearts. After she has thrown it down, we go back to my townhouse with the delicious winter all ahead of us, and I plan the final seduction, *the coup de grâce*, for the week after Christmas.

'I survive Christmas. Just. My wife's relations arrive in droves, and we spend our days in a fug of mulled wine and spiced puddings. Finally, it is over. We – Juliet and myself – are to meet at my townhouse on a date agreed upon before Christmas. I arrive at the appointed time, but Juliet is late. I don't worry. There are often complications. I light the fire and set out the wine glasses and cakes. I go to the window and look up and down the street. The street is empty. I start to fear she won't be able to come. Perhaps she's ill. I wait longer, but impatiently. I draw the curtains and light the lamps and wonder whether to refuel the fire.

'Just as I am about to leave there is a knock on the door. Juliet's manservant is there. I am quite alarmed until he identifies himself, for he speaks English with a strong accent which I believe to be French; besides which, he is uncommonly tall, unbelievably insolent and magnificently scarred. When I have recovered myself, he informs me that his mistress is indisposed. He hands me a basket of sweetmeats. "She sent these for you," he says, and then disappears into the darkness. I am disappointed. I sit down by the last embers of the fire and consume a large portion of chocolate fudge and almond shortbread.'

I swallow hard. I have come to the most difficult part.

'That is the last thing I remember. After this, there's a period of time of which I'm completely oblivious. During this oblivion, I was discovered down at the docks, dragged from there by several constables, and eventually deposited here. Not in this exact spot, of course – I was put in the curables' wing for a time and given treatment. *That* is a story in itself.

'For a long while, I had no idea at all how I came to be at the docks where I was apprehended; and the cause of my fugue was never adequately explained. But as I lay on my bed in the curables' wing, I came to suspect Juliet's husband. I lay there and found myself returning again and again to the same old tangle.

'How did Juliet's husband find out about the townhouse? Presumably he had her followed. It is the only solution I can – could – ever think of. Perhaps she had been acting oddly at home, singing around the house, laughing a little too readily, forgiving more easily, seeming somehow younger, and prettier. Perhaps we were seen together by her servants on their days off, by her husband's friends or mistresses. We went boldly out into the world together – although, ironically, boldness is frequently taken as a sign of innocence. But, still innocent we were!

'Well, almost. Our mouths were not innocent; they *would* keep on asking whether indulgence in oral sex constitutes a betrayal. We pondered this aloud as we walked at leisure through avenues lined with burgeoning trees. We pondered this and laughed, while she twirled her umbrella, or her parasol, according to the unpredictable weather; and we carried on with our increasingly lascivious dialogue concerning everything we desired to do to each other's bodies, hers quite the equal of my own untethered imagination. On and on we walked, into the promise of a full springtime, an over-arching summer, autumn's decline, the base metal coming out of our alchemical mouths like the purest gold.

'Nevertheless, Horatio, we had not fully consummated our affair, and were fated never to do so. I was drugged and set loose in the streets. Did I snatch up my map as I went, still cunning enough to realise that to have something of such value would lessen the terrible effects of an intoxicated vagrancy? Alas, I am in chains and my map has been stolen from me. All this for a French kiss, a little Italian debauchery . . .'

～

I wake up. Porlock has staggered drunkenly in with his flask. I notice straight away that it is still raining heavily.

'I heard the apothecary talking about that place again,' Porlock says, while I fill the bucket.

'What place?'

'The place you're always on about. The one in the map.'

'I'm not always on about it,' I reply, feeling irritated.

'Suit yourself.'

'What was he saying?'

'Someone went there – I forget his name – brought back a native. Now he's visiting the King and Queen.'

'Who is?'

'The native is. Can't you follow a sentence?'

'I was just checking that your pronouns were taking you where you wanted to go.'

'Savage.'

'The native's a savage?'

'No, that was his name.'

'The savage was called Savage?'

Porlock titters. 'No, that was the name of the man who brought him back. That's funny, isn't it?'

'I suppose so – like the word bottom is funny to a four-year-old.'

Porlock squints at me angrily. 'I don't have to talk to you, you know. I could just come in here and stuff your food in and sluice you off. I don't have to listen to you. The physician tells me I should ignore you all.'

'Why don't you then?'

Porlock shrugs.

'Perhaps we're the only intelligent company you've got.'

'Look,' Porlock replies in a red-faced crescendo. 'I stood you by the fire when it was cold, didn't I? Wiped you down when you were sweating like a pig. Cleaned up the cell when it was full of shit and spew. What thanks do I get? Not a bloody word.'

'You sound like someone's mother.'

Porlock goes over to the straw bale and melodramatically throws himself upon it.

'Tell me about Mr Savage and the native then,' I say soothingly.

Porlock sulks.

'Has he got tattoos?'

'I don't know.'

'Or have they got him all done up in breeches and grease and hair powder?'

'He wears breeches, of course. How could he go to see the Queen in a loincloth? Anyway, his balls would freeze up and drop off. The apothecary said that Queen Charlotte is quite taken with the handsome fellow. Who wouldn't be after spending your life in bed with a lunatic?'

'Oh, I don't know. Being in bed with the Marquis might be quite entertaining.'

'What Marquis?'

'Never mind.'

'The apothecary says that this Mr Savage is going to put out a little book in the new year. About his travels and things. The native's going back though. On the *Ferret*, the whaler that brought him over here. . .'

'The boat is called the *Ferret*?'

'Yes – what of it?'

'It reminds me of our Earl of Ferret. The one who tried to prove he was insane by a sane defence. Now we have the *Ferret* bringing us a native who's trying to prove he's a gentleman by wearing breeches.'

'You're saying he's not a gentleman?'

'No, I'm saying breeches doesn't prove it.'

'All our gentlemen wear breeches.'

'Yes, and they're a bunch of savages.'

'Bah – you talk like one of those abolitionists.'

'Don't get me started.'

Porlock grunts, takes a long swig from his flask and stands up. He is frowning deeply as he sways.

'Perhaps I'll go out to Port Jackson,' he suddenly announces.

'You think the care of convicts will be better than the care of lunatics?'

'Who cares about that? The weather's said to be better and the food plentiful.'

'You can't live your whole life according to the dictates of your stomach.'

'Why not? My stomach's more reasonable than the King.'

I laugh. Probably he is right.

'Well, free me and take me with you. I could do with a bit of sun and gluttony.'

'What would I want you along for?'

'You might end up in Russia without me.'

'I'm sure the ship will know where it's going. I'm not going to swim.'

'Will you take your wife?'

'That old set of saddlebags!'

'What, you'd just desert her?'

'She can move in with her shiftless brothers. They've always got enough food. Don't ask me how – they never get off their lardy backsides from noon to night.'

'How charming.'

'What about you? You just said you wanted to come with me. What about your own family that you're so bloody desperate to get back to?'

'Of course I'd send for them.'

'And they'd just pack up and go tripping across the world to a convict settlement?'

I sigh. 'No. But I'm not sending for them because I'm not going because you're not taking me because you're not going either.'

But Porlock is no longer listening. He has collapsed on the floor a few feet short of the door.

~

It is still raining heavily. Has been for days. I am both delighted and alarmed. Delighted with the noise, yet alarmed at the puddles of water that have appeared in the doorway. And no sooner does water appear than it spreads. A runnel of water flows decisively towards my naked feet; another flows with equal determination to and underneath Horatio's straw. I watch the dark stain spreading across the flagstones after its passage beneath Horatio.

'Horatio, I don't believe we will drown. Not for a while, anyway. When the water is up to my chin and you have floated off into the drains of this lazaretto, *then* we can panic. For now, I'm going to tell you more about Captain James Cook. I admit, however, that when I envied him his watery escapades, suspension in the filthy water of a dungeon wasn't my idea of compensation. Never mind.

'What's my interest in Cook? you might well ask, if you were less of a laconic type of chap than you are. My answer is that a man can't become fascinated with maps without becoming fascinated with the lands they represent. A map is a trigger for the imagination, as I told that gentleman who was my competitor. I used to look at my map and imagine Jim sitting on the *Endeavour* in Ship Cove, Queen Charlotte Sound, and . . . what?

'I drew a blank. What on earth did it look like? What does he see when he looks out? I think he sees mountains. But how can I imagine the flora? Suddenly I am interested in the specimens brought back by the naturalist, Joseph Banks.

'Jim has watched Joe disappear into the bush for samples – it's thick, according to all reports – and what's he thinking? Again, I've no idea. But surely he must be reflecting on how famous he's going to be back home. And in the future. He's looking at a new country. Well, new to the northern hemisphere – obviously it's not new to the people who already live there. Wouldn't you feel tickled pink? Forget all the upstarts and self-fanciers back home, all the opera singers and composers and poets and politicians and sycophants round the throne – this is the real thing. This is fame on another level.

'So he sits in Ship Cove and begins his ownership with naming. Can you really believe these places don't already have names of their own? He sits there and the sun shines hot on his back, for it is Decemberish and everything is back to front and upside down, and he looks at the steep hills covered in trees and plants he has never seen before, and he hears the lulling sound of the water slapping against his ship, and the melodic calling of native birds, and already he is so in love with the place he plans to produce the most accurate charts the world has ever seen: those in the know about this sort of thing are going to be truly astonished. As they are.

'It's time for Jim's lunch. What's on the menu? Roast native parrots and wild celery and spruce beer? Some special little indigenous delicacy that stops the crew contracting scurvy? For they don't get sick like many others do, Jim's crew. Jim sits down at the table that has been brought up onto the deck and laid with starched linen and silver. It is sunny. The sea sparkles. The mountains rise steeply up out of the water. There is a deep, old, mysterious silence. Jim grunts with satisfaction and helps himself to another portion of roasted parrot. He quaffs another mug of beer. The sun and the drink affect him a little and he goes after lunch for a lie-down.

'He can afford a short rest before the next leg of the trip. Tomorrow he will set sail along the coast to chart the southern island, and then he will go off to the east coast of New South Wales. He lies in his cabin and his mind is full of the images of lush bush and glittering sea and hot sunshine. Yes, definitely he will have to find a way to come back. In the meantime, he will get the ship's artist to make a watercolour so that he can look at it on his other journeys.'

I stop talking to assess the spread of the water. The entire floor is covered with a shallow, rank-smelling tide. My feet are numb. Horatio does not yet float.

'Do you think that Captain James Cook is far away from the expansion of French happiness? He is not. As he is rounding the top of New Zealand, a storm causes him to narrowly miss meeting the French explorer J. F. M. de Surville. Although over a hundred and twenty years have elapsed since the visit of Abel Tasman, two Europeans are suddenly in the same place at the same time, albeit completely unaware of each other.

'They go about the same area, naming and renaming. Monsieur de Surville and crew are currently having quite a pleasant time with the locals. The natives are bringing fish to trade for calico, and the captain has swapped clothing with a chief of the area. The chief now has a coat and red breeches and a shirt, and Monsieur de Surville has the chief's dogskin cloak. Unfortunately, de Surville's crew are not well – many are ill with scurvy and quite a few are dying. They have to go ashore for fresh supplies and are not thrilled with the fern-root staple. They do like the fish, however, which is cooked in an earth oven – I can't recall the name of it – that imparts a unique, somewhat smoky flavour and great succulence.

'But after this it's all downhill, I'm afraid. De Surville alleges the locals have stolen a dinghy that broke free from the *St Jean Baptiste* in a storm, and he punishes them by taking a hostage and destroying some canoes and huts. The hostage leaves New Zealand with his captors, and dies three months later of dehydration and despair. Two weeks after this, on April the 8th 1770, de Surville himself drowns while trying to go ashore at Chilca, Peru.'

I am interrupted by Horatio, who has begun to moan and fling himself about. I look down and see the fetid water is up to my ankles. Horatio is not floating, but drowning – or choking. I stare in horror at the objects in the water: a mangle of drowned rats, a truss of bloodied bandages, a chicken skeleton, an eyeball, a smeared chamberpot, several tarnished spoons, five cracked cupping glasses, an assortment of knives – kitchen, barber and surgical, and the carcass of a threadbare cat.

'Help,' I shout. 'We are drowning in debris.'

No one comes. A large black beetle, legs clawing at the air, is swept on a current towards Horatio's wailing, toothless mouth.

～

I wake up. I must have dozed off. It is pitch black outside. At first I think I'm waiting for the keepers to rescue me, and then I realise my feet are no longer in water. There is now only a thick layer of sediment which I can squelch between my toes. I am not hungry, and my bladder is empty. I look at Horatio. He is lying still and quiet on an irrepressible dark shape which is certainly dry straw.

Then I remember that we were taken from the flood by the steward and several keepers when they carried out an inspection of the lower tunnels by candlelight and barge; that we were chained to a wall in a higher chamber until the water had drained away through the cracks and crevices in our own; that when we were returned, the floor remained covered with a thick brown slime studded here and there with all those objects too large to flow out with the polluted liquid.

'Just get that stinking cat out,' I shouted at the thewless half-cripple who, waving a club, drove me back in a straitjacket to the midden. He muttered something inaudible and went off to fetch Horatio in a wheelbarrow.

Porlock has been absent since the flood. Just as I am wondering what has happened to him, he reappears.

'Where have you been?' I ask.

'Home ill,' he says churlishly. 'I caught a miasma from the thaw.'

'I've been waiting for you.'

'You can hardly do anything else.'

'Porlock, go and find the map.'

'What?'

'You heard me. Look for it and bring it to me.'

'You *are* mad. I told you before, I'll lose my job if they catch me sniffing round the property.'

'It's my map. I authorise you.'

Porlock laughs contemptuously, as I knew he would.

'If you bring it to me, I will give it to you.'

He looks incredulous. 'What for?'

'As payment to help me get out of here.'

'What am I going to do with a thing like that?'

'You can sell it. I will tell you who to go to.'

'How much will it fetch?'

'I don't know. I've lost touch somewhat.'

'What if it's worthless?'

'It's a matter of finding the right person.'

'So, I'm to go dashing about all over town trying to find a buyer?'

'Don't be tiresome, Porlock. You will take it to an address that I will give you. That man will find the buyer. Then you'll get your money.'

'How long will it take?'

I shrug. 'If you were capable of giving me accurate information about the world . . .'

'Who says I can't give accurate information about the world?'

'Porlock, you can't even remember what you had for dinner yesterday.'

'Yes I can. It was bread and cheese and that's all. I've been off work and I had to pay the candlestick maker . . .'

'Look, what have you got to lose? You'll set me free, and I'll make good any shortfalls in your expectations.'

'I get charged for escapees. Against my wages.'

I sigh wearily. 'Just get the map and I will give it to you. You will take it to an agent who will sell it on your behalf. Then you can free me. When you've got the money in your pocket.'

'And what if your agent turns me over to the law for theft? What if you're trying to trick me?'

'Porlock, you are both cunning and stupid in equal measure: cunning enough to suspect a trick, but too stupid to realise that I'd gain nothing from it.'

'There's no call to be insulting.'

'I can direct you to a man who knew that map was mine; I can give you a letter with my signature authorising him to sell the map and give the money to you. Would that suit you?'

'It might. If I could be sure of three things.'

'What are they?'

One, the map is yours and I'm not stealing something belonging to the physician. Two, you're not going to change your story and set the constables on me.'

'And three?'

'Three what?'

'You said three things.'

'Did I?' Porlock blinks. 'Well, anyway, I'd have to be able to find it and take it without a fuss. Last time I was in the offices . . .'

'When was that?'

'Not so long ago. Anyway, I got interrupted by the steward when I'd just opened the books . . .'

'What had you read?'

'I didn't get time to read anything,' he snaps. 'I heard a noise . . .'

'Well you must have seen something.'

'No, nothing, I . . .'

'You can't bloody well read, can you?'

He turns beetroot-red. 'Well, what of it? I can read names and dates. I can recognise a fucking map when I see one.'

'No wonder you're so suspicious. All illiterates are suspicious. They never know whether the letter they hold in their hand is a promissory note or a death warrant.'

Porlock frowns deeply. 'You're not doing your own cause any good.'

'You could show my letter to someone you trust first. To verify its contents. Your wife.'

'That old shrew! She'd steal the document from under the mattress I slept on. Turn it into bonnets and marzipan.'

'I'm glad to hear you've got such a happy marriage.'

'Anyway, she can't read either.'

'Well, your eldest son, or a friend.'

'My eldest son is on a ship somewhere. Probably the bottom of the ocean. And I don't trust my friend.'

We seem to have reached an impasse. But still Porlock can't seem to let it go. His greed works away at him. 'I'll sort it out in my own mind,' he eventually says.

Small chance, I think.

'Then we'll see,' he adds before going out.

～

The clouds lift and the days lengthen. Soon the sun shines every day. The keepers display a holiday mood. They shed their reeking jackets and I am treated to the fetid odour of humid oxter. They are forever salivating and gesticulating over women in their summer scanties, certain that the women's light dress is an invitation, even deliberate provocation.

But summer is a difficult time for me, the period of my deepest resentment. The keepers – drunks, illiterates and failures to the last man – can sling their discarded jackets over their shoulders and walk out whistling into the pleasures of the late sun. For me, the late sun is merely an annoyance that keeps me awake for longer – or would, if I could ever sleep.

The image of a keeper walking, whistling, warm, looking at women, eating and drinking from the streetsellers' stalls, burns into my brain. My brother, a clergyman, always used to declare it an inadequacy to need to find the world outside oneself. Everything a man needs is inside, he admonished. If a man experiences boredom and emptiness when alone, it is because he has become accustomed to being filled up by the world, can no longer fill himself.

Well, it's easy for my brother – he wasn't interested in the world; merely liked to read it the rules, that's all. And he's a close relative, unrelated to me, of the man who said we have to hold ourselves back from the merenessess. But I liked being filled up by the world. What else can a life consist of but this slow, steady distillation? In it goes, drop by drop. What else is there?

'Horatio what do you think the time is? Why won't the sun go down – these evenings are like an afternoon that never ends. Would you like to hear the conclusion to the voyages of Captain Cook, since we are to be awake for half the night? I am sure it will divert you from your empty belly and your boredom, not to mention your lingering disgust at our minders' malodorous bodies and beliefs. Yes? Here we go then.

'It is 1771. Since the great southern continent has not been discovered the government decides another trip is in order. Cook is to set sail in the *Resolution*. Don't you love the earnest names? How can the British fail in the battle with the French, with names like *Resolution* and *Endeavour*? I am twenty-one years old, excited as any young man about the exploration of foreign places. I follow all the news avidly. Joseph Banks storms off in a huff over the standard of accommodation aboard this second vessel, and a new natural historian is appointed, Johann Forster. In 1778 Forster produces *Observations Made During A Voyage Round The World*. Round the world! What a claim!

'But I am getting ahead of myself. Cook has a plan to do three low sweeps into the cold southern waters. Queen Charlotte Sound is to be his rest and recreation base. Between sweeps one and two, Cook goes off to Dusky Sound for six weeks. You probably can't imagine the country, Horatio: Queen Charlotte Sound is at the top of the southern island, and Dusky Sound is at the bottom of the same island but to the west. It is a magnificent fiord and I bought a sketch of it myself. I hope to be able to show it to you one day.

'After these three sweeps, and after failing to discover the great southern continent – or, more accurately, succeeding in proving the nonexistence of it – Cook goes on to Tahiti for the winter. There, he takes on board Omai, a native, who arouses great interest when he is brought back to England.

'The final voyage is in pursuit of another geographical myth, a northwest passage linking Europe and the east. There are two boats, *Resolution* and *Discovery*, and I go off to Plymouth in July 1776 to see them off. I am now twenty-six years old, newly married and slowly realising that all my adventures are going to be rather local and landlocked in comparison to those of the men standing on the decks before me. I stand there wondering at the distance and the danger: cannibals and diseases and storms. But I am still envious. If I could, I would have slung away my safe life to board Cook's ship, to have had Omai's experience in reverse. But I have to watch them all sail away out of sight. They go straight – well, via the Cape of Good Hope – to Queen Charlotte Sound for a nice summer holiday, two weeks in all, from February the 12th to the 25th. I am glad I do not know this as the boats sail off: my envy would be insupportable.

'After Tahiti again, Cook goes on to survey the northern Pacific coasts of America and Siberia. The boats then return to the Sandwich Islands in the northern summer of 1778–79 and our hero, James Cook, dies in a fracas there on February the 14th. I do not believe he was eaten, as Porlock alleges. Porlock's drunken mind has simply got cannibal, sandwich and cook all mixed up . . .'

~~~

'Speak of the devil,' I murmur as Porlock comes rushing in.

'What's the time?' I ask, quite roughly, for I do not wish to be entertained by him at the present moment.

'Gone midnight. I've got it.'

'Got what?'

'The map you told me about.'

'Let me see it.'

He wafts it in front of my nose. It is indeed the one. I'd recognise it anywhere.

'Where was it?'

For some reason I feel a little breathless, as though someone has winded me. It is shock, I think. That I may have been put here to be robbed.

'In the physician's office. It doesn't look like much to me.'

'You have to understand how far away that country is. How young. It's easy to draw a map of a local familiar area. That's not what you hold.'

'Can't see the point myself. I mean, it doesn't tell you how to get there and it won't look like this when you arrive.'

'I doubt that a man with your attitudes would ever arrive.'

'I could go out there if I wanted to. Happens that I don't.'

'This is ridiculous, arguing about such things at one o'clock in the morning. Do you want to proceed with our plan or not?'

'I'm still in several minds.'

'Yes,' I agree, sighing. 'A pity one of them isn't your own.'

'What?'

'It doesn't matter.'

Porlock starts to walk about the cell. 'I'm assessing the risk,' he announces pompously. 'There isn't much money about, you know. What with food shortages and income tax.'

'Income tax was introduced while I was still a free man. I'd have thought people would have adjusted to it by now.'

Porlock looks outraged. 'Does anyone adjust to daylight robbery?'

I decide to change the topic. 'You seem to eat well enough in spite of food shortages.'

'How would you know? I can't recall anything but thin soup and sour ale and old bread for months. There's riots, and the government has had to give out charity to stop us going the French way.'

'You told me that story in 1801.'

'Did I?' he asks, blinking stupidly.

'Anyway, why would the people go the French way? The rich remain rich even when the ordinary folk are starving. And for once that is to your advantage. You have something to sell when there isn't much worth buying. The rich still have to spend – otherwise what's the point in being rich?'

Porlock grunts and continues to walk. He steps over Horatio as if he is a sack of kindling waiting to be put on the fire. Then he comes to a halt directly in front of me and says, 'I will do it.'

'Excellent. You will need to bring me a pen and ink and good paper. There must be a sheet in the physician's office. But you must put the map back until I have written the letter.'

'What? I don't like all this going in and out. It's too dangerous.'

'If you take the map now they may notice its absence before we execute the plan. You will certainly be under suspicion. If it were me, I'd have the keepers' houses searched.'

'Would you, you miserable bugger.'

'Indeed. Now be a sensible fellow and put the map back until I've written the letter.'

When Porlock has gone, I look down at Horatio.

'We are going to be freed!' I exclaim. 'Both of us. I will come back to get you, rest assured.'

I watch his body carefully. Nothing moves. There is not even a twitch of a muscle: indeed, I can scarcely see him breathing.

'There's no one there, is there, Horatio? Inside you, I mean.' I wait for a moan, for anything to indicate his disagreement. Nothing happens.

'Now that we will soon be leaving, I confess I am worried about you – will I have to confine you to a bed on my third or fourth floor, arrange a nurse for you, have you hand-fed and cleaned like a baby? Worse, will I have to carry on telling stories to an absence? Or are you going to snap out of it?'

I stop, still expecting a reaction. Horatio lies as motionless as a corpse.

'On most of our days together I admit I chose to ignore the knowledge of your mental absence,' I tell him severely. 'I carried on, acting as if my talk had some effect on you. And yes, to tell you the truth, I felt that your putative listening made my stories better. I tried harder for your sake, always attempted to assemble them according to the proper method. For myself, I could merely have uttered a string of words, floccinaucinilipilification, chatoyant, sprezzatura, etcetera, for the miracle and the despair to have opened up for me.

'But on the bad days, Horatio – yes, there were some very bad days – I fell silent and knew that it made no difference. You were not amused, distracted, comforted or enlightened. I was alone. No one heard me. Your human essence had wasted away as quickly as the embroidered waistcoat I imagined you wearing in the early days.'

I stop again. It is necessary to give a man a chance.

'I'd dreamed up a whole biography for you, Horatio,' I continue mournfully when Horatio remains silent and still. 'I endowed you with abilities and talents and adventures that no doubt you never had, never even thought of. I do this sort of thing all the time – attribute wonderful characteristics to nobodies, invent exciting adventures for dullards and stay-at-homes. Then I'm jealous of their lives, these lives that are my own invention! I'm also unbearably disappointed when the scales fall away from my eyes and I'm confronted with the bitter truth.'

Then I close my mouth and do not talk any more. Of course I will return to rescue him, but a man who can't even groan at the mention of his own freedom is nothing more than a shell.

~

I wait patiently for Porlock to fetch me the paper. I accept that he must wait until a suitable opportunity presents itself, but he takes so long I fear he has forgotten our plan. A howling wind rises and lasts for days. I look towards the small window and see the first desiccated leaf flying through the air. The autumn will be early this year. I feel a surge of excitement as I realise I will not have to endure another winter in chains.

On the fourth morning of waiting I am about to begin my word search again, purely for amusement, when Porlock rushes in. He is out of breath and all red in the face.

'What's the matter?'

'It's gone.'

'What's gone? For God's sake, stand still and get control of yourself.'

'The map. I put it back and now it's gone!'

'Bah – you probably forgot where you put it. Look in the next drawer.'

'No, don't you understand, there is only one drawer. It's the drawer in the physician's desk. Where he goes over the books and things.'

'Well, did anyone notice you creeping about in there, you old fool?'

'No! I was the only one anywhere near the office. The apothecary is in court today; the surgeon is drunk, and the steward is sick. The two male keepers were with the lunatic in the iron collar, and the female keeper was getting screwed by the coalmen in the linen closet.'

'Not necessarily today, gomerel.'

'I went to get the pen and ink and paper,' Porlock continues wildly, 'and I thought I'd just take a tiny peek at it, and what do I find? Nought. I rifle . . .'

'Riffle.'

'. . . through the papers there, thinking the map has been hidden by something else, but no. It was gone, I tell you. Vanished. Stolen!'

'Come now, I am sure it has just been moved for safekeeping. Somebody must suspect something. You'll just have to lie low for a little while, that's all. Why should anyone suddenly make off with it after all this time?'

Porlock starts to grumble and mutter incoherently.

As he goes out I call, 'And when you find it again, leave it there till we get the letter written, there's a good man.'

~∽

Two days later, Porlock scurries in, breathless again.

'I heard Mr Haslam talking about the map,' he announces between gulps of air.

'So?'

'He told his assistant that it's finally been uplifted. Yes, uplifted – that's definitely the word he used.'

'Has it now?'

'"After all this time," he said. "We've been telling them to come and get it for years."'

'Have they indeed? And did he name the thieving bastards who took it?'

'Yes, he did.'

'Do you still recall those names?'

'Yes. I made a special effort to remember. I repeated them to myself a dozen times or more. . .'

'And what were they?' I interrupt.

'They were Thomas and hearty Miss Lonsdale.'

THE BEGINNING

> *'For some cryen, & lepe, & hurt*
> *& wounde them selfe & other men,*
> *& derken & hide them self in privy*
> *& secret places'*

WHEN I COME TO, I am in a chair. I look around. Everything is unfamiliar. I am about to stand up, seek help, when I notice that I am fastened to the chair with leather straps: leather straps are around my waist and wrists, and my ankles are similarly tied. I look about, apprehensive. I appear to be in a dungeon. The place is quite gloomy apart from where I sit. Indeed, a strange light falls only on me, a light that seems to fall, uninterrupted, straight from the heavens.

And then the deluge hits me. Freezing water hits my head from high above. Tons of dark water. Water as dark and heavy as coal. I bite hard into my own tongue in shock. My neck falters like the weak stem of a flower. The water freezes the blood in my veins, stuns my heart.

As it cascades off my naked body, I look up, only to see the next drowning falling like a dark blanket. It comes down and smothers my face, smothers my breathing. I eat it, drink it, gargle it, choke on it, and then it flows away down my arched spine and braced shins. I don't dare look up again. I try to hunch up, but the effect, given my restraints, is minimal. Down comes the water like the wrath of man: never was a god so angry with the tied and naked, the true innocent.

On and on it goes, water falling like thick blankets, like coal, like gravel, like black hail, like night, like the end of the world. And there is no way to resist or withstand or detach yourself from it: you are present body and soul to the last drop, present to your stomach flying out of your mouth onto the floor, present to your bladder opening onto the chair, and then your bowels give way like a mudslide, and you could wail at the cold liquidity of the world except that your own mouth will certainly drown you. Then you are absent, and a while later you find yourself inexplicably fettered in a bed, but in dry darkness, and anything dry seems like mercy.

~

I wake up. It is light. I find myself lying on a pallet in a cell that is otherwise quite empty except for a chamberpot in one corner. The cell is unheated. I am chilled under the thin blanket. I try to make sense of where I am, but discover that certain necessary portions of connective tissue are missing: one minute I am safe and sound in my own life, the next I am being drenched in a dungeon. Supposing that the drenching is a nightmare, I expect to wake up in my own bed. But the nightmare continues. And I know now that I'm fully awake.

I get up and begin to pace about the cell to stimulate the move-ment of my semi-frozen blood. Absurdly, I feel like crying. Absurd, because I am sure my tears are frozen – and because nothing could be achieved by it but an even greater sense of helplessness, hopelessness. There are some who believe that tears are a catharsis; but I have always thought that the more we cry, the more we find reason to. The hot liquid tears appear to have a life of their own, however, as if they would cry me rather than me them, and they begin to trickle unbidden down my cheeks.

A flunkey enters with a bowl and spoon.

'Where am I?' I cry out.

'Don't you know?'

Before I can answer, he laughs and says, 'Of course you don't. Otherwise you wouldn't be here. You're in the lunatic asylum. Bedlam to be exact.'

'But what am I doing here?'

'Doing? You're not doing anything. You're *being* mad.'

I slump down on the pallet in shock.

'Now, do you want some of this soup or not?'

I shake my head and push his spoon away. In great agitation, I rub my scalp which still retains the flesh-memory of the flood. The flunkey runs to fetch the general factotum. As they come in together, the former is saying, 'He's refusing his soup, sir. If you ask me . . .'

'I didn't ask you, Mr Porlock,' the general factotum replies harshly. He comes over to me. 'Well now, one soaking not enough to drown your mad ideas?'

'Fetch the physician,' I say coldly.

'Listen to him – the lunatic thinks that the physician waits upon *his* pleasure. I can assure you, the physician is not within one mile of these walls. He came yesterday and will not come for another three months.'

'Thank you for that information. Now fetch your superior.'

'And what superior of mine would bother with you, may I ask?'

'I don't know – God?' I answer sarcastically.

'I'll fetch God then, shall I?'

I don't have time to reply before he goes out with great commotion, declaring that the lunatic desires God to be brought to him. I become a little worried at this turn of events. I resolve to exhibit the most straitwaistcoated rationality at the earliest opportunity.

But circumstances are against me. I am dosed by the flunkey

with henbane or hellebore or somesuch, dosed to the point of complete intoxication, and then I am sustained in that state for many days with opium and alcohol. I quite fail to make sense, even when I am intermittently sensible enough to do so. I slur my words, lose track, traction, skid off the sides or ends of my own sentences without coming to a proper stop. My plea of sanity is irreparably harmed.

In the light of my allegedly recurring madness, the deluge treatment is repeated. It is the darkest depths of winter. It is so cold that my breath hangs in the air like an emanation. My teeth chatter while I sit naked and tied to the chair, waiting for the freezing water. I look up to see it flying down upon me like ectoplasm; but when the water hits, it is like something solid. It almost snaps my neck. My head bobs uncontrollably. Blood fills my mouth as my teeth close on my cheeks. As the water drains away, I sense full consciousness ebbing with it. As if I'd have to make a determined effort to perceive things with the usual acuity. A blur, a softness creeps over my brain . . .

～

I wake up. I am again on the pallet in the cell and again cold. And surprised, as if some part of my brain expects to find that the pallet, the cell, Bedlam itself, will have vanished. The flunkey Porlock brings me some tepid soup which I accept with pronounced docility. He says that after lunch he will take me to stand in front of the big fire in the long gallery. I feel a rush of affection for him that's even more absurd than my frequent tears. Here is a man who still remembers that other men need to be warm, fed, comforted.

And in the afternoon he does indeed take me to the fire in the long gallery, and I stand before it toasting myself, grateful as an unrepentant sinner in hell. After a time, I turn my back to the flames and look upon the mayhem in the gallery. In every corner, and also in the centre, each lunatic enacts his own particular lunacy, whether by bellowing like a beast, or tearing at his clothes, or rocking on all fours. And dotted here and there un-mad looking souls are watching these performances with resigned acceptance or mute astonishment.

It does not occur to me in these early days to seek freedom by joining forces with the lucid; I am still convinced that, so far as I am concerned, a mistake has been made which will soon be rectified. I am waiting to be saved. I am, at this point, still a believer in the notion that a man cannot be saved by those enduring a similar plight. In fact, it is only those who share your plight who can be relied upon to take an early interest in its alleviation.

But I wait. I am confident I will recognise the man whom my family will send to save me. Confident that he will recognise me. He will recognise the quality of cloth that I am cut from. I will not even have to speak: from twenty paces, he will see sanity, quality, in my bearing.

My drownings continue at irregular intervals. Nobody, neither the physician nor apothecary, interviews me afterwards to assess their efficacy. The treatment is good because it is done. On the few occasions when I have remained semi-conscious, I have been dragged back to the cell by the keepers and thrown wet into the bed. I have to presume that I get exactly the same treatment when I have blacked out, but of course you can never be sure. Perhaps it is then that the mad-doctors cluster round, noting whether my devils have indeed been frightened away.

I complain about the water treatments to Porlock.

'You object to the drench, do you?' he replies. 'In some places there's far worse. There's the cage where they wind you down unsuspecting into a big tub of freezing water. And to add to the fright, they put the blindfolds on. There's also the bridge that collapses when you walk over it and down you go into a cold bath of surprise. I've seen both of them. And I've heard it said that some lunatics are chained inside a deep well which is filled slowly with icy water. They're half drowned and half frightened to death.'

'I don't doubt that such tortures exist,' I reply bitterly. 'Before I came here, a physician, who was once a friend of mine, acquainted me with the old treatment called *Usque ad deliquum*. He said that lunatics would be suspended head-first under water until their upper parts were drowned. They were afterwards revived – if this was possible. My physician friend said many were permanently drowned, mad ideas and all.'

'Well then,' Porlock says. 'Count yourself lucky.'

'Lucky? When I have fallen into the hands of lunatics? To think that my friend the physician once amused me with his stories! Can you believe that in the treatment I've just been telling you of, permanent drowning was always attributed to fear, or a lack of personal strength? And sometimes water treatments were augmented by shutting the patient up for the night in a church where, alone and fettered, he might be visited by ghosts and spirits, or the blind fear of them, and be driven by pure terror out of his insanity?'

'Yes, everything's much better now,' Porlock comments happily.

I stare at him incredulously. 'So you think the treatment we now endure can be considered an improvement?'

'There is science in it,' Porlock replies.

'Demonstrated by measuring and adjusting the height and the stream of the water? Are we reassured? Too mad to know that a measured and adjusted pondus of water is still a pointless assault upon the shaven head of God's creatures?'

'You're God's creature, are you?' Porlock laughs. 'You crazy bastard!'

⁓

Between treatments, I pester Porlock with questions. But gradually I realise that he has that peculiar failing of the habitual drunk: a memory that keeps on re-arranging itself as it erases the facts. Sometimes an answer he gives fills me with hope; and then that hope is crushed the next time I see him and he disavows all of his former statements. Eventually, I no longer question him about my situation, no longer demand the apothecary or physician at every visit. Then one evening he is watching me eat my soup – if eat is the correct verb for food so liquid – and he mentions hospital visitors. I stop eating, the spoon halfway to my mouth, and look at him closely. He does not appear to be drunk, and so I press him for details.

Yes, he assures me, rich folk pay to view the lunatics. He pulls out a piece of paper from his pocket.

'What have you got there?' I ask.

'A ticket,' he replies.

'A ticket for what?'

'Why, it's a ticket to visit yourselves, the lunatics.'

'Let me see,' I demand. I want proof – proof that these hospital visitors do indeed come to see us, proof that someone who can help me will soon appear.

'The lunatic wants to see?'

'I'm a perfectly sane man,' I retort. 'Not that you'd be able to tell.'

'You're sane, are you? Tell me, then, what year is it?'

'1801.'

'Wrong. It's 1794. Look, it says so on this ticket.'

Porlock comes over to me. He wafts the ticket about under my nose. 'It permits the holder and three friends to visit the madhouse on a Monday or Wednesday between the hours of ten and twelve. Signed by the Governor. I told you there were rich visitors.'

'1794!' I cry as my fresh hope crumbles.

'Not much of an improvement on the days when they charged a penny at the gate on Sundays and any riff-raff could come in,' Porlock carries on. 'And they came in droves – thousands there were.'

'Thousands of visitors?' I repeat incredulously.

'Over a long time,' Porlock explains. 'Many years. Came to see the ladies in the near-nuddy, I reckon. Came to listen to all your mad stories, your claims to be princes or pirates or angels. It was – well, bedlam. So they say. Now only the rich ones come, or the ones with the right connections. Quality.'

'But they still come?' I persist.

'Of course. Why else would there be tickets? And they don't always like what they see, I can tell you. Not that we let them see the worst, mind. Never let them in the locked wing. And we don't let them see the books either, although even the scullery maid knows it's all lies about the deaths.'

'Deaths?'

'They don't write them all down,' Porlock says conspiratorially. 'There's no shortage of bodies, let me tell you. Only a shortage of funerals.'

'It's not 1794,' I tell him after a short silence while I let the truth sink in. 'That's an old ticket. Don't think you can fool me. I was still a free man when the King was executed.'

'King? What King?'

'The King of France. Louis XVI of course.'

'Well, I don't know anything about that. The only king I know of is a madman like the rest of you.'

'Only when he says he's the King, it's not a symptom?'

Porlock doesn't reply.

'And when he says people are out to get him, he's dead right?'

Porlock grunts derisively.

'The year is 1801 at least . . .' I shout, angry that my hopes have been raised and dashed again.

'1802 *actually*,' Porlock sniffs.

'And I'll never believe in your hospital visitors until I see one!'

~

Porlock is the keeper who attends me most often. He's a sturdy fellow with a good heart, most of the time, but he's given to teasing when sober, and forgetfulness when drunk. At first I believe he only drinks at home since I do not often smell drink on his breath, and perhaps this is true at the start. But either my sense of smell becomes more acute or the drinking becomes more frequent, because soon he stinks of liquor at all hours, and his behaviour and memory become infuriatingly unpredictable. Since I cannot have a sensible conversation with him, I amuse myself by lecturing him about treatments and theories I learned from my ex-friend the physician.

'Can you believe it,' I exclaim, as he waits for me to consume another of my rude meals. 'There are rich and fashionable people out there in the world, right now, taking themselves off to expensive and fashionable spas for the water cure. Willingly, all over Europe and England.'

'Are there?'

'Certainly. And if I'm not mistaken in my belief that what's good for lunatics soon becomes good for the whole population, the rich and eminent will shortly be dumping water on themselves from a great height, wrapping themselves in wet sheets, and directing jets of icy water up their back passages. That last is the French way, of course. The Arabs, I've heard, prefer a leech attached to the same part of their anatomies. To suck the madness out. And why their bums you might ask?'

'I didn't ask,' Porlock interrupts.

'Because the Arabs fear that a leech on the neck will suck their souls out instead. As for the French, the efficacy of their treatment relies on shocking, on causing a revulsion in the physical system. Apparently an iced enema does the trick.'

'I'm sure it does.' Porlock replies.

'But the really important question is whether treatment is to be applied to the *seat* of madness – that is, the head – or to distant and diverse sites, as if madness has exploded throughout the body. Or perhaps it is the cure that is to explode through the body, to destroy the seat of madness with small multiple detonations – I'm not precisely sure. Anyway, we, the English, prefer the unexploded theory of revulsion. Mostly. Certainly we can't abide any back-passage nonsense.'

'Can't we?'

'Well, not the *douche ascendante* anyway. Not that anyone can keep their ideas on this matter straight. I mean, is the icy-sheet treatment exploded or unexploded?'

'Who cares?'

I laugh. 'Perhaps it all makes sense in the end, if you excuse the pun. And poetic too, you've got to admit. They like a bit of poetry, the mad-doctors, otherwise they fear losing a sense of themselves as coming from the educated classes.'

'Do they?'

'Still, I'm sure the water cure at a luxury spa is pleasurable if only because one enjoys a full belly, a warm bed, an alcoholic haze and convivial company. Not that I'm truly convinced it's pleasure that is sought. Some of the *curistes* now go to the seashore and have taken to drinking seawater. I always thought salt water *drove* you mad, and that once a man started drinking it, he couldn't stop. But can't you just see them bending over in their fine clothes, their well-fed arses an invitation to Arabian leeches as they collectively lap the briny? Really, there's not that much difference between them and us – except that we are coerced into madness and they embrace it.'

Porlock, who seems to have been mesmerised by the vision of leeches on rich ladies' arses, shakes himself. 'Well, I can't stay here all day,' he says. He picks up my empty bowl. 'Much as I enjoy to hear you going on. And I'm sure having someone to talk to is a comfort for you.'

This comment enrages me.

'What possible comfort is it for me to tell of the lucid deliberately seeking remedies that keep the lunatics mad? What good does it do me to admit of a similarity between the *curistes* and myself, when they are intoxicated with salt water and I am as sharp as the day I was born? What comfort could it possibly be to me to know that the free rich choose seawater and cold wrappings over champagne and erotic love?'

Porlock is held back by this outburst. He stands at the door of the cell looking bewildered.

'Run along,' I manage to say soothingly. 'It is not to men such as yourself that my indignation is directed.'

~

My water treatments suddenly stop. I am left untreated in my cell for weeks. When I question the keepers about this, they shrug. I assume that some wrangle is going on in the outside world – a wrangle that will soon result in my release.

Then one night two keepers come in together and pull me from the bed. I am standing there quietly when one of them comes up quickly behind me. I turn in alarm, expecting the garrotte. He holds out his cloth blindfold and laughs. I remain docile while he ties it on. Then I am led by the arm out of my cell and into the passage, along which we proceed in a straight line for a short distance. Then we begin to turn corners. As we proceed, I am assaulted by the hircine reek of stale urine.

'Where are we going?' I ask anxiously.

'We are going to spin you,' comes the reply.

'What, on a spindle?'

'I told you he's mad. On the gyrator of course. To cure you.'

I tremble at the thought of another cure. I hang back in dread.

'Come on, hurry up,' the keeper says, pushing me. I fall over my own feet which are stuck to the floor as your tongue sticks to the roof of your mouth when you are terrified. But I am bundled along tripping and staggering, and I feel like I am being rushed to the gibbet before a judge has a chance to order a stay of execution.

We stop. A door is opened and I am pushed inside. Although I am blindfolded, an impression of immense light penetrates the bandage. And I sense a kind of spaciousness due to the echo of footsteps on the floor and a cool freshness in the air. For a moment I think that I have been thrust outside, but this is not the case. I hear rain begin on a roof that is high above me.

I am led by the keeper some distance into the room and then I am told to sit.

'Is there a chair?'

'There's one on the apparatus,' the keeper replies, and pushes me down by the shoulder. My backside lands on a hard surface, and then I feel straps being placed round my waist and ankles. I am completely terrified.

'You've made a mistake,' I cry. 'I'm going home. You've got the wrong man.'

'Just let me see,' I beg them, when nobody answers.

'There's nothing to see,' a keeper replies. 'You'll be going so fast everything will appear to melt.'

I hear a crank being turned somewhere off to my left. I hear metal meeting metal. The chair into which I am strapped begins to spin about the shaft to which it is attached. It turns slowly at first, and the first few rotations are not unpleasant, in fact are oddly exhilarating. But the chair keeps spinning and picks up speed. I experience the first rush of vertigo.

'Stop,' I shout, 'I'm afraid I will vomit.'

But they don't stop. The chair spins. I feel the gorge rising in my throat. The chair spins faster. Vomit flies out of my mouth. Three hundred and sixty degrees of vomit is sprayed around the room. The chair spins.

'Stop,' I cry out. 'My system is revolted, I assure you.'

But they don't stop. A kind of blackness begins to descend over my powers of reason. I vomit until there is nothing left. Even then my stomach heaves as if it seeks to throw itself outside my body. The chair spins. I feel something hot and wet on my legs. The spinning has loosened my bladder. The blackness in my brain turns a fiery red. The chair spins. The last thing I remember is the oozing warmth of shit.

~○

When I come to, I am back again in my darkened cell, chained to the bed. I lie there for a moment with my eyes shut, but underneath the stillness I can perceive the relentless spinning of the earth. Like a sailor who still feels the heave and curl of the oceans on dry land, I feel the globe turning around its own axis and also around the sun in the immensity of space. I hear the unlubricated roar of the earth turning beneath the silence.

After only one spinning treatment, I have lost that sense of stillness which once convinced us that we live on a flat and static earth; that sense of stillness which allows us to believe our eyes, and other senses, which deny our true velocity. I shouted, Stop, but who listened? And if I shouted, Stop, now, who would listen? The gods are far too pleased with their little marble.

Porlock comes in. He undoes me and gets me to stand up. I stagger a little, losing my balance on the spinning earth.

'You are all fools,' I say to him. 'You are so infatuated by your treatments, you have forgotten to examine their effects.'

'You pissed yourself, let your shit-bag go, and threw up all over the room. What other effect d'you want?'

'That does not constitute a definition of sanity as far as I'm concerned.'

'It defines, Mr Haslam says, an explosion. And, let me tell you, it is not your place to define sanity. And neither is it mine. I just do what I'm told.'

'Oh yes, the age-old protestation of the innocent.'

Porlock doesn't reply. He sits me on the bed and begins to feed me.

'*Saeva indignatio*,' I hiss, and thrust my face close to his. He reels back as if my breath reeked of garlic.

'Let me tell you,' he growls. 'Your words *are* your illness. Not a symptom. But one and the same. The very thing.'

'You don't even know what it means,' I reply sitting back.

'It has the same meaning as you saying you're the King of England or France or Shangri-la.'

'The King of England *is* mad; the King of France is dead; and Shangri-la I've never heard of. Did you make it up?'

'Who cares? Just learn to talk like the rest of us and you'll be cured.'

'Talk like you? Four-letter words garnishing a completely impoverished vocabulary? Yes sir, no sir, and can I lick your boots or your arse, sir. No thank you.'

'You're raving again. I'm going to tie you up. Then I'm going to tell the apothecary you're no better than you ever were.'

'Yes, tell him I'm incorrigible. Tell him I expressed my indignation at human folly in Latin.'

'I'll tell him you need another spin,' Porlock threatens before leaving.

~

They wake me again in the middle of the night. It is dark outside, without a moon. They do not blindfold me, and I believe from this that whatever they have in mind is not the gyrator. I am wrong. I am ushered into the pitch black and freezing room where I cannot properly see but can sense the malevolence of the apparatus. Several other startled souls are shoved in the door beside me. A flunkey enters with a burning sulphur. Its odour quickly pervades the large room. We are all strapped into the apparatus: two are put in the chair, back to back; myself and one other unfortunate are put into a higher up fixture, in which we do not sit but lie horizontally. I think about my position as I lie there waiting for the crank to be turned. All of my emissions will now be contained by the box as I spin. I fear that I will choke on my own vomit. I close my eyes and think of praying. I see the spinning world, the gods' marble, and decide otherwise.

The bed begins to spin. It is a peculiar, alien sensation, to spin while lying flat. The darkness and the burning sulphur contribute their own nauseating effects. The darkness has a depth that the blindfold did not, and now it is flowing furiously around me like the dark water of a whirlpool. The sulphur makes me feel as if I breathe the vapours of hell. The bed spins, faster and faster. I hear the loud cries of my fellow damned. I hear their loud and copious retching. Mingled with the sulphur, I can smell their defecations. I cry out, throw up, piss and shit myself with the rest, the best, of them. Round and round we go, round and round and round and round . . .

~

I never *experience* it stopping. I wake up later from a terrible blackness which I have no memory of slipping into. I wake up, and when the keeper gets me out of the bed, I stagger like a sailor. The keeper steadies me and I lift my head. A strange man is standing in the cell. He is dressed in a suit, and stands with his hands behind his back and his legs slightly apart. He holds his chin at a supercilious angle. Everything about him suggests a superior being – or attempts to.

'I am Mr Haslam, the apothecary,' he introduces himself.

'I am the King of France.'

The apothecary looks at me piercingly. 'Feeling better?' he inquires.

I don't trust myself to answer. Instead I study him carefully. He has curly black hair and Napoleonic lips. His face is that of a young man, but his body is portly, and he has the aggressively self-confident bearing of a man twice his age. There is something about him that is rather like a bull terrier: something unrelenting, pugnacious, and too close to the ground. He steps forward and I notice he has a large book under his arm.

'Ah, you noticed what I've brought you,' he says, following my gaze. 'Good. It is a poetry book. The physician has recommended that we try the poetry treatment.'

'What?'

'Yes. In some institutions – I can't say we've tried it much here – lunatics have been calmed by the rote learning of poems.'

He places the book on my bed.

'I don't need any treatment. I'm not ill. A terrible mistake has been made.'

'Every day you will select a poem and learn it by heart. One of the keepers will hear your selection each evening. You may have Sundays off.'

'Didn't you hear me?' I ask in a louder voice.

The apothecary raises his right index finger in warning. 'You are shouting so loudly I fear the whole institution can hear you. Please calm yourself at once, or I will have to fetch you a sedative.'

'You mean you will drug me into a stupor again.'

'If we are successful with the poetry treatment, we might continue with music.'

I am alarmed that the apothecary envisages my treatment to be ongoing, as if no one has told him that I am shortly to be returned home. I'm so alarmed I am speechless. Not a single sesquipedalian, Latinate objection enters my mind.

The apothecary and the keepers withdraw, and I turn to look at the book on my bed. I am suddenly afraid that it is an hallucination; that any second it will vanish, and the apothecary will re-enter with his pursuivants and pronounce a different, more terrible treatment.

But when I reach out to touch the book, it feels reassuringly solid. I pick it up and look at the title. It is an anthology, not the work of a single poet. I flick through it. There are contributions by the famous and by several lesser lights, and a significant number by that egregious poet *Anonymous*. This is better than their revolting exploding treatments. But do I start today? If I don't, perhaps it will suggest recalcitrance. I select *Elegy Written in a Country Churchyard*, that favourite of schoolmasters, possibly for ever more. And tomorrow I'll have a go at Marvell's coy mistress.

~

Every night I wake up in a cold sweat, expecting to be taken away and spun. But another period ensues during which, apart from the rote-learning of poems, I am left untreated. The apothecary does not return; the physician has never seen me while I'm conscious. I have given up demanding answers from the keepers. Not that I have lapsed into apathy – merely superficial acqui-escence. I've decided to be more compliant while the process of my release continues outside these walls.

Then one afternoon a keeper comes into the cell. He bundles me along the corridors to a large and fuggy room with an enormous fireplace in which a ferocious fire is burning. The apothecary's assistant is waiting for me. On a long high table close to him is an assortment of bottles and jars and tubes.

'What form of torture is practised here?' I ask, surveying the jumble.

'Cupping. Dry and wet.'

'I suppose that description makes sense to someone.'

'It will make sense to you within a very short time.'

'I want you to know that I'm not going to be the willing partner of a sadist.'

'I am not familiar with that word.'

The assistant sets a tray of small glasses to heat by the fire.

'I made it up. Let's say a sadist is someone who gets sexual pleasure from causing pain. His perfect partner would be someone who gets his pleasure from pain's infliction. I am not your man.'

'I take it you are suggesting that giving you treatment excites me?'

'That's right.'

'Nobody is that mad.'

'*Au contraire*. The French are mightily entertained by it. The Marquis de Sade, one of their most famous criminals and most famous lunatics, both being one and the same man, has written numerous books about it. They are banned from publication, and the French keep him alternately in jail or the asylum, but that doesn't stop people getting a great deal of enjoyment from the secret circulation of his works. I warn you, when the names of the writers of love poetry have died out with their effete mortal bodies, his name will remain. And your own treatments will be described by means of it.'

'Well, what can you expect from the French?' the assistant says disgustedly. 'One of their treatments at Salpêtrière is the *douche ascendante*. An enema by another name, and a perversion.'

'Ah, yes,' I laugh. 'Nothing like a stream of freezing water up your anus to bring back your sanity, eh?'

'I've heard some use hot water,' the assistant replies, looking ever more disgusted.

'Which just goes to prove that all that clysters is not cold.'

'What? What's a clyster?'

'A syringe of physick in the back passage.'

The assistant doesn't even have a twitch of a smile.

'And how has an English lunatic like yourself had access to a mad criminal's work?'

'Copies of the stories multiply. What better amusement for a bored aristocrat than to copy out the works of the Marquis and sell them, or even give them away, depending on the individual's interest in proselytising? In France when I was visiting they were easy enough to get – in comparison to other things my acting group collected.'

The assistant snaps his fingers at the barber who is standing by with his strop and razor, and indicates that he should proceed.

'When were you in France? We are at war with France,' he says contemptuously, and goes over to his glasses.

'I was in France many times before the revolution,' I tell him.

The barber forces my chin down to my chest and shaves my head. The assistant comes back with several warmed glasses and places two on my scalp. It is not unpleasant. He has not accidentally overheated them as I feared he might.

'And what is the purpose of this?' I ask.

'When the air inside the glass cools, blood will be drawn to your skin away from the congested area.'

'That is ridiculous. Do you suppose my head is a cavity filled with loose blood that can go wherever it wants?'

'If you mean, do I think your head is like a bucket – no, I do not. The blood runs through channels – but it can form blockages. The blockages make you mad.'

'And what happened to the notion that the plethora had to escape?'

'Oh, we don't believe that nonsense any more.'

'What do you believe?'

'We believe in the latest theory,' the assistant pronounces. Then he looks a little disconcerted with his own statement and adds, 'Which is the correct one.' Then he busies himself with pulling the glasses off my scalp.

'Is my madness leaving me?'

'There are large welts. I'm sure the congestion is decreasing.'

'And how will this decreased congestion be exhibited?'

'What?'

'I was wondering what sort of behaviour you might be looking for to confirm your theory.'

'Behaviour? I have welts – they are all I require.'

'I thought as much.'

The assistant looks satisfied with his treatment. 'That's all for today. Get the keeper to take him back,' he orders the barber.

I rub my head. My fingers pass over lumps of raised skin that are like scalds to the palate when soup has burnt your mouth.

The keeper arrives and takes me back to my cell.

The welts go down soon enough. As far as treatments go, cupping has a lot to recommend it. It is annoying but not painful; it is free of the more gross bodily evacuations that have accompanied several of my earlier treatments; it is even sociable, allowing one to converse pleasantly with the staff. And a brief respite in a warm environment is always to be welcomed.

I pick up my poetry book and read till late.

~⌐

Porlock comes in with a candle.

'What on earth are you doing here? It's the middle of the night.'

'I've come to hear your poem.'

'Now?'

'I forgot, earlier.'

'Go away. You woke me up.'

'I've got to hear it. I have to report to the apothecary.'

'Well, just tell him you heard it.'

'I need a title.'

'What?'

'He might ask me what it's called.'

'Well, make one up, for God's sake.'

'I can't. I'm not poetically minded.'

'Of course you can. Anybody can. Think of a topic.'

'Flowers?'

'Flowers will do. Now think of some attributes of flowers.'

'Um. Red, thorns, dewdrops . . .'

'There you are. There's your title. Now clear off.'

'I can't call it that.'

'Why not?'

'It's not . . . poetry.'

'How would you know, since you're a self-confessed philistine?'

Porlock stands over the bed, his anxious candlelit face shining grotesquely forth one minute, then melting back into darkness the next.

'Stop swaying,' I order him. 'And call it *Roses* if you want. I don't care.'

'How did you know it was about roses?' Porlock exclaims.

~

I am taken again to the cupping room. Of course the assistant cannot warm the glasses in my own unheatable cell. When I am seated, he announces, 'Wet cupping today.'

'Perhaps it's just me, but that sounds lascivious.'

'It is just you.'

The assistant snaps his fingers at the barber who advances to reshave my head. After he has finished, he quickly makes several small incisions in my scalp. I push him away angrily.

'Do you want the straitwaistcoat?' the assistant demands, equally angry.

'I want you to leave me alone,' I shout.

The assistant ignores me and takes the glasses over to the fire. While they heat up, he busies himself with various small tasks, as if he is avoiding a conversation.

'You don't want to talk about the science of madness today?' I badger him.

'I only wish to do my work,' he replies serenely. Indeed, he is so oddly serene he might have been mesmerised. I mention Mr Mesmer to him.

'That charlatan,' he croaks, in spite of himself.

'Charlatan, was he? Frankly, I can't see the difference between the two of you. He used a magnet to establish harmonious flow of the blood. You use cupping glasses.'

'He gave up the magnets, though, didn't he? Said that animal magnetism flowed straight from his own body into the bodies of his patients. Used it to provoke therapeutic crises. Cracked as his patients.'

'Whereas your therapy is in crisis without animal magnetism.'

'How amusing. You are probably ignorant of the fact that in 1784 a Royal Commission, having listened to the evidence of several eminent people, decreed that Mr Mesmer's powers were all in his imagination.'

The assistant goes over to the fireplace and tests the rim of a glass on the palm of his hand. He appears satisfied and brings the glasses over.

'Interesting experts, weren't they, these eminences? Benjamin Franklin and Antoine Lavoisier and Dr Guillotine.'

'Guillotin.'

'Whatever. How does expertise in head-chopping become expertise in mesmerism? I fear we live in a world where to be expert in one thing is to be expert in everything.'

The assistant applies a glass to one of the cuts in my scalp. 'This will suck the excess blood out,' he explains. 'And what is wrong with that?'

'It smacks of conspiracy. Of vested interests.'

'To be trained in thinking is to be able to apply it to any topic.'

'Ha – as if thinking had no thought and thought had no content.'

'I don't know what you mean.'

'The same old thoughts are applied to every new situation. And that is called thinking.'

The assistant doesn't answer. He is pulling off a glass which is dragging the skin with it.

'Tell me,' I say to distract myself from the unpleasant sensation, 'which war are we currently involved in?'

'We are still at war with France, of course. Against Napoleon. The Maltese didn't want to be given back to the Knights. They were happy with the English as their rulers. But Napoleon didn't like it. He said the Treaty of Amiens had been violated and so we are fighting again.'

The assistant has succeeded in separating the glass from my scalp. He puts it on the table in front of us. The inside of it is spattered with blood. He begins to pull the second glass.

'When was the Treaty of Amiens?'

'March the 27th.'

'What year?'

'This year. 1802. Are you losing track of time?'

'How am I supposed to keep track of it? Every day is exactly the same, apart from the rude interruptions of your vile and worthless cures. Every so often I lose count. And then I have to wait for a gomerel like yourself to restore me to the march of time.'

'Very pretty. And very insulting.' The assistant is inspecting his work. He looks pleased. 'I think you will have some relief from your madness now,' he says. Then he turns and motions to the barber to fetch a keeper.

'Tell me, what privileges – if any – will sanity restore to me?' I ask.

'What did you have in mind?'

'Apart from tipping the scullery maid over the back of a chair, I'd like to go out in the yard. I'd like to see the sky.'

The assistant frowns. 'I'll have to ask the apothecary about that.'

'About what – the maid or the yard?'

'Don't be disgusting.'

I look at him reflectively. 'You must all be in this together.'

'In what?'

'It's a conspiracy. It's as plain as the nose on your face that I am perfectly sane.'

The assistant grunts.

'Someone must have wanted something. Something that I have. Or rather, had.' I look at him carefully. It is the first time this has occurred to me.

'Most lunatics imagine we are plotting against them. That we are trying to poison them or send them to the gallows or otherwise hasten them to their graves. It's just a symptom.'

'Is it a symptom of King George's? Yes? But it also happens to be true. How many attempts have been made on the King's life to date?'

'Two or three, I believe.'

'Well, even if the King believed it to be twenty, or a hundred, it wouldn't change the fact that two or three criminals *were* out to kill him.'

The keeper arrives before the assistant can answer. I notice, however, that he looks quite unperturbed. If there is a plot, he does not appear to be part of it. He is the eternal perfect assistant: one who unquestioningly and uncritically carries out all the orders of his superiors; who even improves on their intentions a little; who sees flawlessness in theories about which even his superiors might have some doubt.

I am taken back to my cell. The blood stops quite quickly. I stand by the small window – it is too filthy to see much – and ruminate on the possibility of a conspiracy. Certainly, it is taking too long for my family, or their representative, to rescue me. Perhaps they do not even know where I am.

Mr Haslam comes to visit me soon after my return. 'My assistant tells me you are much improved after your cuppings. He says you wish to go out in the yard.'

'Does my family know I am here?' I demand.

The apothecary stares at me coldly. 'Is the assistant wrong? You do not wish to go outside?'

'Yes, I would like that, but . . .'

'Very well. I prescribe exercise in the yard to supplement your cupping treatment. An hour on fine afternoons should be sufficient.'

'You are not going to answer my question?'

'I am not in the habit of answering the questions of lunatics. All their questions are the same, and all of them forget what you tell them. Yes, an hour in the afternoons should do.'

'You could leave me out there all day, if you like. I could come in at night.'

'We don't want to overdo it, do we? Some of these treatments are strong.' Mr Haslam's eyes gleam with malice.

'Fresh air is a strong treatment?'

'For the mad, certainly. The outside world is where their madness began, and it never loses its capacity to cause relapse.'

'There is a wall around the exercise yard, is there not? That should be enough to keep the world out.'

'Indeed there is a wall. A very high one. But when a madman can see the sky, that is enough for him to imagine gods and demons and omens. To imagine the end of the world. To fear the unreliability of the sun.'

'And not just madmen either,' I murmur.

'Precisely. So when I prescribe the sky for you, you'll understand why I do so only in small doses.' Mr Haslam smirks. In fact, for him, the sky is psychologically inert. He is proud of his own uninfluencability. He sees it as an indicator of his immaculate sanity. I see it as a sign that he's got a long poker stuck right up his back passage.

～

For the first time since my treatments began, I am let out into the exercise yard. The lunatics are shuffling slowly round in a circle, but I've had enough of circles. I go and stand against the wall, crossing the yard carefully to avoid the human droppings. Everything is grey. The lunatics' faces, their clothes, the sky.

I stare up at the sky, that covering I once used to take for granted. There is nothing pearly about this greyness, nothing mackerel, mercurial, *gorge de pigeon* or moire. It is flat, low, dry, monotonous. But it is a wonder to me. Its changefulness – whether it changes while I am standing here or not – is guaranteed. The sky does not have two or three immutable qualities as does a ceiling, but an endless mutable capacity.

The thought makes me smile to myself. I reflect that all the ways of man are to stymie the changefulness of which the world is made. Yes, some changefulness needs to be controlled or we could not survive; but, as always, they (for I am not *them* any more) go too far with their carapace suits and pocket watches, their lists and timetables and categories and vows.

I look at the poor wretches endlessly circling, mimicking the rotations of the earth. Once upon a time, the mad danced. From the thirteenth to the sixteenth centuries, according to Paracelsus, there was an epidemic of dancing lunatics all over the continent. Nobody thought to lock them up. I can't help but wonder about this change. And if God watches us – I've got my own opinion about that – *our* audience is a man in a frockcoat with a watch and a list, ticking off correct moves in appropriate times; but *theirs* was a capricious monster in a golden cloak who loved to be entertained and sometimes provided the supper.

I look back up at the sky. It is still incorrigibly grey. I wonder how time is progressing. Have I been outside for five minutes or fifteen? How can I stretch out the time, make it seem as long as possible? I understand the absurdity of this, of course: the length of time is not a measure of enjoyment but a measure of boredom: all pleasurable time is short. But if only I could still be here when the clouds part! Then I could be happy for a little while – even until tomorrow.

Will it be fine tomorrow? For how long will I have to cherish this afternoon? Perhaps the weather will be bad for a few days, even a few weeks – it is winter after all. Still, it is the end of winter, and surely the snow is finished for the year. But then there is the rain to consider . . . I stop, feeling sheepish. Soon I will have wasted all my time fretting about pleasure's conclusion and the likelihood of its repetition; about *if* and *when* and *for how long* – all those little words that have terrorised humanity since they were first uttered.

A breeze teases my shirt. I look up at the sky. The breeze shoves a fat white cloud into the field of grey. Then another. In a short while, the greyness is nearly covered over by fluffy white clouds that bounce about like spring lambs. I laugh. Mr Haslam is right – the sky *is* a strong treatment.

Eventually – as it turns out, an hour is a reasonable length of time to stand against a wall looking at the sky – we are all ushered indoors. The evening meal is only a soup but it has large chunks of vegetable in it, thanks less to kindness than to a lazy kitchen-hand, no doubt. Never mind, I am satisfied. Afterwards, I stretch out on my bed and take out the poetry book. *Anonymous* has again acquitted himself brilliantly, even in such illustrious company.

~

I am taken again to the cupping room. I have cuts and blisters and lumps all over my head, but at least I have been outside, have seen the sun, the mutable sky. The assistant inspects my head.

'There is a good thick clot that has formed here,' he announces in a satisfied tone. 'The cups must have drawn it from the blockage that is causing your madness.'

'I think this clot is autochthonous.'

The assistant hesitates before admitting his ignorance. 'I don't know the meaning of that particular word.'

'It means aboriginal. A clot born here.'

'Well, this clot has travelled.'

'Really. Do clots travel?'

'Most assuredly.'

'You think your seduction has drawn the clot from somewhere else?'

'Certainly. From the seat of your madness.'

He busies himself putting the glasses on the tray and then sets the tray before the fire.

'I suppose you're right. Mad clots are always going off to other places where they're not wanted.'

'We *do* want the clot on the scalp.'

'You're a very literal sort of person, aren't you?'

'What do you mean? I don't know what you mean.'

'Think of Napoleon.'

'Oh,' the assistant says with relief. 'I thought you meant me. But I've never been anywhere.'

'Yes, you're definitely autochthonous.'

The assistant frowns, trying to work the conversation back to see if he's been insulted. He gets snagged somewhere and gives up without a struggle.

'You're not much of a word man, are you?'

'What?'

'Words don't excite you. You would consider extending your vocabulary as a waste of time.'

'Words are tools. I have the ones I require.'

'Do you? How do you know? What if a situation arose where you lacked the precise one you needed?'

'I can't imagine that.'

'What if you ended up in Bedlam being cupped by a clot born here?'

The assistant looks bewildered. 'I fear you are having an acute episode . . .'

'Perhaps you have drawn my madness out too assiduously. Perhaps it is here in the room with us and will infect you.'

The assistant tries a glass on the palm of his hand and removes it quickly, wincing. Then he comes towards me with the tray.

'I hope you've cooled those down properly, Lucifer.'

'They will be the correct temperature in a moment.'

'You've given me an idea, you know.'

'What idea?'

'I'm going to go through my poetry treatment book, and find all the words I don't know the meanings of; then I'm going to see if I can discover their meanings through context and cross-referencing.'

The assistant looks alarmed. 'It's not me that gave you that idea. The apothecary won't like it. You'll be dashing about saying all sorts of unintelligible things.'

'Actually, I rarely get to dash anywhere.'

'The apothecary says you have to become calm, achieve insight. He says he doesn't want to hear any more silliness coming out of you. He's against the poetry treatment for that very reason.'

'Is he now. Tell me, how am I to achieve insight without thought, and how am I to think without words?'

'You have sufficient already.'

'Do I? What if my problem is paranoia?'

'Para what? I don't know what that is.'

'Neither do I. I just made it up. But let's agree that it means you think the bastards are out to get you. Except that, because you're a lunatic, you are wrong. Now, wouldn't I need *that* word to gain insight?'

The assistant gives me a long cool stare. Then he goes to the door and calls for a keeper.

'I think you've had enough treatment today,' he says coldly while we wait.

'Paranoia – what a word, eh?' I needle him. 'A word fit for a king.'

~

The weather is bad for several days. The assistant tells me somewhere in the midst of this bad patch that it is the first day of spring. There is much bad weather in spring, he adds, or warns, as if I might not know this, as if becoming a prisoner in an asylum instantly erases all one's former knowledge.

I wait. And worry. So much time has passed, I have given up all hope of being rescued. I begin to realise that regaining my freedom has become my own burden. But I do not know the way out of the building, nor how many locked doors there are between myself and the outer wall.

A fine day finally arrives, as it always does, if only a man can wait long enough. I am let out into the exercise yard. The lunatics circle. I stand against the wall between two coils of dung. There is no part of the yard that is less thickly defiled. The corridors leading to the yard are also liberally decorated, as are the chambers off it. Indeed, the entire structure is an open sewer, which I myself would involuntarily contribute to, were it not for the privilege of the bucket. I am glad to be out in the fresher air. I pull up my ragged shirt sleeves, and the sun is warm and tender on my skin. I turn my face up to it and close my eyes.

The large gate creaks open. I look over. A man has just been admitted to the yard. He positions himself against the far wall and bends down to open a curvaceous leather case. He extracts a fiddle. And then a bow. He takes out his rosin and slowly rubs his bow while looking cautiously all around him. The circumambulating mad people take no notice. He raises the instrument to his shoulder and tries a few notes.

The lunatics stop dead in their tracks. They turn with open mouths to the sound, and the fiddler commences a jaunty reel. The lunatics stand stock still, gaping at him. He finishes the piece and begins a slower, more melancholic tune. The circle begins to break up, and the inmates move towards the fiddler and cluster round. I expect him to be alarmed, but evidently he believes he can cast a spell over them, and so he does. After ten or so light pieces in both major and minor keys, he stops. We watch him pack away his fiddle and bow. We watch him lock up the case. We watch him knock on the enormous gate and then disappear. After he has gone, the lunatics begin to clap wildly.

We do not remain in the yard long after the fiddler leaves. Without warning, a violent rainstorm begins. The keepers rush out to usher us all inside, and what an absurdity it seems to stop us getting wet in the rain while they attempt to drown us indoors.

That evening, Mr Haslam again enters my cell. 'What did you think of your music treatment?'

'That was all?'

'That is a beginning. We will see how it goes.'

'It stopped the lunatics walking in circles anyway.'

'You obviously consider that an improvement.'

'Don't you?'

'If the world fell out of its orbit because of the music of the spheres, would that be an improvement?'

'Possibly.'

'Hah, we would all perish.'

'As I said, possibly.'

'You are a man of the most incorrigible disposition. But tell me, which do you prefer of these new moral treatments – poetry or music?'

'I prefer the non-narrative arts.'

'Oh?'

'Narrative is pabulum, so I'm told.'

'Is that so? And do you not think that music can be a narrative?'

'It can certainly be imposed upon in that way. But it's not necessary. And not desirable.'

Mr Haslam smiles. 'As for me,' he suddenly announces, as if I might care a damn, 'I like a good story. A *true* one. I particularly like the story of human progress. Human progress through science.'

'Yes, that is a good story.'

'I detect cynicism in your voice. But think how our knowledge has improved our lives. Think about our knowledge of the planets . . .'

'Knowledge of the planets is irrelevant to an individual's life.'

'Ah, a modern heresy.'

'As far as I'm concerned, the angels might still be pushing the planets around. What difference would it make to me?'

'You prefer ignorance?'

'A prisoner has other concerns.'

'Such as?'

'The word.'

'The word and not the sentence?' Mr Haslam inquires, looking pleased with himself.

'As I said, I prefer the non-narrative mode.'

'What form of the non-narrative mode, pray tell, is your first choice?'

'The epiphanic.'

'I see that you are still a considerable lunatic.'

'And I see that you are so satisfied by your knowledge of the planets, you cannot see anything in front of your nose.'

'And I see that you are the most wanton recidivist and your new treatments suit you not at all.'

I suddenly feel as if I have gone too far. He is a surly creature, quite capable of depriving me of my poetry and music on a whim.

'In fact, my new treatments suit me very well,' I say in a moderately humble tone. 'I am feeling most . . . refreshed.'

Mr Haslam grunts. 'Let me inform you that it is not sufficient to appear no longer mad in the present. Insight is essential. You have to see, and admit, that you were mad in the past. You have to see and admit what constituted that madness. Can you do so?'

I look at him carefully. He has a strange glint in his eye, perhaps similar to that seen in the judge's eye by the Earl of Ferrets. As if a trick is going on. As if the verbal gymnastics required to answer the case can serve only to prove its opposite. I say nothing while pondering on the Earl of Ferrets trying with all his wit to prove his lunacy while I must attempt to prove my sanity by accusing myself of madness. Furthermore, I must denounce myself to this medical cockalorum in a manner that is distressingly devoid of polysyllables, Latin and contempt.

'Well?'

'I'm thinking about it.'

'Don't think too long. You may have all the time in the world, but I certainly do not.'

'I will tell you tomorrow.'

'Tomorrow I am going to the continent. My spring holiday. The south of France, actually. That will be nice, don't you think?'

'I don't know. Isn't there a war on?'

'Ah – you are not as mad as you pretend to be. In fact, I am not going to the south of France. I am not even going on holiday. I am going to remain here to prepare the summer remedies.'

'I thought you'd get the recipes straight from your grand-mother's cook.'

'Very amusing. Although there are some, perhaps many, who hand down secret recipes from generation to generation, I am not of their ilk. Their secret potions amount to nothing more than quackery. I myself use only known remedies, together with discrimination and judgement.'

'How excellent. What proportion of discrimination and judgement do you usually add to the hellebore?'

~

Porlock, who has been standing in the shadows during my conversation with the apothecary, walks over and looks straight into my eyes, as if he has lost something and hopes to find it there.

'I heard the apothecary say you're not as mad as you pretend,' he murmurs.

'I wouldn't be so gullible as to believe everything the apothecary says. If I were you.'

'Well, you're not me. I decide for myself what to believe.'

'Suit yourself.'

'I always do. But I'm not as ignorant as you think. I know a thing or two about Mr Haslam that might be news to some.'

'Such as?'

'Such as he didn't get his doctoring degree, even though he went to Edinburgh, and some other places I've forgotten the names of.'

'He tried to be a physician and failed?'

'Well, I don't know how hard he tried. The person who I heard talking of it – whose name I can't recollect right at this minute, said a degree wouldn't have been any good to him because he didn't have the money for setting up a practice.'

'No wonder he's so arrogant. Thinks he's physician material, and would be one, but for his lack of material wealth.'

'What are you on about? I can't understand a word you say half the time.'

'Never mind. What else do you know?'

'He makes extra money seeing patients in the private madhouses.'

'Does he indeed?'

'And it's not allowed. He's not meant to leave the premises without permission from the governors.'

'Ridiculous. Does he have to get permission to go home at night?'

'He lives here.'

'Surely not? An educated man shut up in this crumbling ruin like a common lunatic?'

'He has his own apartment here. I've seen it.'

'Good God, what's the matter with the man? I know now why they're called mad-doctors. Who in their right mind would follow a trade that forced them to live in a kennel like this?'

Porlock snickers. 'It's a bit of a palace on the outside. Probably that's enough to make him think he's living like a king. But about this word "trade" – Mr Haslam doesn't like it.'

'Why not?'

'He says mad-doctoring isn't a trade. At least not in the public asylums. He says lots of the keepers of private madhouses are tradesmen. Tradesmen trafficking in lunacy – he says that particular sentence all the time.'

'I'm surprised you can remember it.'

'He has a way of always repeating himself.'

'What else does he say?'

'He says in the public asylums knowledge is what counts. Expertise, he says. It's because of his so-called expertise that he gets fat fees for his signature on the certificates.'

'What certificates?'

'The ones that get the mad rich packed off to the private establishments run by all his greedy cronies.'

'That's corruption.'

'Well, it's just the usual palm-greasing and back-scratching that goes on everywhere now if some starched shirt thinks he knows more than the rest.'

'And what about the physician? Is he in on it too?'

'He's a bloody legend in his own time, that one. I heard someone say he got the equivalent of a year of Mr Haslam's salary for seeing just one rich patient. He used to get the same as Mr Haslam, a hundred pounds a year, just for turning up at the governors' meeting on a Saturday and for two other visits a week. Not that he usually bothered with them.'

'Used to? Have they dropped his pay?'

'No, Mr Haslam's has gone up. Tripled so everyone says.'

'Let me get this straight. Mr Haslam, for his hundred pounds, had to live here and work every day of the week and not take outside work; and the physician got the same hundred pounds for turning up once a week and sometimes more, and was allowed – in fact expected – to have a lucrative private practice?'

'That's right. So Mr Haslam has to pad his pay packet.'

'With?'

'With, what's the word – retainers. Yes, for private referrals and certificates and the like. And he also goes off to the courts to be an expert witness.'

'He gives evidence in court?'

'Yes. For a big fee, not because he's interested in lunacy.'

'But how can a man who profits from referrals be considered an impartial witness?'

Porlock shrugs. 'Who said anything about impartial? It's where he intends to gather his clients. Gets the poor ones sent home with a purge if they're only melancholy, or packed off to Bedlam if they're frantic. But the rich ones get the private workover.'

'Cross-referrals, multiple appointments, multiple milkings?'

Porlock looks amazed and then suspicious. 'How do you know about all this?'

'I know about corruption. It's corrupt.'

'Yes and Haslam knows it. He also says – it's something else he repeats all the time – that the interests of the patients and the interests of the owners of the private institutions are in total opposition,' Porlock mimics the apothecary's 'total opposition' while putting his nose high in the air.

'Yes, I can see that they might be,' I reply. 'After all, the owner makes his profit out of the patient's fee after all necessary deductions for food and physick and minding. So it's in the owner's interest to keep all that small. But obviously not in the patients'.'

'Exactly right.' Porlock nods emphatically.

'Nevertheless Haslam makes referrals and gives certificates for the private establishments?'

Porlock sighs. 'Well, he's the sort of man who says one thing and then does another. Even the assistant grumbles about him.'

'Why do you say even the assistant?'

Porlock sniggers. 'He came down in the last shower, that one. Such an innocent about money and science and everything. Not to mention other people's motives.'

'In what way is he innocent about money and science?'

'He gets this paltry salary but won't take up any private work. He says it will hurt his reputation as a scientific medical man. What's scientific about your jiggery-pokery, I ask him. And what reputation are you referring to? Being Haslam's slave? Don't you know the slave always goes down with the master? He's waiting to be a superintendent, but only an idiot doesn't know those positions always go to the physicians.'

'And how's he innocent about other people's motives?'

'He actually believes Haslam is here because he disapproves of the whiff of exploitation hanging round the private madhouses . . .'

'It's a stench, I'd say.'

'Whatever. But I told him, as I told you, Haslam is only here because he hasn't got the money to set up his own milking shed.'

'How astute of you, Porlock.'

'And the cheek of it – always crying stinking fish about the private places when he benefits so much from them!'

'Your metaphors are so picturesque. Cows and fish together.'

'It's only a manner of speaking,' Porlock says sulkily.

'Yes, metaphors are.'

'Are what?'

'A manner of speaking.'

'Anyway, Mr Haslam keeps on publishing things about his work so he's seen as an expert. In fact, he reckons he's the only expert in England. Says some man called Pinel admires him for his methods and is in complete agreement with them. I asked the assistant who this Pinel was when he was at home. He told me he's some Frenchman high up in the mad-doctoring business. When did we ever give a fuck what the French think, that's what I want to know.'

⁓

I am let out into the exercise yard for a third time. I am both grateful and fearful in equal measure: grateful for my time under the sky, fearful that each time will be my last. The lunatics begin treading the circle again. I stand near the gate and hope for the fiddler.

It is a beautiful day. A warm spring sun shines down on our shaven heads. The sky is perfectly blue. In my mind's eye I see a wood carpeted with bluebells and daffodils. Perhaps it is better that the fiddler doesn't come: it seems an extravagance to have a fiddler *and* the spring. When cold and silence is all you have had, music or warmth, one at a time, is a sufficient luxury. I am anxious lest all possible pleasures be exhausted in a single afternoon.

Then the fiddler is admitted. Behind him – I can hardly believe my eyes – comes a child. The fiddler takes up the place he took on the previous visit and the girl moves in close to him. He takes out his bow and rosin, and by this time I have ascertained that he is drunk. His face is flushed, his movements are uncoordinated. When he puts his instrument to his shoulder he staggers forward a short way, as if the act has unbalanced him.

He plays a note and in a sudden rush the lunatics gather round. The child steps back behind him, exclaiming, *Papa!* He begins a tune and the lunatics inch closer. I walk over flapping my arms at them and they move off and settle at a less threatening distance. As I walk back to the wall, the child and I stare at each other. She has a bold, cool, clear stare, unsullied by the confusions that cloud adults' eyes. I have often seen this look in children, not least my own. As if they see the world for what it is.

Of course she does not see the world for what it is: does not see that her father is drunk; that the man charged with protecting her through the streets has probably forgotten her every time he has entered another ale-house; that she is only with him now because of her own watchfulness, running to his side as he staggers out, drunker, from each succeeding establishment. And now she stands here with him, a little body of trustfulness, hiding behind an oak which might well crash over right in front of her, leaving her exposed to all the madness in the world.

Although the fiddler plays a jaunty tune, I am overcome with sadness. The fiddler's child will leave these grounds with her father, will go and take her chances, or be given them rather; and who knows, maybe luck will be on her side and nothing will swoop down and pick her off as she skips along behind him; it may be that she will make it to adulthood with no inheritance from his slipshod parenthood apart from a similar ability to play a fine fiddle. Maybe he ruffles her hair at night and gives her a kiss and promises her a doll, and would never let her go away from him by design, even if such a thing eventually occurs by neglect or accident.

I look up at the small high windows on the facade of the asylum. I know that in there, somewhere, are the children who have been sent deliberately away into the care of others, the idiot and mad children, to be made well by the cold, and poor diet, and treatments and slaps, the only mercy for whom is to be truly stupid, truly insane. But how many peep out at their prison through recurring lucidity or cumulative growth in their intellect? And how many are then driven mad by what they see? I shudder at the thought. Everywhere there are parents who would give their children up to the compassion of institutions, to the mad-doctors' enlightened scientific cures.

The fiddler plays longer than usual and the little girl eventually relaxes or gets too bored to hide, and she sits down on the ground to play with some stones. She throws them up and catches some on the back of her hand. She throws those she caught up again, and catches some, a smaller number, in her palm. She sets aside those she has caught except for one, and then proceeds to toss this in the air while, one by one, she picks up the stones she has dropped.

I walk over to her. I feel immensely tall as I stare down at her.

'That looks like fun. What is that game called?'

She shrugs without looking up. 'I call it Jackstones.'

'And why is that?' I notice that my shadow looms over her like a giant's.

She looks up and smiles slightly. She points to the fiddler. 'That's *his* name.'

'Your father is called Jack Stones?'

She nods.

'Do you play it a lot? When out with him? While you wait for him?'

She nods again.

'Hey, you!' the fiddler suddenly shrieks out at me. He has been playing with his eyes shut, but now he has stopped and his face is going purple. The lunatics stop and everyone is staring at me.

'Calm down,' I say, striding away from the child as quickly as possible.

There is a moment when it seems anything could happen. The

fiddler's rage has communicated itself to the lunatics who are now
bellowing and gesticulating wildly. But the fiddler is too drunk to
sustain his anger, or perhaps to recall what provoked it, and he
soon begins to play again, a maudlin piece that sucks the passion
out of everyone. By the time the keepers come, rather later than
usual – the clouds are already preparing for the sunset – the
lunatics are docile and the fiddler and his daughter long gone.

Deliquium

I AM TOLD IT is May. I am told that it is a wonderful May this year, warmer and finer than usual right from the start. I enjoy my time out in the yard. The fiddler comes, not always sober, but he plays simple tunes well enough. He doesn't bring his daughter. I am just beginning to think that life is improving when, one late afternoon, Mr Haslam appears in my cell. I am sitting unrestrained on the bed, lost in one of my many plans of escape.

'What do you think of the weather?' he asks me with a pleased smile, as if he himself were responsible for it.

'Very pleasant.'

'Yes, isn't it? Owing to the unseasonably fine and warm weather, we have decided to bring the summer treatments forward this year.'

'Summer treatments? I thought music and poetry and a view of the sky were my current treatments.'

'Life isn't all poetry and fiddling, even for madmen. It is our custom here to apply medical treatments to all of the curables every summer, all at the same time.'

'I've had a number of your so-called medical treatments. They made me ill.'

'These will make you better. It is not enough that we might

have a rational conversation together from time to time; there is still a nerve in you that, when plucked, vibrates with a lunacy all your own.'

'Oh, and what nerve is that?'

'It is difficult to describe precisely. But it speaks Latin, lacks insight and sometimes claims to be a king.'

'That nerve is educated, refuses to be bullied and understands a complex metaphor.'

'That nerve is arrogant, deluded and doesn't know its place.'

'I don't feel like having this competition.'

'Good. You realise the wisdom of not doing so. We will begin your summer treatment tomorrow. We begin with bloodletting, move on to vomits and vesicants, and conclude with purges.'

'Thank you. That sounds most enjoyable.'

'During this time, if you are well enough, we also might use plays.'

'*Use* plays?'

'As a treatment. It has been reported that play-acting has produced calming effects on the lunatics in some asylums. I assume it is because they are all bored rigid. But the physician is keen to try it anyway.'

'So we are to stumble round throwing up and shitting ourselves while declaiming *to be or not to be*?'

'You remain a very coarse man.'

'Well, who knows – it might be an improvement. I always thought a prince having such anxieties was a flagrant self-indulgence. Much more fitting for lunatics who can't control their guts or their bowels to put the eternal question.'

'I see you are familiar with Hamlet.'

'I'm familiar with all of Shakespeare.'

'I despise the theatre.'

'I thought you might. I rather went off it myself. Too much dross. It's become difficult for an intelligent man to be entertained these days.'

'Too much immoral muck. And an actress is as good as a prostitute.'

'Better, I'd say.'

Mr Haslam draws his mouth in sourly and motions to the keeper to unlock the door. 'I hope your treatment cleans up your mouth,' he says, pausing in the doorway. 'Your talk is frequently a gross pollution.'

When he has gone, I notice with a pang that my poetry book is missing.

∼

I am scarcely awake in the morning when the assistant to the apothecary comes in with a bowl and draws off a large amount of my blood. I am alarmed at the volume in the bowl. I am already ill nourished, and I fear that the loss of blood will weaken me still further.

'Can I drink it?' I joke.

'Are you a vampire?'

'I am the King of . . .'

'Spare me,' he interrupts. 'I've got a busy morning.'

'Making blood sausage?'

He gets up and leaves without replying. I decide to conserve my strength by spending the morning on my bed, but a short while later the barber appears. He makes me sit up and reshaves my head. I am about to thank him when he whips out a large sharp blade and starts to cut into my scalp. Angrily, I push him away. He goes out and comes back with two keepers. Together they hold me down and the barber completes his incision, a long one from just above my nape to just above my eyebrows. In the incision he inserts some small, round, hard objects, pulses of some sort, and then applies a stinging ointment. They tie me to the bed and leave.

I am disgusted. I have always had a deep revulsion to surgical invasions of the body. The barber carries his filthy knife from patient to patient, probably uses it to cut his meat at lunch, to cut his bait when fishing; and I fear, superstitiously, that infections might enter through the portal he has made, in much the same way that the humours or vapours or other theorised contumescences and obstructions exit. I am afraid that I will become filled with pus from the scalp down and die of the inspissation.

The next day I am bled again.

'This is making me impossibly weak,' I remonstrate.

'You can have it all at once if you like,' the assistant says coldly.

'What? Take all my blood?'

'We would replace it.'

'What with?'

'Why, the blood of a calf.'

'You're joking of course.'

'Indeed I am not,' he replies indignantly. 'I've seen it done. It doesn't always work, admittedly. Some live, some die. They're not sure why. Perhaps the calf is sick.'

I shudder. 'No thank you. I'll stick with this.'

'Anyway, there's only a few more bleedings to go. At the end of the week we begin the vomits. Although the apothecary says we might give you a leech.'

'A *leech*?'

'Certainly. We attach it to the nape of your neck to suck out the obstructions.' He drops his voice. 'Certain foreigners think it sucks out your soul when placed in that particular location. They always apply the exploded theory. We tend to use the unexploded.'

'Yes, someone already told me. But I don't think I fancy a leech, no matter what theory it's attached to.'

'You don't get any choice in the matter,' he reprimands me. 'But you'll prefer a leech to the seton, mark my words. The physician says a seton for you, for certain.'

'What's a certain seton?'

The assistant smiles rather cruelly. 'It's a thread put through a fold of skin to keep it opened up for discharges. Now let me look at your incision so I can see how it's progressing.'

I bow my head, speechless.

'Good. It is quite purulent, and discharging your disease nicely.'

'It hurts and stinks and I don't have a mental disease, least of all in my scalp.'

'The patients always misunderstand the theory,' he replies mildly.

'That's because it doesn't make sense. Do you think it's pus running through my mind now? That's all that is coming out.'

'Mr Haslam thinks you do have pus in your mind. Why else would you keep on about unnatural passions?'

'What unnatural passions are you referring to?'

The assistant blushes. 'I'm afraid I can't say.'

'Oh, *those*. Goodness, you lot are squeamish. I keep on about unnatural passions as you call them to illustrate a point.'

'And that point is . . .?'

I take a deep breath and speak slowly. 'That the way we think about things changes. Do we bury buggers alive any more? No, we don't. We believe that they are mad and act accordingly. And whether you like it or not, your own treatments will one day be seen as the gross equivalent of burying sodomites alive.'

'Mr Haslam says you just want to talk dirty. And I doubt that our treatments will ever be seen as you describe. Ours are scientific. Science is the truth that never changes.'

'Science is the story with a thousand endings.'

'Mr Haslam told me you are determined to be ignorant.'

'Not so ignorant that I have to refer to sodomy in Latin.'

'I don't think there is anyone here who knows the Latin for that particular act,' the assistant replies smugly.

'*Peccatum illud horribile inter christianos non nominandum.*'

The assistant stares at me quite menacingly. 'Mr Haslam also says that your display of Latin and English words that no one else knows the meanings of is highly symptomatic.'

'Does he, the poxy cretin.'

The assistant purses his lips at this, but his eyes display

satisfaction with a communication more at the expected level. He puts away his equipment while I look with a sickened covetousness at the bowl of blood. 'You'll get your seton at the end of the week. In the meantime, the play-acting is about to start.'

'I don't want to go in a play,' I say petulantly.

'Why ever not? Mr Haslam tells me you know quite a lot about plays.'

'In a former life I used to be a theatre critic.'

'How many former lives have you had then?'

'I didn't keep a tally. I am the kind of man who is always giving things up.'

'Pity you can't give up madness, eh?'

'If my madness is constituted by my use of language, as you allege, I think I'll stick to it.'

'Or it will stick to you. You always speak as if you have a choice.'

'Tell me,' I say, wishing to change the subject, 'what play will we perform? Or will it be an unrecognisable pabulum, all the women Lady MacBeth and all the men King Lear?'

'What difference would it make?'

'I myself fancy something a little French, in an asylum or prison, say, Bicêtre or the old Bastille or Charenton. We could all be ourselves.'

'And who would you be? The pervert?'

'Yes, why not? I'll be the Marquis.'

'What Marquis?'

'Sade, bien entendu.'

'Him again.'

'Yes, I can just imagine it. The lunatics all dancing round and ripping their rags off, and the Marquis performing sane soliloquies in their midst.'

'And what would these sane soliloquies be about?'

'Torture.'

The assistant shakes his head while I chuckle away. 'Torture's not sane,' he says.

'My point exactly. Please hasten to tell Mr Haslam that you and I are of one mind and there's to be no more treatments other than the arts. For personal reasons, I'll stay out of the play-acting. I'm sure the high quality will only over-excite me.'

The assistant picks up my blood and leaves, muttering inaudibly.

~

In the afternoon I am taken to the long gallery which has been cleared of the usual human flotsam and where there is gathered together a group of twenty or so alleged lunatics of the more or less lucid variety. I find myself standing next to a woman who has managed to look quite clean and tidy despite our conditions. Her brown hair is drawn back into a neat bun – she surely has access to a brush or comb. She has intelligent brown eyes and I am immediately certain that when I address her, she will respond completely rationally.

'I believe we are to be inserted into *The Tragedy of Dr Faustus*,' I remark, although I have no such belief at all.

'Do you know this play?'

'Yes. Quite well in fact.'

'Is it good?'

'It is good, but not true.'

'All of it is lies?'

'Dr Faustus sells his soul to the devil in exchange for knowledge and pleasure.'

'And what is the untrue part?'

'He has no soul, there is no devil, and knowledge can't be bought.'

'And pleasure?'

'His nonexistent soul is to buy him twenty-four years of pleasure. But if you were to take all the pleasure in the world and squash it all together, I'd say it would only fill up a week.'

'Are you a cynic?'

'Not at all. Pleasure is one of my favourite things. I only deplore its rarity. I would happily mortgage myself to Mephistopheles if I could find him.'

'You do not think he is all around you?'

'No. It's simple human evil that is all around me. It's impossible to profit from.'

'I believe there are many who profit from simple human evil.'

'Of course you're right, but it never has the grandeur, the pay-off, of a pact with Clootie. Still, the peasants are easily pleased, are they not?'

'Are you mortgaged to God then?'

'Certainly not. Whatever made you suggest such a thing?'

'He is easier to find.'

'Ah, you think so. That is not my opinion.'

'You are an atheist?'

'He can exist if he wants to. I don't mind. But I am mortgaged to human beings.'

'I'm afraid I don't understand you.'

'I dearly want to sell my putative soul to Mephistopheles. But really, he doesn't want it. Who is puny enough to want my soul? Who feels sufficient doubt about his own power to need mine? Not God, surely? Who is willing to promise me anything to prove his own puissance? And who is all around me, thoroughly real and believable, with money in his fist?'

'So, you've sold your soul to man?'

'Oh I didn't want to. I'll never get my week of pleasure out of it. I'll be lucky to get an hour.'

'A little while ago you said there is no soul.'

'And neither there is. In fact, it was something else I sold. My heart. And many times.'

At that moment, a man walks into the gallery and claps his hands theatrically. 'Over here everybody. We're going to begin.'

'I hear we are doing Faust,' I call out to him.

'How absurd,' he cries. 'We're going to do a comedy by Molière,

The Physician in spite of himself. I have here a few copies of the work translated into English. You'll have to share, so gather round.'

The twenty or so lunatics in the room form a circle around the director. He is one of those people who accompanies every word with an overly flamboyant gesture and a facial contortion which he imagines to be expressive. As if he is being watched from twenty yards away. It is quite tiring watching his arms and eyeballs and lips all slaving away at odds with each other. And his trained voice, slithering up and down the octaves even while speaking, makes me dread to hear him sing.

'I know this play too,' I say to the woman who continues to stand beside me.

'Is it true?'

'Absolutely. No souls, no devils, just the foolishness and vanity of man.'

The director, whose name is Ahn-Tuan (you say it the French way, he tells us), passes round some handwritten copies of the play.

'Now, for those of you who don't know the work, I'll quickly summarise. A gentleman's daughter has become mute since he refused to allow her to marry the man she's in love with; he – the gentleman – is now looking for a way to cure her. He sends out a couple of his servants to search for a doctor, and they come across a woodcutter's wife. The woodcutter's wife has just been beaten by her husband and is thirsty for revenge. She tells the servants that her husband is really a doctor and he cuts wood only as a cover for his true profession. The servants beat him into admitting the truth of his wife's story, and then he is dragged off to cure the master's daughter. Any questions?'

'How does he convince the master he's a doctor?' I ask, although I already know the answer.

'Well, that's the amusing part,' Ahn-Tuan explains. 'He uses lots of Latin phrases sprinkled with idiotic references to the spleen and to humours. In short, medical gobbledegook.'

'Excellent word. But I never heard it before.'

'I made it up.'

'Does he cure the girl?' someone calls out.

'Certainly,' Ahn-Tuan replies. 'The woodcutter finds the girl's lover and dresses him up as an apothecary. Then the fake doctor prescribes that the fake apothecary should give her a dose of flight and two drams of matrimonium. Now who will be the woodcutter-doctor?'

'I will,' I volunteer. 'I even know some of the lines.'

'Do you?' Ahn-Tuan looks surprised.

I step forward and begin to declaim loudly and pompously: *'I think I'll stick to doctoring for the rest of my days. It's really the best trade of all. You get your money whether you cure the patient or not. A bad job never reflects on us: if a shoemaker ruins a piece of leather, he has to pay for it; but a doctor can spoil a man for nothing.'*

There is a ripple of laughter amongst the assembled lunatics. Only then do I notice that Mr Haslam has come into the gallery and is watching us. I advance towards him theatrically. Then I look him straight in the eye unwaveringly and quote my favourite lines, *'So these vapours pass from the liver on the left side to the heart on the right and combine with the vapours of the shoulder-blade; and as all these vapours are malign due to the influence of the acrid humours, they are the direct cause of your daughter becoming mute. Or, expressed more fully in Latin: ossabandus, nequeis, nequer, potarinum, quipsa milus.'*

'A more concise explanation I couldn't hope to hear,' Mr Haslam returns, *'I'm surprised however by one thing and that is the position of the liver and heart. You seem to have got them the wrong way round. I always thought the heart was on the left side and the liver on the right.'*

'Yes,' I say, *'that was how it was once. But we've changed every-thing now. The whole science of medicine is run on a completely new system.'*

The lunatics burst into wild laughter and applause. Mr Haslam smiles sourly.

'For a man who despises the theatre, I am surprised that you know Molière so well,' I remark.

'I certainly know his play better than he knows his medicine.'

'You don't think he has a point?'

'None that I can see.'

'Come now. You claim to be an intelligent man. His point is as plain as a pikestaff.'

'Every person who takes the degree of doctor becomes, in consequence, a learned man. A doctor may be blind, deaf, dumb, stupid or mad, but still his diploma shields him from the imputation of ignorance. It is libellous to call him ignorant.'

'Why is he always changing his mind, then?'

'Medical science rests on a firmer foundation than it once did. We won't be changing our opinions again.'

'Won't we?'

'Not in my area of expertise.'

Mr Haslam has drawn himself up to his full height and has put out his chest. The lunatics wait expectantly.

'You can rest assured that insanity is uniformly accompanied by diseases of the brain,' the apothecary declaims. 'We can safely conclude that such organic infections have produced the incorrect association of ideas that is characteristic of the lunatic. A human spirit is immaterial, incorruptible and immortal, and not subject to the gross and subordinate changes of matter.'

'You deny any metaphysical cause of insanity?'

'Correct. And I despise all metaphysical cures. They are all quackery. I am especially against the use of the eye – the attempt to reduce ranting and raving by the moral force of one's gaze. It is said that Mr Willis did it with King George, but I never saw it done unless the furious lunatic was already in a strait-waistcoat.'

The lunatics have by this time gathered around, and are listening in an interested and respectful fashion. Mr Haslam suddenly becomes aware of them and coughs in an embarrassed way.

'What d'you think you're doing? Get on with the treatment at once!' he orders Ahn-Tuan.

Ahn-Tuan walks into the middle of the room, clapping his hands and ordering the lunatics to take their places. Mr Haslam and I stare at each other for a few more moments, then he turns on his heels and stalks out.

∼

A few mornings later, the assistant to the apothecary brings with him the surgeon, who is assistant to the physician. It seems the assistant takes his status from the master.

'Get him ready,' the physician's assistant orders the apothecary's assistant, who quickly and meekly obeys by pushing my shirt from my shoulders. The physician's assistant takes out a scalpel.

'What are you doing?' I cry, feeling sufficiently assaulted by the incision in my scalp.

'I am here to make the seton. If it is of any concern to you.'

'Of course it is a concern to me. It is I who must endure it.'

The apothecary's assistant rolls his eyes apologetically. As if he can't make his share of the lunatics behave themselves.

'Can't the disease escape through the hole in my head?' I ask.

'What was the point in doing it then?' I carry on when nobody answers. 'After all, if it can't get out of the hole in my head, how is it going to get out of the hole in my . . . where are you putting the seton exactly?'

'In your shoulder.' And the physician's assistant grabs my shoulder and cuts a circle in the skin. He has already done it by the time I have formed the intention of punching him.

'Now it has to be kept open,' he says, and draws out his needle and thread.

The apothecary's assistant makes an attempt to hold me, but I shrug him off violently.

'I am not having any more of your holes in my body. You think that the mental diseases get out, but it's only the physical diseases that get in. How do you know it's not the coughing disease that comes in this way?'

'Get some keepers,' the physician's assistant orders the apothecary's assistant, who dashes out as ordered and returns with Thumbscrew and Strappado. Together they hold me down on the bed while the physician's assistant sews around the incision to prevent it from healing up.

'Bastards!' I hiss as they all make ready to leave.

The assistants go out, but Thumbscrew and Strappado hang back.

'Did you hear what he called us? Was your father married to your mother, Strappado?'

'Most assuredly. How about yours?'

'Absolutely.'

'I don't think he checked his facts, do you?'

'Can't have done.'

'Still, I don't think I'll beat him up this time. I'm sure my father did have a few bastards – it's just that I wasn't one of them.'

'What man doesn't have a few bastards, eh?'

'Absolutely. I'm sure I've got a few myself.'

'Got to be sure the equipment works before you're wed.'

'And got to keep it in working order after.'

They do their noisy shoulder-slapping routine and go out the door laughing.

I lie down gingerly, trying not to cause any disturbance to my scalp or shoulder. The back of my head is now severely inflamed and my shoulder has started to throb. Disturbingly, my startled heart beats noisily, as if it fears excision from its proper cavity. I sink into despair when I realise with sudden clarity that all my escape plans are completely wild, unworkable.

∼

I am left alone for a few days to ripen in the lentous heat. At first, I believe it's warm because of the summer weather; then I realise it's the warmth of suppuration. As the pus increases, my temperature rises, until one morning I wake up in a frank and liquid sweat.

'Fetch the apothecary,' I order Porlock when next he comes in. 'I don't feel well.'

'The apothecary isn't here,' Porlock replies.

'Well, when he gets back then,' I say, struggling to sit up.

'You're all wet and shiny. What's the matter with you?'

'I'm melting. From the heat of putrefaction.'

'Don't melt too quick. Mr Haslam won't be back for a day or two. He's moving out.'

'Moving out? Resigning, you mean?'

'God no. He's going to live out, that's all. He's got himself fixed up over at Islington.'

A bead of sweat runs down into my left eye. I wipe it away with an exhausted hand.

'Don't you know?' Porlock continues. 'That's where the new asylum's going to be. This place is going to fall down on top of us all one day, turn us into a brick sandwich.'

'Lunatic sandwich would be more correct. You don't say bread sandwich, do you? You say what is in it.'

'Sandwich *royale* then,' Porlock says sarcastically. 'There being so many fucking kings and queens in it.'

'I think I'll have to lie down now,' I tell him. I stretch myself out carefully on the bed. I feel a little better lying flat. 'It's not very convenient for Haslam to be living over there. It's not very convenient for us.'

'Well, his apartment as it is now, you couldn't put a dog in it.'

'They could put some patients in it then.'

Porlock ignores me. 'Did you know this place was built directly on the old city ditch? They filled the ditch in with just any old muck, and then the brickwork was set down straight on top of the soil. God only knows what vapours and miasmas are poisoning us all.'

I dismiss his raving with a wave of my hand. I am too tired to care about miasmic putrefactions without when I am decomposing within.

'So, there won't be any mad-doctors with us,' I manage to say. 'What's the point of keeping us here?'

'To stop you infecting the rest of us of course.'

'Madness isn't infectious.'

'Some of the physicians think so.'

'That's ridiculous. And it's absurd to confine us for cure and then allow the physicians to spend their days elsewhere.'

'Well, we can't have lunatics loose on the streets, can we?'

'Why not? We always used to.'

Porlock doesn't answer.

'And why doesn't the government have us sent to the private madhouses if all the marvellous doctors are there all day?'

Porlock looks shocked. 'You can't have the paupers in with the gentlemen,' he protests before leaving.

Porlock does not bring the apothecary. He turns up a few evenings later with the supper and buckets. He appears to have forgotten all about my request. Fortunately, I have cooled down somewhat without the benefit of further physick. I have been lying on my pallet dreaming of the move to new premises, of the break in the summer treatments, of a chance to see the outside world, of – who knows – perhaps a chance to escape, to dash off down an alley in my straitjacket and throw my suppurating self on the mercy of one of my former friends. But Porlock informs me that the move is off, that the governors didn't pay when they were expected to, that the Drapers company which offered the land went to the courts, or said they would, one or the other, but it amounted to the same thing because they withdrew their offer and we are all staying put. And so, all the crashing that I hear in the night, the tiles and bricks falling from the building, this will continue, as will the torture.

~

When my temperature is back to normal and I am again on my feet, I am taken to the long gallery for another session of play-acting. I immediately go over to the woman with the bun. I like her. Of course she is too serious, too self-controlled, to duck into a broom cupboard with me, but pleasant conversation is also lacking from my usual day-to-day activities.

'Are you being treated?' I ask her.

'Oh yes,' she sighs. 'I'm being bled every morning. What with the treatments and the poor food, I'm always exhausted.'

'I hear we are to go on to vomits soon.'

'They always try to bring our madness out through our mouths.'

'And our backsides. The purges are after the vomits. Although they continue to assert that anything involving that part of the anatomy is the French way.'

She blushes attractively. 'Where is Ahn-Tuan? He is late today.'

I shrug.

'Last time we were together you talked about mortgaging your heart. Do you remember?' she asks.

'Yes, I remember very well.'

'I wish I'd thought to sell mine. I just gave it away. That's why I'm here. I was once a teacher of languages and I was happy. Then I met this man and we married and had a child . . .'

I try to appear thoughtful and interested even though I am still thinking about the broom cupboard.

'The child, a girl, was born dead.'

'Oh!' I say, startled out of my fantasy. 'I'm sorry to hear it.'

'There was no time for grieving because he wanted a son. But I . . .'

I wait.

'I couldn't seem to get over the dead girl. I had a kind of childbirth fever such as some new mothers have. But I think I would have recovered spontaneously if it hadn't been for his philandering. I'd given my heart, as I said, and it was jealousy that brought me down.'

'What did you do to him?'

'I set him alight in his bed.'

I am impressed – and shocked. Perhaps not the best companion for the broom cupboard.

'Oh, he didn't suffer too horribly. He is not disfigured. He poured the chamberpot over himself.' She stops to laugh quietly. 'He said I was mad with grief and took me to the doctor. I went to a private institution first. But he said he couldn't afford the cost. Really, he just wanted me out of the way. There were too many cures in the private establishments for his liking.'

The lunatics let out a cry of excitement as Ahn-Tuan rushes in the door. He's a man who obviously loves an audience, even an audience of madmen. He calls us together and then distributes the scripts while strutting about in an outlandish parody of Molière's physician. Some of the lunatics cannot recall the parts that were assigned to them in the previous practice, and several arguments break out simultaneously. Ahn-Tuan does his best to arbitrate, but soon a large long-haired creature who looks as if he should be carrying a club pushes over a runt of a man with a stoved-in head. In a trice all of the arguing lunatics are at each other's throats. Ahn-Tuan throws up his hands and rushes off to get the keepers.

'I too am part of a fix-up. Or so I am coming to believe,' I say to the woman with the bun who is still standing near me. We have both stepped backwards from the melee to avoid being knocked over or punched. 'But then, in a way, we're all part of a fix-up, aren't we?'

'How do you mean?' she asks.

'Life. Life is a fix-up. It's against us, right from the start. It's out to get us.'

'Oh, do you think so?'

'Certainly. You're perhaps too young to know it yet. Perhaps you think only your own life has gone wrong, rather than the thing itself. But it's the thing itself that's all up the pole. All these people struggling against each other. Against themselves. There's no respite from it.'

'People struggle needlessly,' she replies as the runt is sent flying across the floor by the caveman.

'Well, they can't help it. They are born with their obsessions already present. Tiny homunculi waiting to grow into powerful enemies. Tell a man to resist what is inside him and he must spend his whole life fighting or praying.'

The runt is picked up by his opponent, dangled by the scruff of the neck for a brief moment, and then flung into the fireplace where, mercifully, the coals have not yet been lit.

'A life of prayer would perhaps be better,' the woman replies.

'A life of prayer is an insult to God. It's like bringing bread and water to a feast.'

'One minute you say life is up the pole and the next you say it's a feast. Which is it to be?'

I laugh. 'Yes, don't listen to me. I'm a lunatic. I declare and assert things all over the place, but I have no idea about the truth. That's why I contradict myself.'

'I don't think you are very mad,' she answers. 'No madder than I am, anyway. And nowhere near as mad as Ahn-Tuan.'

We both turn to look at the director who has come in again with as many keepers as he can find, and who is now screaming hysterically while they break up the fights. When order has been restored, when the caveman has been led away to a straitwaistcoat or worse, when the runt has been stretchered off to the apothecary or better, we calmly read through the play again as if we were all leisured gentlefolk in a luxurious drawing room.

~

Between sessions in the long gallery I am confined to my cell, sometimes tethered to the bed, sometimes left to wander freely – six paces from the bed to the wall and back again, three paces to the grimed-over window where I stand trying to make out the weather. A certain effulgence tells me when the sun is out, but apart from that I can decipher very little. I am frequently bored.

One afternoon I am amusing myself by catching insects in a corner of the room when Mr Haslam enters. He orders me to sit on the bed, and begins to inspect my running sores. The pus is now oozing out of my scalp like a thick lava; the open wound created by the seton weeps a discoloured syrup, like a tree giving up its sap. He seems pleased.

'Today we begin the vomits,' he announces. 'The assistant will give you antimony, or perhaps camphor. Even camphor and opium. I haven't quite decided yet.'

'On what will you base your decision? Your mood?'

'I am not going to engage in another prolonged conversation with you this morning. I have a great many patients to see to. All the curables must be vomited.'

'Tell me how I can become an incurable so I can escape your stercorarian treatments.'

'You think the degree of madness is a matter of personal choice?'

'The degree to which madness is exhibited is a personal choice for the sane.'

'In my experience the sane don't wish to exhibit madness.'

'We certainly don't. But some people see mad things in us. As for myself, I only wish to influence their conclusions a little — towards deciding I am not worth bothering with.'

'You would perhaps regret that intention. The incurables are kept apart and fully restrained. Here you have the freedom of your cell and the galleries.'

'An odd notion of freedom – a cell and the confines of the galleries in a madhouse.'

'Freedom is a relative thing.'

'Yes, I'm sure even King Louis realised that at the last.'

'I'm glad we are in agreement. But now I have pressing duties to attend to.' The apothecary turns on his heels and goes out.

In due course the assistant brings a bolus. I do not ask what it contains. It is no doubt a reliable and strong emetic. I swallow it. In a short while I start to feel nauseous. Soon after I am retching violently into the chamberpot. When it is full, I retch on the floor, continuing until all I am bringing up is a clear, slightly viscous liquid, very much like drool. The tears pour down my cheeks, both from the effort and the sorrow.

After a night of stomach cramps, I am given another emetic, one smelling strongly of camphor. I am sick all day. Then the days run together as I stagger in a nauseous stupor round my cell; each day I am administered a new poison, perhaps mixed with a narcotic, I do not know, but my disorientation would indicate it. I vomit, sweat, shiver, shake. I see fleeing shadows in the daytime and inexplicable pulses of light at night. My body is alternately rubber or stone; I walk and vomit, huddle and vomit, lie down and vomit. I am more dead than alive when I see Mr Haslam's distorted face above me.

'Good,' he pronounces. 'Tomorrow we will start the purges.'

～◝

The next day, when I am so drained I could not manage to be mad even if I were, the assistant comes in with a small glass of physick.

'What's that?'

'It's the purgative.'

'But what's in it?'

'I'm not sure. Mr Haslam concocted it. Perhaps digitalis. But there's certainly white hellebore.'

'Hellebore is a poison.'

'That's what they all say. It's part of the madness.'

'Don't you get tired of uttering that particular platitude?'

'What platitude?'

'Attributing everything a madman does to his madness.'

'Are you going to swallow this or do I have to fetch the keepers?'

I take the medicine glass and swallow the contents. The taste is vile. The assistant smiles grimly, and leaves. I sit on the edge of the bed waiting for the worst. In a short while I begin to feel nauseous. I begin to sweat. I grip the bed ends. My stomach starts to turn over and my bowels feel loose. Soon I am retching over the end of the bed. Then I lose all control of my bowel. I evacuate solids, then liquids, then only gas and rotten air.

I am frightened because the spasms in my stomach make it difficult to breathe: after each violent retching, my breathing stops. And frightened too because of the painful straining of my bowel against its unnatural emptiness, as if it seeks to expel something, anything, even the little red-hot demon of the apothecary's imagination. Then suddenly I am not quite there any more; the cell becomes a blur as a twitchiness overtakes my muscles . . .

I wake up. Mr Haslam is peering at me. I become aware that I am sweating pungently, profusely.

'He's back with us,' the apothecary announces, and then I notice other figures clustered around the bed.

'You did well. Your body was violent enough to expel the very devil.'

There is a short whispered conversation between the apothecary and one of the other figures, then the latter withdraw.

'I believe you will only need a few more such treatments . . .' the apothecary begins.

'What? How many devils are in me?'

Mr Haslam smiles. 'That I cannot tell.'

'I am too hot,' I cry out.

'Yes – it is the after-effect of the evacuant. I'll get the keeper to wash you down with a cool pledget.' He clicks his fingers at the assistant, who goes off dutifully. The sweat runs down my forehead and into my eyes.

'Tell me how to be incurably mad and I will do it,' I beseech him.

'Do not fuss so. You will be incurably mad soon.' He walks over to my little window. 'You do not have a good view from here,' he murmurs. 'Indeed, you have no view at all. The window is too blackened.'

'Why should I care a fig about a view?'

'There's to be a public execution today. You can't watch the crowds from here.'

I make no reply.

'Yes, another wretch who plotted to kill the King. So they say.'

'Why do they not send him here? He could have a field day,' I say with considerable effort.

'I see you are returning to your usual self. They do not send him here because he is not mad. He is a criminal and will be treated like one. A shame, in my view. The King is just another lunatic. The country would be better off without him. Without any king, in fact. Look at France.'

'How can I look at France?'

'Napoleon is doing a fine job – for the French. We need our own Napoleon.'

Mr Haslam continues to stand by the window.

'I won't be going, of course,' he adds.

'Why not? You could have a toffee-apple.'

'Very amusing. It is not street theatre.'

'Isn't it? What do they all go for then?'

'How should I know? I expect it's to see the power of the law.'

I wipe away the sweat that is collecting on my forehead. It is an effort to speak but I am determined. 'The power of the law is better seen in the courts. They go to see blood. They love the atmosphere of delirium that follows the spilling of it. They go to see people doing what nobody else is allowed to do. It is like watching public fornication. Toffee-apples are perfect.'

This exertion exhausts me. If Mr Haslam continues to argue, he will soon have the better of me.

'Where's that wretched keeper I sent for?' is all he says.

The next moment, Porlock rushes in with a bowl. Mr Haslam watches while Porlock removes my rags and begins to wash me. He wrinkles up his nose in disgust. As the stench of sweat and soil pervades the cell, Mr Haslam takes his leave.

'Christ, what have you been doing to yourself?' Porlock asks.

'What have they been doing to me, you mean. They've been torturing me. Making me swallow poison. Cutting me open so I will turn to pus. Purging me till I have tenesmus.'

'They do that to all of you. But you stink worse than the rest.'

'It's the stink of my rage.'

'Now don't you carry on like that.'

'Tell me what the difference is between myself and an incurable,' I beg.

'That I can't properly tell. Some of them are insensible, and some of them are violent. They are all fully restrained.'

'I will become violent then. Bend down so I can punch your head.'

Porlock finishes washing me, and helps me to put my rags on again.

'Thank you, I feel better,' I tell him.

'Well, don't be feeling too good,' he warns. 'There's to be more of the same quite soon.'

∼

Before the next purgative is administered, I am taken to the long gallery for play therapy. Or whatever they call it. The usual crowd is assembled. The woman with the bun no longer has it; she has been shaved and bears a weeping scalp incision similar to my own. She also looks quite haggard, as if she has spent a month in the broom cupboard. She comes over to me, and together we wait for the arrival of Ahn-Tuan.

'I don't know why we need a director,' she says. 'It's not as if we will put on a performance.'

'Yes, and thank God for that.'

'I heard you were once a great fan of the theatre.'

'Did you? Yes, a long time ago, I was a theatre critic. When I gave it up, I was a street actor for a time.' I feel something thick and slow and damp sliding down my forehead. I put my hand up, expecting to find a slug that has transferred itself from the lugubrious walls. Instead my fingers encounter an unexpected spreading viscosity. The woman's eyes follow my fingers and then drop in embarrassment to the floor. I take my hand away and wipe my fingers hastily on my rags. 'Our troupe,' I continue with much feigned dignity, 'all rich and useless men like myself, made use of the stock characters from an old Italian form of street theatre called *Commedia dell'arte.* Do you know anything about it?'

'I'm afraid I don't.'

'I'm sure you will recognise some of the characters. There's Harlequin, the valet, witty and cunning and acrobatic, always searching for food and women. Pantalone is the merchant who dresses in Turkish clothes to hide his age and procure women. Pulcinella is the bad egg, always coming up with outrageous schemes to satisfy his cruelty and lust.' I stop to wipe a gobbet of pus out of my eye. 'Then there is the doctor. Like Molière's wood-cutter, he uses meaningless Latin phrases to demonstrate his superiority, and he is always suggesting dangerous remedies for other characters' imagined illnesses. Apart from these character attributes everything is improvised. The beauty of it is that the audience knows what motivates each character and can always quickly get a grasp on what is going on, but each performance adds a new twist to the theme. Excuse me.'

I turn aside from her and use the remains of my shirt to wipe my head. When I have finished, it looks as if I have used it to clean up egg yolk. I notice that the woman takes a small involuntary step sideways.

'I was always the doctor,' I carry on. 'The room for satire was enormous — but think how witty and wonderful I could be after my time here. I obviously never went far enough with my ironies and sarcasms. Imagine if I'd had Mr Haslam to model myself on!'

The woman laughs. We wait a few more minutes in silence, but the director fails to arrive. I try to move my body inside my soggy shirt to make myself more comfortable, but the fabric has now adhered to the weeping wound of my seton.

'I loved being the doctor,' I say, and try to smile nonchalantly, but my mouth sets in a rictus. 'How many opportunities are there in daily life to utter meaningless Latin phrases? I made quite a few esoteric jokes which anyone with a classical education could have a good laugh at. I prescribed many dangerous remedies for many imaginary illnesses. Who knows how many in the audience went home and tried them?'

I laugh and then stop as my shirt suddenly breaks free of the phlegmonous injury to my shoulder.

'But who would have thought it? I believed I was improvising, and in reality I was rehearsing. Hard to know whether to laugh or cry, isn't it?'

'You were rehearsing the wrong part. You should have been rehearsing the part of the patient.'

'Yes, that's true.'

We wait in silence. The crowd is becoming restless.

'A short while before I became unwell, I saw a performance of Molière's last comedy, *The Imaginary Invalid*,' the woman says. 'It's about a hypochondriac who fears the ministration of doctors . . .'

'Yes, I know it. Delicious. Imagine being in that particular cleft stick: driven to the doctor yet terrified. And do you know what happened in the first week of the first performance?'

She shakes her head.

'Molière himself played the leading part, and in the opening week he was stricken ill on stage and died a few hours later. Can you imagine the stunned audience? It's a new play. How are they to know that the main character becoming sick, really sick, isn't part of the play? Perhaps they're all guffawing loudly while he's in his death throes.'

'Grotesque.'

'And the irony of the title! Don't you see a parallel of sorts between my rehearsals in the streets and Molière's death during his own play? It's as if we are mocking fate, mocking our own futures. Look at me, Molière cries, able to mock the fear of illness, to publicly ridicule it! And look at me, I also cry, able to laugh at the dangerous pomposity and ignorance of doctors! Well, well. Molière was struck down and I was hung up. Molière met fatal illness and illness won. I met scientific medicine and it is having its indecent way with me.'

The woman shakes her head, but says nothing.

'Am I saying we should never poke fun?' I carry on with mounting passion. 'Not at all. Not on your life. It is life's capacity to deal these humourless blows – these blows that are determined to miss the point, that show us that right in its design, life is not going to laugh along with us – it's this capacity that most deserves human derision, human mockery.

'For here we are, sensitive little souls all of us, stupidity and brutality notwithstanding (and not forgiven), and look what we have to deal with: Commedia dell'arte characters who turn out to be real; imaginary illnesses that kill the leading man. What are we going to do if we don't stand up and give the finger and hoot, Rotate? We are going to go mad. Really mad. Absolutely bananas.'

A keeper bursts in and announces that Ahn-Tuan has sent a message that he's too ill to direct today. The crowd emits a collective bellow of disappointment. The keeper goes out and fetches two other keepers to herd us back to our loculi. I give the finger and shout Rotate! all the way down the corridor.

Reliquiae

THE PURGES CONTINUE. I lose track of time. During my short periods of recovery, I am so weak I'm incapable of joining in the acting therapy. Indeed, I have only a dim recollection of the final session, as if it were a decomposing scene from my past life, or a purulent dream.

'None of them are acting now,' Porlock says when I mention it. 'They're all reduced to your own stinking condition. The apothecary is happy though – he doesn't like the artistic treatments. Says it's all modern fiddle-faddle.'

'How long do the treatments usually last? All summer?'

'The physician will be coming tomorrow. He'll be the one to say. It's not the apothecary who'll decide.'

'He's coming to see me then?'

'It's possible.'

The next day I wait for the physician. I am determined to be declared either sane or incurable. I wait all day, until the sun starts to set. When Porlock comes in with my evening soup, I ask him where the physician is in his rounds. He tells me the physician has gone away again. Before I can react, Porlock informs me that the physician has discussed my case with Mr Haslam, who told him I was improving. My heart sinks. My improvement can only falsely support the efficacy of his treatments.

'Then I heard him, the physician, say no more purges,' Porlock tells me.

I brighten considerably.

'But, here's an interesting thing,' Porlock continues. 'The physician said – I heard him distinctly, even though I was restraining a bellowing idiot at the time – "Just get him out of the way." Meaning you. Yes, that's exactly what I heard. And he didn't mean through the front door either.'

'Why on earth would the physician want me out of the way?'

'How should I know?'

When Porlock leaves, I spend a considerable amount of time mulling over this piece of information. I can come up with no satisfactory answer to the question of why the physician should want to dispose of me. If I have been sent to the madhouse as part of a plot, surely it is enough that I am kept here? Why should I need to be hidden as well, unless someone is looking for me? My heart jumps at the thought of it.

Later that evening the apothecary appears at the door. He comes over to the bed where I have again been tethered. He looks down on me for a long time without saying anything.

'I haven't been out in the yard for a while,' I say tentatively. 'I'd like to go out in the yard.'

'What?' he replies. 'You are being purged. Do you expect us to walk behind you with a shovel as if you were a king's horse?'

'I hear the purging is finished.'

'Where did you hear that? It's not finished at all. Except for yourself. In your case the purges are not bringing the expected results.'

'And so?'

'And so we will stop them.'

'Is someone looking for me?' I ask, trying to take him by surprise.

The apothecary blinks. 'Why, no. What made you think so?'

'Something a keeper told me.'

'Ah, you shouldn't listen to the keepers, you know. Some of them are madder than the inmates.'

'This keeper heard the physician speaking.'

'Some of the lunatics hear God.'

We stare at each other for an extended moment.

'How did I get here?' I ask quietly.

'You were brought. Like all the others.'

'Brought by whom?'

'Myself actually. Yes, I went and rescued you from the dark room you'd been shut up in. Now, no more questions – or should I say, no more answers.'

❧

Late the next morning the assistant comes to the cell to remove my seton. He draws the thread out of the thick gum that surrounds the wound and holds it up to inspect it. He puts an ointment and a bandage on my shoulder, and wipes around the dressing with a filthy rag drawn from his apron pocket. He then tells me to bow my head, and begins to remove the dried peas from their putrid soup.

'That is that then,' he says with satisfaction.

'That is what?'

'That is the conclusion of this particular treatment. Until next year. Or earlier if you become acute.'

'Tell me, was this treatment exploded or unexploded?'

The assistant hesitates. 'Don't waste my time,' he finally says. Then he picks up his instruments and ointments and leaves.

Porlock comes in with the lunch.

'Guess what?' he says immediately.

'You're mad and I'm not?'

'No more treatments for you.'

'Why not? Who said?'

'The apothecary has just now told the steward. I over-heard him.'

Soon after lunch, the apothecary himself arrives. He stands by the bed and looks down at me thoughtfully.

'I have said it before and no doubt I'll say it again – insanity is always a matter of degree,' he says.

I look up at him. 'What are you trying to convince yourself of?'

Mr Haslam puts his hands behind his back and starts to walk about the cell. 'The treatments are not my idea, you know. In fact, many of them I don't agree with at all.'

'Why do you perpetrate them then?'

'The physician decides the treatments.'

'Which in particular do you disagree with?' I ask, since the apothecary seems to expect it.

'Well, I think emetics are useless. I prefer cupping to venesection. Camphor and opium are not much good – others swear by them, but I do not go by the opinions of others.'

'I hear that the physician is in attendance very little of the time. How is he to know if his orders are carried out?'

Mr Haslam does not answer. He goes to stand by the grimy window.

'I am doing some research,' he says presently. 'I am looking at the brains of lunatics who have died. All show pathological changes, but here's the thing: the changes are exceedingly various and are uncorrelated with mental symptoms.'

'What are the mental symptoms of death?'

The apothecary grimaces, stiffens and falls silent.

'What do you conclude from this review?' I persist.

'Some people think,' he continues a little aggressively, 'that a scientific way of treating madness would require close attention to the way the mind works. On the contrary, I am concluding that we must pay attention only to diseases of the brain. Organic infection produces the incorrect association of ideas that we call lunacy . . .'

'Yes, you told me once before.'

'It is of little importance which particular incorrect association is displayed as a result; it is the underlying cause – organic disease – that is important.'

'So we are all suffering from pus on the brain?'

'Not at all. I have examined many venereal brains, for instance, without finding any venereal pus whatsoever. The infection is not pus. It is something else. But not something metaphysical; I cannot conceive of a disease of the mind. And if there were such a thing, which there is not, how could we cure it with corporeal remedies?'

'Perhaps you would have to *talk* a madman back to sanity.'

'Well, that would be folly, wouldn't it? I never saw a lunatic who could be talked out of his mad beliefs. No, you have to forget about the metaphysicians. Management is the key while you cure the brain pathology – if you ever can.'

'Management?'

'Kindness, gentleness. In conjunction with proper presentation of the self. Charisma.'

I burst out laughing.

'What do you find so amusing?' Mr Haslam asks me coldly.

'Are shackles an example of kindness, gentleness and charisma?'

'Some lunatics are incorrigible.'

'If I too am incorrigible, as you would seem to imply, why do you come in here and discuss with me the relative merits of the explanations put forward for the causes of insanity?'

'I do not expect that you will keep it straight in your mind. In fact, I do not expect that you will even remember any of it by morning.'

'Why come then?'

'Actually, I came about a different matter altogether. I came to tell you that we find you incurable. Tomorrow you will go to the incurables' wing.'

'Thank God for that.'

Mr Haslam smiles. 'I wouldn't celebrate too soon. All incurables are fully and permanently restrained. Forget about play-acting in the gallery. Forget about walking around. Forget about lying down. Forget about poetry books and your *copia verborum*.'

'You sound as if you relish the infliction of chains upon a man.'

'Why should I care?'

'In my experience, many relish such an infliction.'

'For me, everything is quite logical and straightforward. An incurable is too mad to suffer from being restrained. And curables are treated, not tied up. At least, not on a regular basis.'

'Treatment and restraint seem very similar here. The curables are restrained by their treatment.'

The apothecary refuses to take up this topic of conversation.

'I will escort you to your new position myself,' he announces. 'We wouldn't want you getting lost down there – you might meet the Minotaur.'

'Excuse me, I already have.'

'Your new apartment is even now being prepared, and I have selected for you the most perfect companion.'

'I am to have company?'

'Yes, of course. Few of the incurables are kept alone. But do not look so alarmed!'

'I don't always like company.'

'You will like the company of this man, I am sure. He will never disagree with a thing you say.'

'Have I given the impression that *that* is all I care about?'

Mr Haslam puts his nose in the air. 'You do not care for reciprocity in your social relations.'

'It always alerts me when you refer to such things as reciprocity in my relations. I conclude that you are alluding to relationships of mine which you should know nothing about.'

Mr Haslam raises his nose even more alarmingly. 'I know more about you than you could possibly imagine.'

THE END

The King of Rien

SO THAT'S THE STORY of my treatment. I am put under the deluge. I am spun in the Herculean chair. I am given the apothecary's carefully concocted poisons. I am cupped and cut. I act, walk in the yard, listen to music and read poetry. Between times I find myself standing in the long gallery, before the fire if the weather is cold, by a small window if the fire isn't lit. And standing thus, looking high above the hoi-polloi, I miss the only opportunity for escape I ever had. My only possible saviour has begun his gradual deterioration.

Already, while I am gazing into the middle distance, Porlock has forgotten the name of an item he ate for dinner. He has been enthusiastically recounting this repast to another keeper and suddenly he breaks off. He is standing there, clicking his fingers, hoping to recall the name of the food. It doesn't come. The other keeper supplies the name, and looks a little surprised. It is a common enough item, because common food is all that is available, and in ever-decreasing quantities, owing to the wars and agricultural failures. And look at the prices! No wonder Porlock starts to eat less. And, as more of his available pennies are needed for alcohol, his nutrition increasingly suffers. He loses weight. He loses words. It is so gradual, I myself hardly notice.

Anyway, my concern isn't really with Porlock. I am anxious. Where is the man who will save me? I am less confident than I once was. I crane my neck. I look for signs: fancy carriages in the driveway, tall hats in the hall, cigar butts on the floors of the corridors. Nothing. All the while Porlock drinks and starves, shrivels physically and mentally, becomes the cretin who cannot recognise what is in his own best interest, as I am the cretin who cannot recognise what is in my own, even without the drinking.

My treatments continue. All this time I wait, with decreasing hopefulness and eventual dejection. All this time Porlock deteriorates. Then one day it is too late. The apothecary pronounces me incurable. I am taken from the solitary cell where I am only occasionally tied to the bed, and ushered into another wing. I am thrust into the cell where Horatio lies supine on his straw and I am chained by the legs and arms. When Porlock arrives with my first incurables' soup, a liquid even thinner and cooler than that of our curable colleagues, his once-straight back is hunched over, and he has forgotten who I am. He soon remembers, after several promptings, but I have received quite a shock.

'What are you staring at me like that for?' he growls.

'You've changed,' I mumble.

'Changed? You sound like my wife.'

'What does she say is different about you?'

'I don't think it's right to tell you. But apart from that, she says I'm not affectionate enough. Don't dance attendance like I used to once upon a time. Well, that's marriage I tell her, like it or lump it.'

'You didn't know who I was,' I accuse him.

'How can a man remember every lunatic? Particularly when someone's always moving them about?'

'Tell me what you had for dinner last night.'

'I didn't have dinner last night.'

'Why not?'

Porlock screws up his eyes. 'Well, now that you ask, I don't rightly know. Perhaps the old goose forgot to cook it. Or she ate up everything in the larder for her lunch. I had some beer – that I do recall. She probably saw me drunk and tricked me out of my share. So she can get fatter and more abdominal than ever.'

'Your wife is fat and abominable?'

'All wives are.'

'Well, why did you marry her then?'

'She wasn't fat at the start. She was as slim and sweet and affectionate as any bride. She only turned into a sow after she'd got her babies.'

'How many children do you have, Porlock?'

'Too bloody many to count. But they're all gone now, thank God. Now I only have to worry about *her* gaping maw.'

'Don't you like any of your children?'

'Like? What's like got to do with it? What choice did I ever get?'

'Some people like their children.'

'Huh. They arrive all pale and sappy, and turn themselves into porkers at the father's expense. What's the bloody use of them?'

I sigh. Not only has Porlock deteriorated, he has become quite churlish. He has become the kind of person who no longer helps anybody because it pleases him more to hinder. I watch him go out muttering, looking more wizened than ever. And the next time I see him, he again fails to recognise me.

~

But all that was many years ago. How many years have Horatio and I spent together now? I don't know. I confess that time moves queerly for me. The seconds are slow, excruciating, like droplets of water forming on the end of a stalk: we wait and wait and finally they fall, only to be replaced by another tedious formation. But all these droplets together have formed a river of years, a river that has flowed relentlessly, unstoppably, past us.

When did I first begin recounting my treatment to Horatio?

An aeon ago. We were interrupted so many times: by illness, sleep, despair, accident. We were interrupted by other stories that came and went, by all those words whose pathways I had to explore. We were seldom interrupted by mad-doctors; as far as I can remember, the apothecary has come to see us only once. I woke up from a doze and there he was in the doorway, malevolent as a cloacal spectre.

'They tell me you've been making a racket,' he said.

'On and off,' I replied carefully, although the memory of my doing so was stale, as of something that happened very long ago. 'My cell-mate is sick. At least, he *was*. He doesn't seem to have got any worse in recent times.'

'He looks all right to me,' the apothecary replied from the door.

I studied carefully the barely concealed malice in his expression.

'You can still be treated if it pleases us, you know,' he warned. 'True, we don't usually wish to waste the physick. But do not think you are free in here.' He stopped to laugh noisily at his own joke. 'There is still the chair,' he added with dark pleasure.

'You've heard about the chair, haven't you?' he persisted when I said nothing. 'It is designed to remove all movement, even all sensation. You are tied to it, chest, arms and legs, and your ankles are bound, and then a box is placed upon your head, padded so that it cuts out all sound and light. The padded box is designed to render your head immobile, and there you sit for hours or days or years, with a chamberpot beneath you, and defecation as your only entertainment.'

I looked away to avoid the apothecary's peculiar enjoyment.

Then he stood there as if he did not know what to do or say next, as if he had time to waste or fill in, an hour or two before a dinner or a ball. While he loitered, I was determined to know something of the outside world.

'How is the extension of French happiness progressing?' I asked.

The apothecary looked surprised, startled even, as if he had forgotten that anything existed beyond these crumbling walls. Then he recovered himself and smirked. 'It is progressing alarmingly through Europe, but has had some defeats in the colonies. Napoleon had to sell Louisiana to the Americans. He'd planned a large colonial empire there, but events were pressing at home.'

'And what about the Antipodes?'

'What about them?'

'What is winning: French happiness or English melancholy?'

'Scottish dourness, I believe. And drunken whalers from Port Jackson.'

'And is Napoleon closer to England? Will we become manic instead of melancholic?'

'Goodness, you are out of touch. Nelson saw him off. October the 21st. The battle of Trafalgar.'

'October the 21st? Which year was that?'

'1805. Now England has mastery of the seas.'

'Last year was 1805?'

Mr Haslam frowned copiously. 'It is currently 1808.'

So much time? I wondered.

'And is everything you have just told me generally considered to be good or bad?'

'You can't seriously think the French are fit to govern the English? Good God – a nation of moral degenerates.'

'I quite liked the place myself.'

'That's because you are a degenerate also. Imagine, we would all be speaking French and . . .'

'Having continuous *soixante-neuf*?'

Mr Haslam frowned so deeply his face became geographical. 'I do not know what you mean.'

'But you can guess, surely? Let me help you: a sex act with heads at opposite ends.'

'You are still polluted I see,' the apothecary replied through virtually clenched teeth.

'Oh, get away with you. What do you dream of in your strait little cot? Conjugal duty? Not on your life. So what's your fancy? English muffin, French tart or American pie? Exploded or unexploded?'

'I beg your pardon?'

'Do you prefer the treatment to be given in the seat of passion or the opposite end?'

'I'm going to fetch you some camphor,' Mr Haslam declared, and he turned on his heels and went towards the door.

'Fetch me what you like,' I called as he went out. 'You'll never shut me up. I know all the secrets of the body.'

Camphor is an odious poison that causes nausea and brings on strangury, but I half-hoped he would return so I could have another go at him. He didn't.

But now the memory of that visit is itself stale; and the apothecary has not come again. Horatio continues to cough and writhe at odd intervals, and I boom on in the silence.

~

'Horatio, I am now strong enough to return to the subject that concerned us immediately prior to the story of my treatment. Do you recall it? We had just suffered a terrible blow. We had settled on a scheme with Porlock whereby he would sell a certain map for me and then keep the money in return for facilitating our escape. Before we could put the plan into effect, however – horror! My own children came to uplift the proposed merchandise. They came and they took my map without even visiting me.

'The first question we must ask ourselves is: who sent them? Obviously, it can only have been their mother. The authorities here would not deal directly with children. The second question is: did they know, or not know, that I am buried alive in this mausoleum? Well? Would their mother have sent them here in complete ignorance? I think it unlikely, for the simple reason that the physician or the apothecary may have found cause and opportunity to speak to them of me, and their mother would have wanted them to be well prepared, would not have wished them to receive such information like the fall of the guillotine. So, my family has abandoned me. Not just my wife, as I thought in the beginning, but the whole accursed lot of them.'

I become silent for a minute or two. Then I clear my throat and carry on.

'Do not think, Horatio, that I am about to go mad now. I have been living with the pain of this betrayal for quite some time and I have become accustomed to the sharpness of it. A man gets to the point where he rejects those who reject him. Rather than returning to the family fold he starts to have different plans for his freedom, should it ever be granted. Do you remember the country which my map depicted? When I am freed from here, I've a mind to start again there. I'd like to see the cabbage trees, and the flax swamps, and the tangerine and emerald mountain parrot, and the green sea so clear they say you can see the fish suspended in it. There's no need for a map of course. As Porlock so rightly said, the captain of the ship will know the way.

'After my property and income have been restored to me, I will board a vessel as a passenger, as I should have done at twenty-six when I went to Plymouth to watch James Cook sail off the edge of the world. Do I now disown my children? Will I disinherit them? Will I allow my weak and manipulable wife to sink into poverty? Of course not. They all gave me pleasure in their own ways, despite their eventual betrayals. But I have a lot to make up for now, and I do not wish to spend my remaining years chewing over their wrongdoings. No, I will sail off into the sunset, or rise, and put all this behind me . . .'

Porlock interrupts my speech with the lunch.

'This soup is even more watery than usual,' I complain as he feeds me.

'I pissed in it.'

'You're too mean.'

'A sheep died in it.'

'Oh? It will be much more nutritious then. Give me more.'

Porlock snatches away the spoon. 'You've had your share, funny man. I'm giving the rest to the sad-sack.'

When Porlock has gone, I look down at the huddled bundle that is Horatio.

'Where were we? Ah yes. Do you recall what I once said to Mr Haslam, my friend? I told him that I prefer the non-narrative mode. In fact, I enjoy a good narrative as much as the next person. But I wanted an opportunity to sneer at him, to say narrative is pabulum in that particular tone of voice. As someone once said it to me.'

I look out of the tiny window and see snow falling – the first of the long hard winter. I have a moment of panic at the thought of the biting cold, the extended darkness.

'What are we going to do all winter, Horatio? How are we going to keep our spirits up? Of course, you already know. It's my stories that keep us sane, isn't it? Narrative is pabulum only when it's badly done. So, what say I make a start?

'Once upon a time . . . what the hell does that mean? I never knew. No matter. Once upon a time, everyone knew the function of a story. After the roasted boar, someone told a story because it was hours till you could all go to bed and fornicate. That's how it was, Horatio. You knew what you'd had, you knew what you were going to get, and you just had to fill in the time between. All so straightforward.

'Of course, some of the stories were better than others, and that was good. But then some fool comes along and tries to make some rules. Before you know it, storytelling to stem the boredom is over. It's now a display, a virtuoso performance of the application of the rules. And competitive. If you don't want a knife in your back, better not open your mouth.

'True or false, Horatio? How should I know? I'm too tied up at the moment to go and research the history of storytelling. But whatever the truth once was, the freedom has gone out of it. The story is now its own prison. You begin – you mistakenly think you can begin with anything – and the beginning is the ball and chain. You carry on – already limited by your initial mistake – and soon the walls are up, constructed out of plot and character, both of which increasingly define the space allowed.

'You look back longingly at the beginning and wonder how you could have started differently, better. Obviously, it's not true that you can begin with just anything. What, then, are the rules? Start at the end and work back, a seemingly marvellous process of loosening, of unknitting? But what are you working back to? To nothing.

'So you get craftier. You think about the final effect you want – the thing you really want to say. You have to have something to say beyond the story. That's part of the rules. By this you will be judged. You'll work back from there, mentally, and then you will tell the story forwards. But what constitutes a final effect without a plot or character already defined? By this time you are mixed up and very irritable. And all you wanted was the requisite flourish and aptness, and then serenity. Oh, and beauty. You wanted it to be beautiful, to pay homage to the world that you can't have, can't hold, can't even touch . . .'

Horatio lets out a long loud groan, almost a bellow, and I fly into a panic. I shout for a keeper, rattle my chains, yell madly at the top of my voice. But no one comes. Horatio starts to cough blood clots onto the flagstones.

~

Porlock staggers in later with the buckets.

'Fetch the apothecary,' I cry. 'Horatio is sick again. He is coughing up blood.'

'Don't tell me what to do, lunatic,' Porlock replies angrily. 'I've got everyone on my back today.'

'Fetch him or I'll . . .'

'You'll what?'

We glare at each other.

'Settle down, lunatic. You might start imagining things again. Like you've got something to sell – a map or somesuch.' Porlock bursts out laughing.

Rage implodes in my stomach.

'I'm not ordering, threatening or bargaining. I'm pleading.'

Porlock looks pleased. 'Well then, I just might. You never know.'

He busies himself cleaning up Horatio's straw. 'They say Napoleon's invaded Russia,' he informs me as he works. 'Five hundred thousand frogs have gone in.'

'Well they'll all croak, mark my words.'

Porlock cackles. 'It'll be the end of that silly little man. The Russians'll see he's all hat and stallion.'

'And what's the year? What year is it?'

Porlock rolls his eyes. 'It's 1812, for fuck's sake.'

'So late,' I murmur. Then, 'What's that terrible stench?' I ask, as a thoroughly noxious miasma assaults my nostrils.

Porlock discovers that one of the buckets contains the morning soil rather than the evening sustenance, and he leaves the cell to search for the missing slurry. I look down at Horatio.

'Didn't I tell you the years have flowed by, my friend? I can hardly remember what the date was when I last knew it. 1808 rings a bell, but I don't know why.'

We wait. Porlock forgets to return. My stomach rumbles a few times and then gives up. It has learnt not to waste its energy in protest.

'I didn't get a story started earlier, did I, Horatio? I spent a certain amount of time pontificating morosely, and then we were interrupted by your crisis. The sad truth is that after all these years I've run out of stories. Without any new experiences, I've nothing left to tell. Perhaps I should return to my word game and hope that an intriguing word will be a stimulus to my tired imagination. But not right at this moment. I'm so hungry I could only present you with a long list of comestibles.'

I open my eyes from a dream of a banquet hall crammed with grotesquely overladen tables.

'Horatio, are you awake?'

He doesn't move. I wait for a moment and plunge on.

'I can't possibly sleep with this hunger. So, if you don't mind, I'll carry on where I left off. The fact is, words aren't a life. No, not even for the man who has nothing else. Why should I not just give up? Succumb to an existence of raging and incontinence? At least then they'd give me some straw to lie on. What do I get while I hold myself up and in? Nothing. *Rien*.

'Horatio, excuse my sudden chuckle there when I slipped into French – I reminded myself of something. Did you know that on the day of the storming of the Bastille, King Louis XVI wrote *Rien* in his diary? Imagine that! First that a king keeps a diary – is this believable, I ask you? Second, that a king with everything and everyone at his royal command should ever sum up a day with *Rien*. Nothing fit for a king, or really nothing – nothing like ours? Third, that a man surrounded with spies and seers and oracles and God's whispers should have so little prescience. And fourth, the most unimaginable, that a man with all the freedom in the world should ever care to fit little nothing words to days. Why is he not on his horse's back, his mistress's back, his wife's back, his own back? A sin. A crime. Got what he deserved, I say. Now he'll know what *Rien* is.'

I stop to chortle out loud.

'Horatio, what do you think Louis wrote in his diary on the day he first saw a hot-air balloon go up? I will come right out and admit that I have no idea, but it's an amusing thing to speculate about. On this particular morning, in September 1783, Louis gets up, dresses grandly, and with Marie Antoinette proceeds to a field where the balloon waits. He is excited perhaps. The French are about to conquer the air. Joseph Michel and Jacques Etienne

Montgolfier, the inventors, are standing by. They will light a fire of wood and straw which will heat the air in the balloon and, if everything goes according to plan, they will perhaps soar even higher than the six thousand feet of the test flight. Alternatively, they might provide entertainment for the royal couple by going up in a conflagration. Yes, they themselves will go up in the basket, along with a duck, a sheep and a rooster.

'What does the King think of the ridiculous little cluster of passengers? I don't know. Why are they there at all? This is the question that interests me now. Do the inventors believe that their king is a child, more amused by the presence of harmless animals than by the marvels of science? Anyway, all goes well. The fire is lit, the huge balloon carries the duck, the sheep and the rooster aloft, the King claps excitedly, the Queen reapplies her rouge. All the King can think of are the surprised looks on the faces of the dear little sheep, the plucky duck and the cocksure rooster. Why, they are French heroes!

'Is that a muffled guffaw I hear from you, Horatio? Perhaps now we have a clearer idea why the Bastille business, when it happened a few years later, did not amuse the King. Did not even interest him. When you can watch God's fluffy, fleecy and feathery creatures ascending to the heavens!

'Of course, you'll say I've made him ridiculous. I have, haven't I, with my selective accounts of his love of small animals, his *Rien*. We can put this skew on anyone we want to. So why put it on Louis? To serve my own ends, of course. His *Rien* was always another man's ruin. And eventually, up they rose, his subjects, and chopped off his silly head. The way I've described it makes it seem justified, doesn't it? Did him a favour. Did themselves a favour. Well, did they? Did you know that some political wit said that the notion of happiness began with the French Revolution?'

~

I wake up. Someone has forgotten to bring the morning bucket. I know this because my bladder is about to explode. And I am also dying of thirst. I'm always furious when such occasions arise. The keepers come in and abuse us because we piss our rags and straw: 'You're the only incurable with a bucket,' the half-cripple roars. 'Fuck knows why. And you can't even fucken wait for it.'

This particular morning I am about to give in when Porlock arrives and saves me. He staggers out with the sloshing bucket and returns quite promptly with the gruel. It is still warm and I slurp it off the spoon greedily. Then he goes over to feed Horatio. One of the advantages of Porlock's poor memory is that, having forgotten when he last fed Horatio, he compensates by feeding him more often than the other keepers do. By the time Porlock leaves I am feeling almost contented.

'Horatio, I am not going to work today. I am having a day off. I want to explain something very important. I told you the full story of myself and Juliet, but I left something out. I never explained why I approached her in the first place. So, are you settled comfortably and ready to listen?

'Last night I said some political wit claimed that the notion of happiness began with the French Revolution. He must have been referring to the happiness of the peasant, of course. Or perhaps your average textile worker. It's understood by the lower ranks, who have a tendency to equate money and the giving of orders with happiness, that the rich and influential have always been happy. But the rich and influential, even the moderately well off who hope to persuade, are secretly relieved to share the burden of happiness with the peasant and the textile slave. The burden of happiness has been gladly handed on and down, like some awful parcel that is all wrapping and no content.

'You don't agree? Of course you don't. It's preposterous! But I have taken it upon myself to convince you that the notion of happiness is indeed a burden. When I say it was shared gladly I have no proof at all. I am being ironic – for who would share a burden and be miserable? But now the peasant and industrial flunkey have to secure bread *and* quality of life. It's a wonder we can't hear them groaning from here.

'They weren't immediately aware of all the problems, of course. They took their knitting down to the scaffold and were mightily entertained to see the heads roll. If this was to be the new order of things – the King's head on the block, while their own remained safe and sound and chortling upon their shoulders – why, happiness could be guaranteed. But too soon the new order became the usual order. A few on top, many underneath. Same story, different names. Did they cry in the new bread queues? And crying, did they not feel robbed twice? For now they lacked both bread *and* happiness.

'Once the peasants and textile workers have been permitted happiness, they are also responsible for it – or rather for the lack of it – in their own lives. In this they are finally equal to everybody. They must shoulder the full weight of the burden. Every day they must slog after bread and happiness, the satisfaction of the former requirement no longer a substitute for the latter. Every first minute of the day they must ask themselves, *Am I hungry?* and every second minute, *Am I happy?* They have two worries where they formerly had one. Eventually, they will have to answer the question: If a full belly no longer makes me happy, what will?

'And so they slip into the permanent unease of the rich and the middle classes, into that twilight of anxiety where every action, indeed every plan, must be scrutinised for its capacity to produce and eventually maximise happiness. One thing after another must be discarded, one plan after another abandoned. The sheer choice becomes frightening. What if you choose the wrong course of action and are never as happy as you might have been? By what criteria are you to select one thing over another? Will you know it when your hand finally closes upon the one thing that will bring everlasting, gold-plated happiness?

'A great determination now overtakes the peasant: he *must* be happy. At all costs. First, necessarily, he must be rich and give orders. But getting rich is problematic – and exhausting – and the minions he gives orders to are always trying to overthrow him in their own pursuit of happiness. Then he must express himself, because hitherto he has always been told to keep his mouth shut, and this is a freedom which will surely lead to much personal happiness if money and power are still out of his reach. Temporarily, it is to be understood. And so he spews out his arid and uneducated opinions all over the place, and is troubled to find he gets a fist in his nose and a boot in his arse and that happiness has been startled off, only to settle down a little further ahead. The clever ones begin to suspect that the freedom to be happy is another slavery, although, curiously, a slavery to oneself. And how is one to overthrow the despotism of the self, Horatio?'

~

'Raving again, are you, lunatic?' Porlock scoffs from the door.

'Ah Horatio, here is the peasant now. But what is he doing here? No doubt he's forgotten he's already seen to us this morning.'

It quickly becomes apparent that Porlock is drunk, despite the earliness of the hour. He staggers about the cell, raving incoherently. Then he falls across the straw like a felled tree. He eructates loudly. I am pleased when he suddenly sits up, interruptively clutching his head and groaning. Talking about the pursuit of happiness is almost as wearying as doing it.

'Tell me, Porlock,' I taunt as he looks for the flask he didn't bring. 'Are you tired out by the pursuit of happiness?'

'I'm tired out by lunatics.'

'But when you are not here, do you pursue happiness?'

'What – like I would a rabid dog?'

'Yes, with a weapon.'

Porlock staggers over to me and narrows his eyes. 'I can't be bothered with it. I've got to worry all the time about money.'

'So if you were rich you'd be happy?'

'Certainly. An unhappy rich man is an idiot.'

I laugh. Porlock can always be relied upon for entertainment of this kind.

'Mercifully, a poor man can find happiness in a bottle,' he adds.

'You're happy when you're drunk?'

'Of course. An unhappy drunk is the idiot's brother.'

'So you'd say sober happiness is only for the French, perhaps for the Americans?'

'What?' He screws up his wizened face and looks quite irritable. 'What have those two got to do with each other?'

'They both had revolutions.'

'Well, I don't know anything about that. But we've had some revolutions. I believe,' he says a little uncertainly.

'We certainly have. And now we have the steam engine. And so happiness should be on its way.'

'Yours won't,' Porlock declares. 'Lunatics can't be happy. Mr Haslam said so. They are up or they are down and either way their judgement is affected.'

Then he begins to stagger about the cell again, muttering and hiccoughing.

'Do you know a little game I play with myself when I'm really bored?' I ask, because I cannot bear to watch him – cannot bear to watch how the peasant makes the most of his freedom.

'Is it self-polluting?'

I ignore him. 'I try to work out which, of eyesight or hearing, I'd give up if I had to choose between them. For a man who loves music this is more difficult than it is for the man who is indifferent to it. How can we choose between Mozart and the sight of the sea?'

'You can stick both of them arse-wise as far as I'm concerned.'

'But if you *had* to choose . . .'

Porlock frowns. 'I like to see my money. If you couldn't see it to count it, you'd get swindled. How could you trust anyone else to count your money for you?'

'Why do you make yourself a slave to money when freedom's the only thing that matters?'

'Because I want to eat. Because I like to go to the whores down by the docks. Because I might want to go to New South Wales. Now keep quiet, lunatic. I feel sick.'

Porlock weaves back to the straw bale and sits down. He makes a number of unconvincing dry retches and then announces his stomach is a little settled.

'I bet you have a little hoard that you wouldn't dream of spending on food or fannies or flight. That you keep for its own sake,' I continue.

'Well, what of it?'

'I bet you're obsessed with that little hoard. That's why you keep coming here to empty pisspots and hose off bums.'

Porlock groans loudly, breaks wind, and finally manages to say, 'Look, funny man, money doesn't matter to you because you had plenty, so you say. But freedom doesn't matter to me because I can't do anything with it.'

'We should change places then. I could do things with it.'

'What things?'

'Well, nothing. Or nothing in particular. It would be enough just to walk around. Lie down.'

'You'd soon get sick of it. Everyone gets sick of what's no trouble to have. Then you want more.'

'I think I've finally learnt only to want very little.'

'Well, that's easy to say when you've got nothing,' Porlock sneers. 'Your expectations soon go up again.'

'Yes,' I agree with him. 'That is the great flaw in a human being.'

Porlock sits on the straw and gapes at me slackly for a short while, then rouses himself. He gets up and goes over to Horatio. He lifts him up by the armpits and props him against the wall. I turn my head away while Porlock irrationally searches for his flask in the space vacated by Horatio's body.

'Yes, by all means, hand the burden of happiness to the peasant,' I intone while he hunts. 'I'm sure he will always be able to treasure it. Even when he's no longer the peasant who works the soil but simply the dumb sod, no longer the textile worker but the rough cloth that is worked over, no longer the toolmaker, merely the blunt tool.'

'Who're you calling a fucking tool?' Porlock growls.

∼ↄ

'Where were we?' I ask Horatio when Porlock finally leaves. 'Oh yes, I'd just asked you how we are to overthrow the despotism of the self. Well, we can't. Or I couldn't. I tried when I took up archery, but the despot was too strong and forced me to give it up. Now, here we are at the beginning of my own story of happiness, Horatio. You didn't really think I was only interested in the peasants and textile workers of the revolution, did you? No. Since I am a human being, I am far more interested in myself than in absolutely anything else.'

I stop for a moment to look at Horatio. He is lying quietly and breathing evenly.

'Think, Horatio, before we came here, of all the small defeats there were in the average day. Though individually none of them might amount to much, collectively they were like a pack of wolves: they could bring your life down with their sharp teeth and relentlessness. Did you not feel that the pack of small defeats munched away at your life till it could no longer stand up, could hardly get to its knees?

'I know I did, and from time to time I would take to my bed for a week or two and pile the blankets over my head, simply to try to regain my strength and carry on. I wasn't mad, as my wife often feared. She would hover around me, wringing her hands, and I admit I had some sympathy for her: when you are married you are in the same boat – if you'll excuse me for going from wolves to boats so untidily – and it's very alarming if half the crew looks like he's going out of his mind from all that sea and salt.

'In my bed, accompanied by rich broths, soothing custards, mulled wines, peaty whiskies and good books, I got control of myself, regained my perspective with regard to all those sharp little teeth. Oh, I know I had fewer wolves in my pack than most. The possession of money alone was enough to ensure that. But still, there were always onerous little duties baring their fangs.

'For example, there was the education of my sons and daughters. They all had to be educated. I had an endless struggle with the ballet of tutors. Entrances, exits, everyone out of step. The mathematics tutor would be too harsh and the girls would cry; the French tutor would be too soft and the boys would fight. The music tutor would say So-and-so had no talent and he was wasting his time; the English tutor would read a bawdy tale and the children's mother would come to me red and trembling and allege he was debauching our daughters. Then I would engage a governess for the girls, and their fine minds would slip away into poetastry and embroidery.

'On and on it went. And I remember well the looks on the tutors' faces whenever I had cause to speak seriously to one of them: a hurt pride behind the polite demeanour, as if I were guilty of unjustly taking my children's or wife's part against him. To hell with them all, I'd think periodically; but such defiance can never last in family life. If a family is nothing else, it is at the very least a set of problems to be solved, and unsolved problems always accumulate, form a pack.

'The tutor problem was but a refined version of the servant problem. Maids, cooks, butlers, gardeners, coming and going, drinking and fornicating, fighting and bellyaching. And there wasn't any silent reproach when you had to give one of them a talking-to: no, there was screaming and hissing and swearing and shove-it-up-your-arse-then. The servants stupidly believe that the rich man has it easy, but the rich man has to deal with *them*.

Fortunately, they do not have to deal with themselves, and thus they are freed from one of life's nastier vexations.

'The fact is, Horatio, as long as your stomach is full, life's most difficult trial is dealing with other people. And not just the likes of servants and tutors, errant children and anxious wives, but peers and superiors and heroes and phantoms. It's no surprise, my silent friend, that the transcendent effect of *eros* is such a relief.

'I might as well come straight out with it: I wasn't very good at being happy, Horatio. I made a pig's ear of it. In our current circumstances, I'm quite ashamed to admit to my failure. Happiness should have been easy. When I was much younger, say about twenty-five, it was certainly easier. When things went wrong, as they often did, I could wave the glorious future like a magic wand in front of myself, and the present would be sorted out in a trice. The real trouble began when the future seemed worse than the present.

'This catastrophe occurred when I turned forty-eight. On my birthday, two of my teeth fell out. Teeth fall out all the time, you say. Agreed. But they were the first of mine to drop, and all at once I began to see the future as an inexorable process of decay. For the first time I stopped looking at old people as though their dodderiness and slowness were self-willed, a state they somehow preferred to intellectual acuity and physical competence. And I realised this horrible business of cumulative deterioration would be thrust down on *me*. It wasn't a matter of deciding to have it otherwise. I saw that one began life with grand hopes – to be rich or famous or in some way splendid – and ended just happy to take a few steps and breathe.

'Something else happened when my teeth fell out, and it was perhaps even worse. Do you remember how I told you about the chains of a story? That in a story you think you can say anything, but then plot and character and all the rest of it start to form a prison? The event that occurred around my forty-eighth birthday, when I was ruminating excessively on my new toothlessness, was my sudden recognition that this process had happened to my own life. I myself was the main character, and I was being ever more rigidly defined and delineated by the situations I found myself in. My life was the plot, and no matter how much I tried to direct it, to create new situations where other character traits could emerge, *one thing led to another!*

'I was shocked. All the choice I'd had at the start was gone. There could be no more change or development. The walls were up to my neck. The shackles were on. And in real life there's no hope of any fiction tricks – hysteron proteron, or working backwards, or repeatedly starting again. You're stuck with it all.'

I fall silent for a minute or two so that each of us might reflect on this bitter truth.

'And do you also recall my telling you that our inheritance from the French Revolution was that every action, indeed every plan, must be scrutinised for its capacity to produce and eventually maximise happiness? That everything must be sorted according to this goal; that, as a consequence, one thing after another must be discarded, one plan after another abandoned?

'But now, in my own tale of happiness, I am suddenly forty-eight with two teeth missing, and old-man's breath, and everything seems to have solidified around me. I have come to the end of possibility. How can I be happy when I cannot endlessly sort and discard according to happiness's fickle dictates?

'Well, we've had wolves, teeth, the servants' dance, sailing boats. The freedom to sort and discard has just become an illusion in my own life. I am forty-eight, all tied up, and my tongue won't stop poking around in the wounds in my gums. I am miserable and the future is bleak. In a sense, my life is over.

'Well, Horatio, we both know what happens next. One summer morning, I get up and my wife reminds me that we must again attend a party. I am cross. I dress, reflecting that at least it's a garden party – probably I will have a chance to sneak away on the pretext of admiring the landscaping. Indeed, I have just decided to do exactly this when my attention is first drawn to Juliet. She is statuesque with sable hair, ivory skin and full lips, but although these physical attributes are attractive to me, they are not very important. I don't mean to boast, Horatio, but I've had many beautiful women. No, this time there's something else as well: an indefinable quality, something that shines. Or perhaps it's just the nimbus surrounding an ageing rogue's last chance for gold-plated happiness. Because that is how the rogue sees it: William Lonsdale is going to be happy – at last!'

~

I wake up in a dazzle of moonlight. My leg is burning, and my old itch is again screaming to advance.

After the Big Flood, when I stood in an excrementitious scum for weeks, I developed a patch of scaliness on my smallest toe. My chains allowed me to scratch it only with the big toe of my other foot. I scratched, and the skin turned bright red and then shiny. I scratched, and scratched, thoughtlessly, heedlessly, giving in to that intense pleasure when the scratch finds the unslakeable source of the itch. My toe began to bleed.

I was alarmed. I tried not to scratch, but the urge was overwhelming. I gave in, even though scratching now produced a lasting, burning agony. The skin fell off my toe in flakes, and the itch fled to its neighbour. Soon my whole foot was a mess of dried blood and scabs and peeling skin, and the itch was advancing up my leg to the shackle. But my other foot could not reach to scratch there, and the disease halted. I conscientiously avoided any movement which allowed the shackle itself to abrade the itch or there would have been no stopping it. The itch would have roared up my body and I would have rubbed myself mad and then dead on the greasy walls.

I now look down at my lower leg and notice that it is also swollen; the shackle clutches me in a way it has never done before. And I am drippingly hot, as if I've been given one of the apothecary's medieval cures. Very soon I am also feeling nauseous and weak. I sag against my chains as my strength – what little I possess – is driven from my limbs by a mounting fever. I fear that the poisons have travelled from my diseased leg and are now attacking my vital organs . . .

I again open my eyes, but instead of moonlight I see sunlight streaming in the small window. Then I see the apothecary is standing a little to my left and staring at me.

'Ah, you have come back to us. You nearly died,' he informs me when he sees me looking at him. 'But once we chopped your leg off . . .'

I look down in alarm at my legs. Both are present and complete, although the diseased limb has now been released from its prison. The apothecary watches me and laughs. 'Just a little joke, Mr Lonsdale. No, the physician ordered an infusion of foxglove for your fever and a hot poultice for your swelling.'

'Cured yesterday of my disease, I died last night of my physician,' I quote coldly.

'Ah, not only have your swelling and fever abated but your sense of humour has returned. I will inform your wife.'

'My *wife*?'

The apothecary tries and fails to suppress a smile. 'Naturally we had to inform her of your imminent demise.'

'My wife knows I nearly died? She has visited me here?'

The apothecary sighs with exaggeration and shakes his head.

'Why not? Why has she not visited me since she knows where I am, knows I might have died. . .'

'Your wife was at your trial,' Mr Haslam interrupts me soothingly. 'When you've built up your strength, I'll tell you all about it.'

Noting that I am too shocked to reply, the apothecary sticks out his chest, full of the importance of his secrets, and leaves.

For several days I am given a fortifying diet, and at regular intervals the apothecary's assistant assiduously rubs emollients on my diseased leg. I notice, however, that though it has returned to its former size, and the surface of the skin has healed considerably, the itch still hovers, as all itches do. An itch is an accursed thing to get rid of.

Eventually the apothecary arrives to inspect the assistant's work. He squats down and rubs his hands over the skin with much feigned interest. He is making me wait for what I am so impatient to hear. A kick twitches in my lower leg.

'About your trial,' he finally says, standing up and assuming his usual stance, legs apart, hands behind his back, as if he's about to give a lecture. 'Your wife was at your trial as I recently said. In fact, contrary to what I once told you, your wife instigated it. Once the constables had tracked you down, of course.'

'And why would she have done that?'

'On the grounds that you were displaying fiscal irresponsibility and wantonness. You were giving away large sums to another woman – a former actress, wasn't she?'

The apothecary is now looking at me very carefully. For the first time, although it is now years too late for such an intuition, I sense danger. Danger rather than the usual culpable stupidity. Then another old memory comes back to me.

'You referred, another time when we spoke of this, to other interested parties at my trial.'

Mr Haslam looks surprised. 'Indeed I did. Your memory is excellent and correct.'

'To whom were you referring?'

'Witnesses were called.'

'Ah.'

'You are not going to ask me who these witnesses were?'

'I was allowing myself time to think it out.'

'Thinking is tiresome when there is someone else who already knows. The witnesses, the interested parties, were some relations of your friend the actress.'

'Yes, I had begun to form that conclusion.'

'They were able to recount certain extravagances which seemed, shall we say . . . inexplicable?'

The apothecary raises his eyebrows interrogatively. I make no reply.

'When one gives away large sums of money to a woman, it's not unnatural to expect a little kindness in return, wouldn't you agree? And there's the rub. It would appear that the kindness was never extracted.'

'Indeed it was.'

'Yes. That was rather her husband's view. He accused his wife of lying about her chastity with regard to yourself. Whereupon – not in the court, you understand, this was a private interview – the poor woman became quite hysterical and . . .'

'This is where you came in.'

'Excellently concluded.'

'And what did you do with her?'

'Why, nothing. She remained at home with her husband. And although he secretly believed you to have cuckolded him, he went to the court and was witness to the fact that a patent madman was paying his wife money while entertaining no dreams of seduction.'

I almost laugh.

'You find this funny?'

'I certainly didn't fuck her. . .'

'Oh, please!'

'Although I certainly intended to,' I carry on, ignoring the apothecary's grimaces and gesticulations. 'I had it planned for the week after Christmas.'

'The very week you went out of your mind,' Mr Haslam murmurs. 'A strange coincidence.'

'A very strange coincidence, now that you mention it,' I agree.

We look at each other. The apothecary appears to be on the verge of confessing more, but changes his mind.

'Now, I don't want to tire you out,' he says maliciously, for when did he ever care if I were tired?

'You are not going to explain this strange coincidence to me?'

'Another time,' he replies, as if it were a matter of no importance at all. Then he turns and saunters from the cell. When he has gone, I realise I've forgotten to ask him to help Horatio.

~~

Three nights later I wake up to find the apothecary standing in front of me in the dark.

'Why are you here in the middle of the night?' I ask in a hoarse whisper. 'Am I your sport?'

I cannot see the expression on his face.

'There are other men here who I loathe far more than you,' he declares. 'One in particular has been the bane of my existence, always writing manuscripts about me and reading them aloud to anyone who would listen. You probably think I have taken pleasure in neglecting you, but I can assure you, all my attention has been taken up by this other madman . . .'

'Tell me more about my trial,' I interrupt.

'First, tell me what you wanted from the actress.'

'Am I foolish enough to tell you? A man who knows her family?'

'I don't think anybody has ever considered you a fool. Apart from the cretins in the jury. A particularly poignant and paradoxical case of *it takes one to know one,* wouldn't you agree?'

'No, I wouldn't agree. I've never liked alliteration.'

The apothecary sighs. 'There you go again. Displaying your habitual arrogance.'

'You said witnesses plural. Who else testified?'

'The prosecutors were able to obtain some of your little cast-offs. Very nice some of them were too. Very toothsome. And very voluble. Especially when they discovered the price discrepancies. Really, a cherry should be a set price, don't you think, if we are not to risk upsetting the feminine order of things?'

'I don't mind putting a fixed price on the fruits of pucelage. I think you'll find, however, that most young ladies regard their cherries as priceless.'

'Be that as it may, picking cherries certainly had its price for you. And your wife went bilious green. Absolutely.'

'Let me get this straight. I was allegedly out of my mind, and the court produced a procession of streels as witnesses? Why, every man in the city should be in Bedlam.'

'The court produced an *array* of women to whom you had given money who all vouchsafed that you had had carnal relations with them. The point being . . .'

'Yes, I understand the point.'

'I don't think you do. The court wished to show that the seduction of women was quite in accord with your previous and *normal* character. Your behaviour with the woman in question looks decidedly peculiar in comparison. Furthermore, until these ladies were produced, your wife could not be prevailed upon to give a certain portion of her own evidence. Which was that you had had several attacks of melancholia in the past . . .'

'Indeed I had not.'

'That during one such attack you had given up the theatre and taken up archery. . .'

'That, like the affair of which we have been talking, was a quite sane and calculated decision.'

'That on another occasion you took to your bed for weeks and ate only soup and custard . . .'

'I had had a personal setback. I was merely recuperating.'

Mr Haslam smiles conspiratorially. 'As a matter of fact, I believe you. We all do. Does that surprise you? Stop for a minute and admire how the pieces fit. Ask yourself: what was the best course of action for a cuckolded husband? How could he believe, after seeing this parade of deflowered and otherwise violated female flesh, that you did not intend to seduce his wife? Had not already done so, in fact? And then, being a man who dearly loved his wife, what did he want most? Revenge, of course. And was he to effect revenge by accusing you of being merely another Lothario – of which, as we both know, the world is so miserably full? No. This man was cleverer than that. He accused you of abnormal and perverted passions; and you corroborated by spitting and foaming and yelling. He flung the mantle of lunatic at you, and you snatched it up.'

'You are saying it was a conspiracy then?'

Mr Haslam stands in front of me and looks serene. 'Of course. With yourself as the chief conspirator.'

'How could I conspire when I was in a state of fugue?'

'Tell me, how do you think this alleged fugue came upon you?'

'I've no idea. The last thing I remember was arriving at my townhouse a week or so after Christmas.'

'Seduction week.'

'I walked in expecting to see the woman in question and . . . yes, her manservant arrived instead. He told me that she was unavoidably detained, and produced some baked morsels which Juliet had sent to me. After he left, I ate them. That is the last thing I remember. Although Porlock, the keeper here, tells me I was discovered down at the docks trying to board a ship.'

'*That* was some time later.'

'You appear to know rather a lot about this.'

'Indeed. You were trying to board a ship to the Antipodes, although none have ever left from the place you selected. You seemed to be of the opinion you had to get as far away as possible. You had some rather rare documents with you, if I recall correctly. But no money.'

'What documents? And now that you mention it, what became of them?'

'I know nothing about it. I can offer you only one thing, Mr Lonsdale. The action, stripped of the identity of the actors. That is, I can tell you what happened – to ease your mind, bring you to an understanding of your true position – but I cannot divulge to you the names of those involved. This is all I can offer you. In return, I wish to know what it was you bought from the lady in question. Call it curiosity.'

'Call it spying.'

'I can assure you, her husband has no further interest in the matter, since he believes you to have carried off the main prize already. Anyway, it was years ago now. Nobody really cares any more.'

'I'll think about it.'

'Think hard. Think about the time that elapsed between that Christmas week and your reappearance down at the docks. Think about the unfolding of events at your trial. Think about your inexplicable and sudden delirium. Think why a gentleman of your standing did not go to a private madhouse in your own town – a warm bed, sufficient food, an absence of chains. Lastly, think about why you remain here, lucid, completely in charge of your faculties, overseen by confabulating drunks and casual sadists – to use your own word.'

Mr Haslam smiles at me and then, to my utter astonishment, first winks and then taps the side of his nose. It is such a gesture of knowingness and insolence I summon a large gob of spit into my mouth and eject it at him. It misses. He turns and goes out laughing.

As soon as he leaves, the hoofs of rain start across the roof. And my heart gallops with them, down the eaves and across the courtyards, under the gates and out into the streets. It arrives, dripping, exhausted, at Juliet's door; clambers, shy, awkward, foal-like, up the stairs, and looks down at her asleep in her bed. What is there to know but that she is here, safe? That in the morning when she gallops on real horses across her own sodden fields her heart will race to me as mine has done to her? What is there to know but this?

～

I was in shock after the apothecary's revelations. That is why my heart galloped off for solace. In fact, there is much to know beyond passion. It is not sustainable, wears itself out by expressing itself. It is a weak poet, always beginning with dramatic and overheated phrases that stress its potency over time and distance; but in the end it peters out before the finish line.

If I now tell Mr Haslam what it was that I purchased from Juliet, will he graciously tell me that I was first poisoned, then imprisoned in my own townhouse and repeatedly drugged, permitted to escape in a frenzy, caught down at the docks by the constabulary, brought to trial in a narcotic rage, denounced by outraged strumpets, set up and done down by the poisoner, and finished off by my own jealous wife? Is that what he will tell me?

I decide to decline his very generous offer.

～

Eventually the assistant pronounces me cured. My shackle is re-attached and my diet returned to its former level of inadequacy. In the autumn, with a supreme effort of will, I avoid scratching, and by the first day of winter my skin disease has reluctantly shrunk to the size of a pinprick on my left small toe. The snow falls, then melts; the rain falls, the sun shines, the temperature rises. The keepers strip and sweat, drool and leer. They make rutting motions with their hips and go off to the halfpenny whores, the only receptacles that take all comers. By late spring my itch is but another bad memory. Horatio coughs and intermittently disgorges blood clots onto the flagstones.

'The phancy of one person may,
by means of some subtile intervening fluid,
bind the phancy of another . . .'

I WAKE UP. A strange man is standing in my cell. We look at each other. He is very well dressed. His waistcoat is of many blues and greens, and ocellated, like a peacock's tail. He has an abundance of grey hair and keen blue eyes.

'I thought there were two men in here,' he comments.

'That is a man there,' I reply, nodding in the direction of Horatio, who today looks more like a sack of wood than ever. 'He is in permanent humicubation to scientific medicine.'

'What is his name?'

'Nobody remembers.'

The man begins to walk about the cell, his hands behind his back. He looks out of the tiny window, kicks his boot at a loose flagstone, regards the ceiling.

'I am Edward Wakefield,' he announces at last, stopping in front of me.

'I am the King of *Rien*,' I reply.

'What – another king?'

'We're all kings in here.'

'Actually, I've met a few queens today.'

'Lucky you. I wish I could meet a few queens today.'

Mr Wakefield snorts, a little amused.

'That man there – I call him Horatio – is very sick. Can you help him?'

Mr Wakefield walks over to Horatio and looks down at him thoughtfully. 'What is the matter with him?'

'Coldness, hunger, cruelty, and bleeding from the mouth.'

'A very perspicacious list, sir.'

'We have time for perspicacity here. We have time for all sorts of things.'

'Such as?' Mr Wakefield asks, and walks back towards me to hear my answer.

'Such as experiencing a very slow, but still very deadly, crucifixion. Such as chasing polysyllables through the moonlight, hoping to catch a word that explains the world.'

'You think that a single word can explain the world?'

'I'm certain of it.'

'That word would be God then, wouldn't it?'

'I doubt it.'

'You don't think God explains the world?'

'I think the world explains God.'

Mr Wakefield laughs. 'A good answer. But blasphemous.'

'On the contrary. Humankind is so enchanted with the Earth and its manifold wonders that it attributes all existence to a divine creator. Rather a compliment really. Undeserved of course.'

'A man in chains thinks the world is wonderful?'

'Only a man in chains can think it.'

'I fear you are not as mad as you seem.'

'You fear I seem as sane as I am.'

'Seeming is in the eye of the beholder, sir,' he admonishes, and begins again his peregrinations of the cell.

'That may be so,' I reply. 'But the truth isn't –'

Mr Wakefield stops.

'– although I can certainly imagine a world where every man has his own truth, each his own little piece ripped off the carcass, which he fights for against every other man. Can't you?'

'Truth is a carcass?' Mr Wakefield asks, raising his eyebrows.

'In that world they will think it is.'

'It is not my prerogative to imagine other worlds.'

'Let me hasten to correct myself then – other times.'

'And when will this time be, in your opinion?'

'I'd say around the end of the second millennium.'

'Hah, but that's a long way off. It needn't concern us.'

'But already the scraps are being torn off. I tore one myself when I said that the world explains God.'

'I've never approved of the seductiveness of metaphors, sir.'

'You're right. They are harlots in the convents of thought. But, like their embodied counterparts, essential for entertainment.'

Mr Wakefield smiles a little disapprovingly.

'If, as you allege, the scraps are being torn off now, then is truth already dead?' he finally asks.

'Why no – it is being eaten alive.'

'And how did this begin, in your humble opinion?'

I laugh. 'I have no humble opinions. All of my opinions are arrogant. It began with the French Revolution, of course. With the peasants and textile workers. They think that because they have been poor and oppressed they are now the only repositories of proper thinking. It passed straight from Louis' head into theirs with one chop of the guillotine.'

Mr Wakefield laughs and slaps me on the shoulder. 'You're a fine fellow,' he says. 'And I'm going to get you out of here.'

'Oh, and how are you going to do that? Have you a file?'

'I have something better than that. I have a pen. I'm going to write to the papers.'

~

Later, Porlock comes in with the bucket and supper.

'What have we here, lickspittle? There's meat in this boiled water.'

'It's probably a rat.'

'Well, it's tasty anyhow.'

'Yes – why should a lunatic care if he eats rat or pork?' Porlock agrees sarcastically.

'I hope they've cooked the plague out of it.'

Porlock doesn't reply but continues to shovel in the soup.

'I had a visitor today,' I announce when he's finished.

'Yes, I saw there was a governor here.'

'Not just a governor. There were several other men – one an MP, I hear.'

'I met them all,' Porlock replies darkly. 'Prancing round like princes, demanding this, that and the bloody next thing. Unlock this, unlock that . . .'

'The one who came to see me was called Mr Wakefield. He said he's going to get me out of here.'

'Did he now.'

'What do you think about it?'

'I don't think anything.'

'What if you lose your job?'

'There'll be others go before me,' Porlock growls. 'We see what goes on here.'

'We who?'

'The keepers.'

'You *are* what goes on here.'

'Don't get funny with me, madman.'

'Who carries out the day-to-day care of the lunatics? Do the blows and insults come from the doctors? Are the doctors continually drunk?'

'The doctors prescribe firm treatment.'

'I'm sure they don't mean you to act like sadists.'

'The lunatics are unmanageable. But it's our job to manage them. Then all the do-gooders come in here and criticise. No straitwaistcoat, no leg-irons! they cry before going home for a cream tea. Use charisma and the strength of your gaze! order the physicians before going off to their private patients. Well, fuck them all, I say. I'd be murdered if I listened to any of *them*.'

'You can't tie up sane men in a madhouse and leave them to rot,' I object.

'That's right,' Porlock replies with unusual cunning. 'And do the keepers sign the certificates? No, they don't. At the end of the day, it will all boil down to who was sane and who wasn't. The brutality that no one will forgive is the imprisonment and treatment of the sane lunatics. What the keepers have done to the true lunatics will be like nothing.'

'Sane lunatics? How quaint you are, Porlock. As to your assertions, I wouldn't be too sure about them at all.'

'Well, we'll see – if it ever comes to anything, which I doubt. These hospital visitors are all the bloody same. They just want a cheap thrill. To see the mad ladies all undone down the front, and grown men howling like dogs. They've been coming for years and what's ever changed?'

'These particular ones haven't been coming for years.'

'What's the difference between one powdered wig and another?'

'You're such a peasant, Porlock.'

'What d'you mean?'

'It's so plebeian to see all authority figures as indistinguishable in character. It makes you irretrievably lower class.'

'Well, thanks. For once you haven't insulted me.'

'My pleasure.'

Porlock picks up the bucket and the food, and walks towards the door, muttering.

'Before you go, Porlock, remember what you said about the apothecary's assistant in your more perspicacious days.'

'What was that?'

'You said, the slave always goes down with the master.'

'Did I?'

'I recommend you take note of your own singular wisdom, if it's not too late.'

'Bah, what the hell would you know?'

~~

Mr Wakefield comes into my cell. He does not pace about but comes over to me directly.

'Good afternoon, your Highness.'

'How is the revolution?'

'You're now the King of France?'

'The King of France is dead.'

'Quite so. And now the Emperor has abdicated.'

'Emperor?'

'Napoleon.'

'Made himself an emperor did he, our Mr Bonaparte? Now there's a good carcass-ripping sort of name.'

'Hah, you reiterate that the rot of the third millennium begins with the French Revolution.'

'It's true that every man deserves justice,' I repeat, just to make sure Mr Wakefield understands me. 'But merely because the peasants finally receive justice, it doesn't mean they know the truth – although everybody will begin to think so.'

Mr Wakefield smiles, sadly it seems, but makes no reply.

'It's afternoon is it?' I say querulously. 'Porlock has forgotten the lunch. Again.'

'Mr Porlock has been temporarily relieved of his duties. Pending the results of an inquiry.'

'Oh? And so we are not to be fed?'

'You are not interested in the reasons for his suspension?'

'I am not interested in anything on an empty stomach.'

'I will see what I can do then.'

He turns to go.

'Wait . . .'

'Yes?'

'Can you tell me the date?'

'Of course. It is June the 28th.'

'The year. What year is it?'

'You don't know?'

'Have I a calendar?'

'It is 1814 of course.'

'Why of course? Is there something inevitable about it? What's the date according to the Manchu Dynasty?'

'I'll get your lunch directly. I'm sure it will improve your humour.'

Mr Wakefield returns with bread and cheese and porter. I am amazed. I haven't tasted cheese in more than a decade. As I eat, as he feeds me, I begin to get excited about these two sudden changes – the disappearance of Porlock and the reappearance of cheese. And a moderate amount of alcohol without the addition of opium is a true pleasure.

'So, tell me now, why has Porlock gone?'

'You could see for yourself, he wasn't fit to look after the sick.'

'That never bothered anybody before. He vacated his mind years ago.'

'Well, it bothers people now. It bothers me.'

'I don't mean to be rude, but who are you exactly?'

'I'm a hospital visitor.'

'Oh. You do exist.'

'I believe so – but let me pinch myself. Ah yes, I do.'

'Porlock always said you did. But I could never be sure. All manner of things existed for Porlock that had no reality except in a drunken mind. I tried to bribe him to bring you to me. I tried to bribe him into bringing a relic – a glove or cigar butt. But he never did.'

'Relic is an interesting word in that context.'

'You find your saints where you need to. In fact, he finally produced a visitors' ticket. But it was so old I feared the visitors had lost their interest.'

'On the contrary,' Mr Wakefield splutters. 'We had the most trouble imaginable gaining admission to see you. We first came on the 25th of April. The current rules require that we be accompanied by a governor, and so Alderman Cox came with us. Unfortunately, his feelings overwhelmed him even before we came to the men's wing, and he had to go and rest in the steward's office. We were then required to leave. The second time we came, May the 2nd, we brought a less squeamish governor. But Mr Porlock had lost the keys. Or pretended to. It was only upon my own continued insistence that we were finally admitted to the locked wings. And what did we find . . .'

'What did you find?'

'The unfortunate Mr Norris. Other lucid men and women in chains. Excrement, starvation, nudity, consumption . . . and then yourself. It's simply appalling.'

'Is this Mr Norris more unfortunate than the rest of us?'

'He's a sane man who is locked to his sleeping trough by iron bars. They are around both his neck and his body. He has been in that very same spot for more than twelve years. He is also physically sick. I cannot imagine a worse fate than such confinement.'

'Indeed. But in the end, what does it matter whether it is iron bars or chains or physick that restrains a man? The cruelty is in the imprisonment, not the means.'

Mr Wakefield looks a little uncertain.

'Tell me,' I say before he thinks to argue, 'how did the letters to the papers go?'

'Well enough. Questions were raised in the House of Commons. Consequently, the governors of this institution met and read aloud to each other the stories that ensued in *The Times* and the *Morning Chronicle*. A subcommittee was formed to inquire into the allegations. They interviewed the physician, the apothecary, the steward and the attendants.'

'I am impressed. Are you such a powerful man then?'

'Obviously. But don't be too impressed. The physician and the apothecary said there was no foundation at all for any charges of cruelty. They focused particularly on Mr Norris, alleging that he is unusually dangerous, that he had repeatedly attacked both attendants and patients. On one occasion, they said, he had attacked a keeper with a knife, and on another he had bitten off a patient's finger. Unfortunately, the subcommittee found all this quite satisfactory. But I am not satisfied. I have some plans to take this further.'

'Such as?'

'I am going to approach an MP of my acquaintance. He is an old friend of the King.'

'Oh no, a friend of a lunatic. Can this be helpful?'

'The King is the top lunatic in the country, sir.'

'Oh yes, I quite forgot.'

'I hope to secure an inquiry which is much less biased. In the meantime, I will continue to visit you, if you should like that.'

'I should. But why would you want to?'

'You are a most engaging conversationalist, although I'm not sure whether I quite agree with anything you say. Your opinions are too much your own. And I'm certain you are an inveterate blasphemer.'

'I think it's having my own opinions that makes me a good conversationalist. The single bonus of my predicament here is that I'm free to believe anything and say anything. It's hardly a ladies' sitting room. There is not a single restraint, not even of decency or sense, on the reach and roaming of my mind.'

'Except that of new material.'

'Not even that. I can imagine everything I need.'

'There is always the problem of accuracy.'

'Well, there is no one to check my accuracy. And this is the last place where anyone cares about such a thing.'

'I think it ought to be the first. How can you determine if a man is a lunatic otherwise?'

'To be here is to be insane.'

Mr Wakefield signals his disapproval with a series of noises. Then he begins to walk about the cell. 'It's a lovely day,' he announces. 'We should talk about more pleasant things.'

I stare at him coldly. 'I have nothing pleasant to talk about. I am nearly always bored. My friend is getting sicker. Nobody helps him.'

'I have informed the physician of his situation. I am sure he will be attended to very soon.'

'The physician?' I repeat, feeling a little hopeful. 'Do you think he is as irresponsible as the apothecary?'

'He is not allowed to be. He is in charge of the entire establishment.'

'Then you will probably find he is the most irresponsible of all.'

~⌒

It is mid-summer. The days are too long. I daydream about tall windows with an expansive view of the sea. Sometimes it occurs to me that all I now wish from freedom is an opportunity to change my surroundings. To walk into a new and different room and lean out of the windows while strangers whisper at my back. To take the mossed stone steps down to the forest, or the well-trodden path to the marketplace. Instead, for novelty, I can only tell my secrets.

'Horatio, when a man is a collector he is offered, or discovers, all sorts of wonders. He soon comes across items closer to his heart than those which he is reputedly collecting. He realises, however, that his known and public interest serves as a useful cover for his real desires. That is to say, the price of maps goes up when he is around, but the other things, the things he really wants, the prices of these remain magically fixed.

'The dealers in documents spread everything out before him. There are maps, of course. But he has a chance to run his eye over the entire merchandise, to note without being seen to note the presence, or otherwise, of the objects of his more emotionally laden avidity. It's not that he doesn't like maps: they are beautiful, stimulate the imagination and frequently increase in value. It's simply that words are closer to his heart than pictures are. He, with one eye, always pays great attention to the maps: yes indeed, he likes them. He nearly always buys one if it's rare and of satisfactory quality.

'Meanwhile, his other eye is quickly appraising the exuviae of poets and playwrights; he is trying to see signatures, recognise handwriting styles. Before allowing the dealer to put away the merchandise, he always says, "And have you anything else of interest to show me?"

'The dealer picks up fulsome letters by the famous to the famous, or the diaries of tedious generals. Then he says "Of course, there's some snippets of Molière here. First-draft stuff. But I don't suppose you'd be interested in those. The investment value of these things is quite unpredictable."

'"Who's this Molière? A Frenchman? What has a Frenchman done to deserve our attention?"

'"Written plays."

'"Are we to collect material written in French?" I thunder.

'"Quite so," the dealer agrees, obsequiously if I have already spent a good sum; with resignation if I've bought nothing and seem unlikely to do so.

'I visibly soften. "Well, who knows? A man has to take a few risks in his life, otherwise he is not a man. Show me this Molière flummery. Perhaps I can purchase some for a friend. I know a man who's a theatre critic and a rank bibliophile. I can't see the point myself – he'd be better off with dirty pictures."

'The merchant quickly produces his snippets and I always get them for a good price. Trading in this way, I finish up with a barrowload of Molière's manuscripts and papers. I believe I held the largest extant collection – larger than any reference collection in France. I reasoned that if one wishes to reconstruct the mental life of the literati in terms of their scribbles, then the more the merrier. What good are odd scraps? So, I settled on Molière and bought other scribbles only to buy and sell. They themselves ended up forming quite a significant portfolio, I must say.'

I fall silent and shut my eyes, remembering again the first winter Juliet and I spent together. We are looking out at the snow from the window of my townhouse. We have had our afternoon tea and she is thinking of going home. I want her to stay, and am looking at a poignant little curl on her neck that has escaped the careful hairdressing. Why poignant, I don't know. Perhaps all little freedoms are poignant.

'Would you like to see something secret?' I ask her.

'I've already seen that today, William.'

'No, no, not what is written on my heart. Something that is expressed a little better.'

'What is it?' She smiles, but is obviously a little impatient, perhaps anxious to get home before she is missed.

'Wait a moment. I will fetch the box.'

I go out and fetch the large box containing my collection. I open it in front of her with the little gold key. She is not so stupid as to suppose that the box contains a locked collection of blank sheets of paper. She immediately snatches up a sheet and skims over it. Then she delves again into the box and takes out another piece to read. I watch her face closely. Her mouth has dropped open in amazement.

'Where did you get all this?'

'Everywhere,' I reply.

'Is it very valuable?'

'It is to me.'

She continues to snatch pieces up from the box. 'I made my name with Molière,' she tells me. 'I know screeds of it off by heart, even now.'

'Then the early versions of his work will certainly amuse you,' I reply.

'We will read one of the plays together after Christmas,' she exclaims with delight.

'Not now?'

'I have to go home. My husband will be back before me and then I will have to make up another lie.'

'You don't like lying?' I feel she ought to be prepared to do anything on my behalf.

'I have no moral objection to it. I just fear that one day I will become too complicated and implausible, or I will contradict myself.'

And so off she went to her family Christmas, as I did to mine. I was a little disappointed that my booty had not convinced her to stay another hour or two, and concluded from this that she had been interested, perhaps covetous, but not so fascinated that she could completely forget her familial obligations.

After Christmas – and what an oddly lonely time it was – we met again in the townhouse and had a splendid reunion. Of course, we did not think about plays for quite a few meetings; we did not even think about wine and cakes. Eventually, however, the intellect gets bored with flirting and fluttering, and seeks more subtle amusement. We fetched the box – I showed her where it was hidden and where I kept the key – and we glutted ourselves on Molière. My Juliet demonstrated herself most erudite, frequently pointing out where the original differed from the final versions. She had a particular affection for the *School for Wives*, and one afternoon while snowflakes fell slowly and softly outside the window we drank champagne and performed the first draft of the play.

A tear rolls down my cheek. It is as if this blissful memory is covered in verdigris. 'See, I am not tough, Horatio. Despite my onomatomania, I am nothing more than a sentimental old fool.'

I close my eyes, and unexpectedly feel myself beginning to drift off. There is something about giving in to self-pity that is so relaxing.

~⌒

I wake up. It is morning. I can tell by the temperature in the cell that there has been a sudden severe change in the weather. I am cold and stiff. I fear if I bent over I would snap in half. I hear a keeper coming noisily down the hall with the breakfast buckets. I am surprised when it turns out to be Porlock. He is dressed in innumerable layers of clothing. His head pokes out of them like a turtle's, scrawny and bald and undersized in relation to his body.

'They've let you back, have they?' I ask.

Porlock doesn't reply.

'So, you managed to pin the blame on those above,' I persist. 'What did you say? I only kick the lunatics' arses because the steward tells me to?'

'When did I ever kick your arse?'

'It's true, you didn't. But I've seen you kick others'. I've seen all the keepers punching and slapping utterly helpless wretches.'

'Just as well they won't ask for your opinion then.'

He goes over to Horatio.

'Uh-oh,' he says.

He had grabbed Horatio by the shoulder, but has now let go of him. He stands there looking at his hand as if it has been burnt.

'What is it?'

'I think he's dead.'

Porlock bends down and begins to examine him. He stands up.

'Well?'

'Yup. Dead as a dodo.'

'Are you sure?'

'Quite. I've seen a lot of stiffs. Probably swallowed his tongue.'

I feel a terrible rage overtake me. 'Go and fetch someone, you ignorant old prick,' I shout.

Porlock turns and looks at me uncomprehendingly. 'What for? It's too late.'

'Are you just going to leave him here?'

'No. But what's the hurry? Where's the fire?'

I realise I have gone into an unnecessary and inexplicable panic. Without my seeing, during the cold night or even while I was talking to him, Horatio slipped away. I didn't even see him go. And I was his last witness, the last person to see, care, whether he lived or died.

Porlock is now leaning against the wall and sighing copiously. 'I can't drag him out on my own,' he grumbles. 'I've just remembered the other keeper didn't come in today. I've got to do everything myself.'

'Get the apothecary's assistant! I don't want to spend the day with a corpse,' I bellow after him as he goes out. This is something that even Porlock can understand; but really, what I wanted to say was: I don't want to spend the day with my own failure. As if it adheres to Horatio's body, together with the strange smell that is now starting to burden the air.

I spend the day with a corpse. Porlock goes to get help – I assume he intends to – and doesn't return.

I look down at Horatio's body. He doesn't appear any different. Of course, only his spirit has gone. But was it such a poor spirit that it could depart without leaving any visible change? And where do such impoverished spirits go after death – up to heaven to sit with more ample souls for eternity? Wouldn't it feel rather provoking to be – to have been – so short-changed? Bad enough in life, but in the everlasting hereafter. . . Or maybe simple and reduced souls are amplified in heaven, brought up to the full guinea as it were, and wouldn't that make for an interesting dialogue with the creator: 'What d'you mean *guilt?* Why'd you do such a piss-poor job, that's what I want to know.'

I feel glum. Horatio went and couldn't even say goodbye. As he rose from those prostrated rags, did he send a warm emanation in my direction, a flow of affection? For the first time I see him as elegant: he wears a wide-brimmed hat with a feather in it, and skin-tight breeches, and he walks like a dancer. He is witty in his gestures and facial expressions, and he's off to heaven to have it out with his miserable creator. I rattle my chains: come back and take me with you, Horatio.

'What are you crying for, you old fool?' Porlock says from the door.

'Horatio's dead.'

'How can you tell?' Porlock sniggers.

'Get the body out of here,' I yell.

'All right, keep your bloody hair on.'

'What's all the racket?' The apothecary unexpectedly fills the doorway.

'There's a man dead in here and this idiot won't get him out.'

'I only just discovered him,' Porlock snarls.

'You were in here at breakfast, gomerel. You found him then,' I snarl back.

'Now, now,' Mr Haslam interrupts. 'I'll sort it out. Mr Porlock, go and get the steward. You – be quiet.'

Porlock scuttles off as ordered. The apothecary and I glare at each other in silence.

'You have blood on your hands,' I accuse him coldly.

'I do not.'

'You should have come when he was ill.'

'No one told me he was ill.'

'I did.'

'That was years ago. And you are not fit to judge.'

'It is your responsibility to find the illness.'

'Hark, I am being told my responsibilities by a lunatic.'

'You cannot expect the keepers to decide when the doctor is required.'

'I do not expect it. But his recent symptoms were not reported. What am I to do?'

'As I said, you could make inspections.'

'That man has been inspected. Did you see any change in him? Did he stand up or begin to talk? No. Am I to walk round all day inspecting the vegetables to see if they are rotting?'

'How would you know if he was a vegetable? You have only spent time with his corpse.'

'That is where you are wrong. That sack of incontinence has been here a very long time. Since he was a child, in fact; and I have frequently examined him. He was a cretin then and a cretin he remained.'

'He has been here all his life?'

'Nearly. His parents brought him in. They thought he'd been born without a brain. Not surprising, I thought, considering *they* didn't seem to have one to share between them.'

'Well, what could he do then? Could he walk? Could he talk?'

'He could only lie on the floor and foul himself. He did that all his life. Have you been trying to have an intelligent conversation with him? Did you think you had company that had been misunderstood?'

'Everyone subject to such contempt is misunderstood.'

'He is not cognisant of our contempt. It doesn't affect him.'

'It affects us.'

'Oh? In what way?'

'We are made too harsh by it. And the harshness expands to others – to others like him and others less like him and others not like him at all.'

'Well then, such people should avoid stimulating our contempt.'

'Or you should avoid feeling it.'

Mr Haslam snorts. 'Are you one of these egalitarians who thinks happiness should be shared out equally to all? That God made us all equally worthy and capable of it?'

'I'm not sure about the God portion of your question. And as far as happiness goes, most of us seem to be unworthy and incapable. I merely wished to point out that your contempt was under your own control. I never felt any contempt for Horatio.'

'Horatio?'

'Yes, that's what I called him. No one ever told me his name. No one here even seems to remember it. He was fine company in my opinion.'

Mr Haslam regards me with narrowed eyes. 'There is a very simple reason for your enjoyment of his company. Owing to your staggering arrogance, you require only that a person should uncritically absorb all your absurd opinions. It is a kind of megalomania. There are many here who suffer from it, but you are the worst.'

'You seem to have caught quite a bad dose of it yourself.'

'It's not catching.'

'The arrogance that one is the only sane person in a world of fools is, however. You could catch that quite easily here. We could catch it from you.'

'Excuse me, a lunatic is free to talk rubbish all day if he wishes, but I am not. I have no desire to continue this conversation.' He goes to stand at the window with his back to me.

Eventually Porlock rushes in with the steward and a keeper from the curables' wing. They are all holding rags up to their noses. A strong smell of serpolet permeates the cell. Then, under Mr Haslam's stern supervisory gaze, the steward and keepers drag Horatio's remains out on a piece of sacking.

'You'll have to come back and fumigate the cell,' Mr Haslam orders as they disappear.

'I would like to come to his funeral,' I call out.

'Don't be ridiculous,' the apothecary replies as he goes out the door.

～

I wait. Wait for the funeral, wait for some — any – ceremony dedicated to the knowledge that Horatio lived and died. The days pass. Eventually I have to conclude that he has been thrown into the ground or the furnace, or sent off to the medical school, without any of the proper formalities. I do not know how it can be concluded that a lunatic is less in need of a funeral than any other man, since all are equally dead. But there it is. Then I no longer wait. The days pass.

One afternoon, Mr Wakefield appears again.

'Where is Horatio?' he exclaims, looking around.

'They took him away.'

'For treatment?'

'For the best treatment there is.'

'I'm glad to hear it. I was beginning to think the physician would never act on my complaints. I will have to investigate the treatment, however; with the poor food here, Horatio is surely far too weak for the physician's bag of tricks.'

'You do not need to worry about the treatment. It is perfect. He is being given the final colliquative.'

'You seem to know rather a lot about it,' Mr Wakefield says in surprise. 'What exactly is the final colliquative?'

'Do you know what colliquation is?'

'I'm afraid I don't. I am not a medical man.'

'Do not be ashamed on account of that. Colliquation is a wasting away of the body, accompanied by excessive fluidification of bodily humours, especially the blood. And the disintegration of tissue into pus.'

'The doctors are turning Horatio into pus?'

'Not the doctors. It is the earth on the lid of a long box that will do it.'

Mr Wakefield looks at me a little uncertainly. 'Death is the final colliquative? Horatio is dead?'

'You never know when you might need a word,' I carry on lugubriously. 'You never know when you might be called upon to name the horror. Or the blessed release from it.'

'Don't go off on that tangent,' Mr Wakefield replies grumpily. 'I am very upset that this has been allowed to happen.'

'Fitting the proper words to things is not a tangent. If he had been called sick rather than mad, he would still be with us. They would have given him the correct medicine instead of anointing his backbone with the balsam of earthworms and bats.'

Mr Wakefield looks horrified. 'They did that?'

'No. They did nothing. What I described was once a treatment for madness.'

Mr Wakefield frowns deeply. 'This will certainly have to be brought before the parliamentary inquiry, should it ensue,' he says at last. 'It is scandalous that a man can be confined in such a way and yet receive no treatments for his maladies.'

'Yes, he would have been happier lying on some dock where the sailors could kick him and the rats could nibble his toes.'

'Do not joke with me.'

'I am quite serious. On the docks the sun can come out and warm him. He can hear the music of the sea. He can sniff the fresh air braced with salt. But there is a price for all pleasures, and we must pay it willingly.'

'Why must we?' Mr Wakefield asks irritably.

'Because otherwise we will be in danger of believing that for happiness our freedom must be absolute. No rats, no sailors. If we come to that conclusion, we will watch out for rats and sailors and never notice the sea or the sun.'

Mr Wakefield sighs. 'I am sure there is some sense in there somewhere.'

'Enough for a lunatic, anyway.'

Mr Wakefield starts walking about in a state of agitation. 'It is all inexcusable,' he fumes. 'I am going right away to make my displeasure known to the physician. If I can find him. He is forever trotting from one institution to the next.'

'Well, he has to trot after his money.'

Mr Wakefield turns to go.

'By the way,' he says on his way out the door. 'After I've seen the physician, I'm afraid I won't be able to visit you for a little while. I am going on my annual holiday.'

Nil admirari

THE DAYS PASS: morning bucket, noon bucket, evening bucket; gruel, slurry, pabulum; sun up, sun down, sun up. The temperature rises again after the brief chill interlude that saw Horatio off. It stays light for an interminably long time after the last bucket of the day. I am depressed. The last blow has fallen, the one after which I can no longer raise myself up.

I cannot bear to be so alone. I think back fondly to my perfect companion. Would I have bothered to talk out loud but for him? And if I hadn't talked, hadn't organised my thoughts for a decade or more, what sort of mess would I have got into?

For a few days after he died, I sensed Horatio's presence rather than his absence. As if he hovered incorporeally about me, trying to console me. As if he knew that when he passed over, or relinquished himself to the earth, I would have no one. And in those few days I still talked fondly to him, told him of my feelings, apologised for my faithlessness when I briefly caught the scent of freedom.

Then I no longer sensed the hovering spirit of Horatio. The summer air became thin with absence. Now I cannot bring myself to talk aloud, to act as if his absence makes no difference. I wake up with the bucket and hose. The keepers feed me. Their visit is short because there is only me. They scurry back to their card games or maid-poking or nose-quarrying or whatever it is they do to fill up their day. I stare at the walls. My jaw is locked shut. My mind has gone blank.

I remain thus until Porlock – usually it's Porlock – comes in with the lunch. He cackles and goes cross-eyed and feebly kicks up his heels in a pathetic attempt to jolly me up. I remain unjollied. He goes out again, muttering, and I am left to the mercy of the long afternoon. Sleep often overcomes me, since I do nothing at all to keep my mind occupied; and then, after the evening bucket, I must face the cruelty of the long sleepless night. My mind dozes like a dog with half-open eyes.

It is evening. A shaft of late sunlight falls across the floor. Outside the small window I can see the edges of a hot pink sunset. I can't bear to watch these remnants of a summer day disappear, knowing that I have been denied another day: another day on which, some-where, someone – perhaps Mr Wakefield – woke up and opened the curtains and saw the whole of a perfect sky and was content; on which, in some orchard at a country house, he came suddenly upon the rich sweet smell of over-ripe summer fruit – plums perhaps; on which, later on, that same someone came home from a walk in the early evening and stood in the doorway of his country house, in the concentrated evening heat, and listened to the deep contented silence of summer. I was such a man once.

Or have I only imagined it?

Many years ago, on the black afternoon when he personally escorted me to the incurables' wing, the apothecary told me a story. He told me there were once two insane men here who shared a cell; one man's delusion was that he believed everyone he met was a king; the second man's delusion was that he *was* a king. 'Aren't you a king?' the first would anxiously ask the second. 'Indeed I am,' thundered the other. 'How dare you ever doubt it!'

Did they not live in a world, Mr Haslam asked sarcastically, where their beliefs corresponded to reality?

'You should have put them in different cells,' I advised him as we trod the dark corridors further and further into the labyrinth.

'I tried that.'

'What happened?'

'They both got a lot worse. The anxiety of the first man increased considerably because he couldn't find the king; he started interrogating even the ants on the floor. The rage of the second did likewise because no one believed him any more. He also wanted to kill all the other pretenders to the throne.'

'What am I to learn from this?' I remember I asked him coldly. He was putting the shackles on at the time.

'You two, yourself and this cell-mate I have chosen for you, are as well matched as they were. As well matched as the only king and the perfect subject.' And off he went, smirking arrogantly, as if he had not only tied me, but nailed me.

Now I stare forlornly at the place where Horatio used to lie. Did Horatio merely serve to reflect my madness back to me? When I told him the story of my life, was it the fact that Horatio couldn't reciprocate, couldn't even answer back, that kept me from perceiving my delusions? Imagine if he had suddenly struggled up and shouted: 'Don't tell me any more about your deluded memories – you've been here as long as I have, all your life in fact, and your mother was a gin-soaked whore same as mine was.'

The clarity of certainty deserts me. A kind of blackness descends upon me. I am smothered in doubt. Could it be that I concocted my former life, this life I so thoroughly believe in, during my fugue? If I say that I was not mad then, but poisoned, and if I allege there was a plot against me, do I not sound exactly like a hundred other madmen? If I use unusual words as entertainment, even make them up to fill the void left by the absence of a dictionary, or to increase my own descriptive accuracy, and if I do confess that such neologisms now occupy much of my mind, do I not slip, thoroughly well greased, into the worst category of lunatic? And if a man utterly divorced from the world can be amused by telling a made-up story to a man who doesn't listen, is he not suffering a special kind of lunacy that has yet to be collared and categorised, and during which, with one single peculiar flash of insight, he appears as mad even to himself?

I can't go on.

'You can't not go on,' Porlock sniggers when I confess this to him.

'It's torture.'

'What? This is what you wanted isn't it? Didn't you say it was the treatment that was torture? Didn't you demand to be incurable?'

'I've changed my mind.'

'Minds change all day long in this place. They don't set any store by it.'

'I confess I am now mad and I wish to be treated.'

'I'll tell the apothecary, shall I? Which treatment would you like best?'

'Human company.'

'Bah, you're as incurable as ever.'

'Incorrigible – but not incurable. Please!'

'Would you like me to hit you on the head with the shovel?'

'I'd like to talk to someone about reality.'

'Well, talk to me.'

'You're an alcoholic.'

'How about the apothecary then?' Porlock taunts.

'The apothecary thinks everyone is mad except himself and God, and he probably has some secret doubts about the latter.'

'Well, the clergyman then?'

'Yes,' I reply gloomily. 'A lunatic and a Bible-basher could have a fascinating talk about reality.'

'I'll tell you about reality,' Porlock says, coming up to me and standing so close I could count the hairs on his hispid chin. 'There isn't one. There's only what you've got. And you've got chains – so get used to them.'

'Just get me some proof of my former life,' I plead as he prepares to leave. 'If I knew that even one detail about my past was true, I could be convinced again of my own sanity.'

'You were starting to doubt it?' Porlock asks incredulously. 'Why, you must be getting better!'

～

I wake up with a jolt. Mr Wakefield is standing right in front of me, looking at me intently. It takes me a moment or two to fully come to my senses.

'Ah, you've come back,' I manage to say, although my frightened heart is beating furiously.

'I returned yesterday from my summer holiday,' he replies.

'And how was it? Warm, lazy, sensual?'

Mr Wakefield looks at me as if he thinks better of going into any detail. 'It was pleasant enough,' he finally says.

'Merely pleasant? What's wrong with you?'

'Pardon?'

'Why were you satisfied with pleasant? Why didn't you make it better?'

'I fear you have lost touch with the exigencies of life.'

'Oh? What are the exigencies of your life?'

'A man can't have everything the way he wants it. At night there were these wretched insects . . .'

'You allowed insects to spoil your holiday?'

Mr Wakefield regards me severely. 'You have forgotten how things are. Snatches of contentment are what I aim for. Between the insect bites and the spoiled soup and the wife's relations. I do not hanker after unattainable ecstasies.'

I smile at him. 'Of course you are right. But I did hanker in such a way. You can see where it got me. Desperate for insect bites and spoiled soup and the wife's relations. Particularly the wife's relations.'

Mr Wakefield smiles and puts his hands behind his back. He begins to pace about the cell in the manner I have come to expect of him.

'How is your search for the word that explains the world coming along?'

'It isn't. I stopped it. I can't think of anything when I have no one to talk to.'

'But you only need a single word,' Mr Wakefield objects good-humouredly.

'The stories that bring the words to mind have all left me. They went with Horatio.'

'What do you do to fill your time, then?'

'I'm trying to go out of my mind.'

'Well, it was an arrogant undertaking anyway. There is no such word.'

'Oh? How do you know that if you don't know it?'

'You are not even clear about what you mean. You won't know the word when you find it.'

'I will make myself clear then. I want a word that helps me to accept my life as it is.'

'Why should you accept it? You're a lucid man wrongly imprisoned.'

'Because I might never get out of here. Not alive, anyway.'

'I see you have no faith in me.'

'I don't want to put my faith in a future saviour. I want to be happy now.'

Mr Wakefield looks at me in amazement. 'You must be saved,' he exclaims. 'You do not have the conditions to be happy.'

'That's what I used to think before.'

'But now it's true.'

I sigh. 'You get on with saving me, Mr Wakefield. And I'll get on with my word. Then we'll both be doing what we do best.'

~

Sometimes at night, I make a temporary peace with life. Then I am almost glad there is no insistent tomorrow. My chains support me: hold me up, rather than down. If there is moonlight, I can waste all I want to. I can spend as long as I please watching the movements of insects and shadows. Sometimes then it seems stillness is the single position, the only perspective, that allows a man a full awareness of being alive. He becomes aware of every tiny moment, each one no longer than a heartbeat. And there is his life beating out, being beaten out, being beaten out of him, moment by moment. Why should he yearn for movement and complexity when this hypnotising, perilous, terrifying rhythm is snuffed out by their futile uproar?

Strappado alone comes in with the morning buckets.

'Where is your support act?' I ask on the first such occasion.

'We can't work together now. I have to do Porlock's shifts.'

'Why doesn't he do his own?'

'They've sacked him.'

'But he survived the inquiry!'

'Yes he did. However, things have heated up again since. Due to your Mr Wakefield.'

'*My* Mr Wakefield?'

'The way everyone sees it, Porlock's been here the longest, so he's seen the most and the worst. That's why them up above want to get rid of him. And the keepers are glad too – he never knew when to keep his big mouth shut. As for keeping a story straight, you couldn't rely on the drunken cretin at all.'

'You mean you couldn't rely on him to keep a story crooked.'

'Don't tell me what I mean,' Strappado says darkly.

He feeds me and goes out. I look out of the small window at the autumn twilight. A curious clutch of interest has taken hold of my insides. Just when I was prepared to stare mournfully all day at the ceiling and floor, I now find my body feels a little . . . well, expectant. As if it knows that any new event may lead to a rinse, a wash, even a flood, of refreshing emotion. I find myself wondering whose head will be next to roll, and whether heads will roll all the way to the top. I feel as excited as a sansculotte.

But the excitement soon abates. The keepers come in, feed me, clean me up a bit, and depart as quickly as possible. Horatio is gone; Porlock is gone. There is no one at all to listen to me.

'What's wrong with you, lunatic?' Thumbscrew asks when I fail to show an interest in my food.

'I miss Porlock somewhat.'

'What was there to miss?'

'The spectacle of greed, gluttony, drunkenness and organic deterioration. Most people have to go to the theatre for such entertainment. I had it all here right in front of me.'

Thumbscrew shakes his head.

'True, I was at his mercy, so in a sense I was more of a character than an audience . . .'

'What the fuck are you talking about?'

'I'm talking about boredom. I'm bored out of my mind.'

'They're trying to bore you back *into* it, lunatic. Now stop going on or we'll never get this fodder in.'

He feeds me and goes out, and I am left to stare into the immensity of cloistered time. Time in a story takes no time, as the saying goes, but I must live through each minute, each and every minute, in the rage that my moonlit truce always drags in its wake.

~

Mr Wakefield keeps reappearing, usually when I have just about given up on him.

'I've come to tell you some good news,' he announces one afternoon.

'Oh, and what might that be?'

'There's to be an official parliamentary inquiry into asylums, public and private. I will be giving evidence.'

'What result do you expect from this inquiry?'

'Why, I expect men like yourself to be freed.'

'And what is the date set down for it?'

'May.'

'May 1815?'

'Well, naturally. May 1814 has already passed.'

'It's rather a long time to wait. It's December or January is it not?'

'Nearly April. The spring is late this year.'

'Spring is not something I'm aware of.'

'You do not notice the longer days?'

'All the days are endless.'

'I'm hoping the inquiry will conclude before the asylum moves its accommodations to St George's Fields. I do not wish to see the therapeutic practices transferred at the same time.'

'I am to be moved?'

'Only the lunatics will go. The lucid are to remain here till they're released.'

Mr Wakefield appears quite sure that I will be among this elect. I am not so certain. I express my doubts to him, and wonder whether we will be treated better now that an inquiry is guaranteed.

'But there have been improvements in your treatment lately, haven't there? The food is better, they assure me. The fires are lit in all the grates. There is generally less restraint. And closer attention to your health.'

'I am restrained as usual. But yes, the food is better. I'm tired of keepers inquiring about my bowels, however. Do I need some physick to loosen them, etcetera? Still, when someone cares if your bowels are working properly, I suppose things must be looking up. But tell me, what will you say at this inquiry?'

'I will tell them the truth, of course,' Mr Wakefield replies, as if I might think he would do anything else. 'Everything is to be looked into: buildings, glazing, the conduct of doctors, keepers and servants; types of lunatics, numbers, admissions, discharges, deaths, recoveries; diet, clothing, treatments, restraint; administration, fees, costs, supervision and inspection.'

'Good God, you'll be there for weeks.'

'I believe there will be several sittings, with many different witnesses, some from as far afield as Scotland.'

'It sounds as if it will be a considerable time before I'm freed.'

'At least there is the hope of it. A very real hope it is too.'

'Almost a promise?'

'No, I can't promise you anything. But the evidence is damning. There are the wrongfully incarcerated like yourself and Mr Norris, and a very unfortunate woman in the female wing . . . she speaks French and other languages and once was a teacher or a governess. She is quite lucid and yet she is chained up by a short tether to a wall on which a half dozen raving incontinent madwomen are also attached, all of whom have scarcely a blanket-gown to cover their nakedness . . .'

'Yes, I met her,' I interrupt him.

'And there is also a locked cell of very small size in which more than a dozen mad and incontinent women are forced to spend the night. I went in there one morning and the stench was intolerable. The walls were covered in faecal matter . . .' Mr Wakefield trails off with a sudden look of disgust on his face. 'It's the disparity between theory and practice that so enrages the common man.'

'The general public know about our conditions?'

'Indeed. Knowledge of them is now quite widespread. Otherwise Parliament might have avoided an inquiry. A quiet sacking or forced resignation here and there would probably have been enough. But we have cracked it wide open. Spilled the beans thoroughly.'

'I would have thought that the theory and the practice were in accord.'

'Not if you read the current books.'

'Which I don't, of course.'

'The modern publications are all about moral treatment; kindness and freedom of movement and the like.'

'Music and plays and poetry?'

'There are advocates of such treatment. But the hospital visitors are not demanding a finishing school. Only humane treatment and hygienic conditions. And proper certificates for those received into the madhouses.'

'And the exploded theory of revulsion – what has become of it?'

'I'm sure it lives on in the minds of some. But there are more scientifically correct beliefs now. And, correspondingly, more scientific treatments . . .'

'Such as?'

'There's the treatment with electricity, I hear.'

'*That* has been going on since 1756. And I hate to tell you, it's the perfect example of treatment according to the unexploded theory. To cause the revulsion to the actual seat of madness. Unexploded pure and simple.'

Mr Wakefield looks disconcerted. 'Well, of course, it's not my profession, mad-doctoring. I don't claim to be an expert in these matters.'

'You don't need expertise to know when a particular way of thinking is wearing a new disguise.'

'I disagree. It's the layman such as myself who cannot see it.'

'I too am a layman.'

'Actually, I don't think so. You are the lucid observer of your own treatment. You could therefore be said to be an informed observer of those treatments' effects. Except that the treatment was designed for lunatics, and so, for you, it is like being treated for smallpox when your disease is consumption. And you could hardly be said to be disinterested.'

'I think it is more like being treated for smallpox when I have no disease at all. But I'll let that pass in the interests of discussing more pressing concerns. In what way is the disinterested observer more reliable than the interested? Does not interest fix your attention on the specific detail of things? Why should the dis-interested care about the complex reactions and feelings of those inflicted with the treatment, whatever it is? In fact, they don't. Only the interested care enough to pay real and close attention. Do not be so infatuated with scientific distance, sir. In the case of the human mind, distance only decreases your acuity.'

Mr Wakefield stares at me for a moment. 'I can't imagine how you came to be here,' he says, shaking his head.

~

My scalp itches. I rub my head on the wall and when I stop I see a hank of hair adhering to the sticky surface. Since the incurables' heads are not shaved, my hair is now very long. It is also dirty, matted and completely white. But I've been reassured to have hair at all, and now that I see it starting to fall I quickly become despondent. I've lost even more of my teeth over the years, and all of my middle-age physique – when I look down at my body it is that of a very old man, shrunken, shrivelled, blotchy – so a fine head of hair was my last vanity.

But everything is to be taken from me.

The days pass. There is nothing between the short visits of the keepers and the irregular visits of Mr Wakefield. I am always pleased to see him, but I am also resentful that he comes so seldom.

'Excellent news,' he announces one afternoon. 'On the 1st of May I took the witness stand at the parliamentary inquiry.'

'Did you?' I reply sullenly. I am holding a newly fallen wad of hair in the palm of my hand. I managed to catch it as it fell.

'Yes. I gave very detailed descriptions of the conditions here, and I concluded with my opinion that the inmates are subjected to treatment regimens that are both indiscriminate and ineffectual, and are then abandoned to their fate.'

'It has all taken so long I've nearly lost my interest.'

'Everybody is busy.'

'Lucky them.'

'I see you are not in good spirits today. My news does not cheer you up?'

'I have been lonely,' I say petulantly.

'Are you more alone than previously?'

'Indeed I am. I was nearly always alone once Horatio died. And then you got rid of Porlock.'

'Frankly, I think he got rid of himself,' Mr Wakefield objects.

'He kept me from talking to myself.'

'Well then, I will come to see you more often. I have been taken up with securing this inquiry, but I see that you find my efforts misdirected.'

'That is not the case. But it seems as if I've already lived a lifetime since you first gave me hope of freedom. And hope cannot last a lifetime.'

Mr Wakefield looks nonplussed. 'You are sinking into melancholy,' he announces.

'I go up and down all the time. Tomorrow I will feel better. Or the next day. Perhaps the day after that. Then I will feel a little worse. I'm sure, if you think about it, you will find this a pattern not unlike your own.'

'I try to keep above my emotions.'

'Is that so? I am not such a man. I never was. What is up there above your emotions?'

'I see you wish to make fun of me. It's generally considered that rational thought is above the emotions. But I am a Quaker.'

'But?'

Mr Wakefield suddenly laughs. 'I'm not sure what I meant by but.'

'Probably that you exist in the rarefied air of faith.'

'I also act in the real world.'

'I also acted in the real world.'

Mr Wakefield looks disconcerted. 'I hope you're not going to become morbidly melancholic just when I'm publicly asserting you're a sane man.'

'Is melancholia to be equated with insanity?'

'Once a man gets down low enough, there is madness in it.'

'I will be better tomorrow,' I assure him. 'Or the next day. The one thing that can be relied upon is that our moods will go up and down quite independently of our daily lives. Next week I might even be euphoric. There will be no reason at all for this, but I will probably say to myself it is because I had cheese for lunch, or because Mr Wakefield took the witness stand at the parliamentary inquiry into madhouses.'

'You really are a most vexing man,' Mr Wakefield replies.

～

But Mr Wakefield turns out to be as good as his word. He comes to visit me more often and I am cheered. My remaining hair remains where it belongs. He brings a chair with him, plants it on the ground with the back towards me and sits astride it. We talk about this and that, jumping from one topic to another, until one day we light on the subject of the physician. Mr Wakefield speculates on his chances of being dismissed, once the parliamentary inquiry concludes.

'I think Mr Haslam, being the medical inferior, will be able to blame Mr Monro . . .'

'The name of the physician here is Monro?' I interrupt in alarm.

'It is. He is the third generation of the same family to be in charge of this establishment. What of it?'

'I knew someone of that name once. An actress. It was her name before she took to the stage. Before she married.'

'It's a common enough name.'

'That is so. But I suspect a connection.'

'An interesting one?'

'Interesting to some, perhaps. It is not the word I would use.'

'What word would you use?'

'Unfortunate.'

'And are you going to tell me of this unfortunate connection?'

'I have no proof of it.'

'Is proof required?'

'A lunatic requires proof. Only the sane do not.'

'Then you do not.'

'A fine reply, Mr Wakefield. But I don't want to be accused of suspicious delusions concerning the physician. I'll only say this: I am not of the usual classes to be incarcerated here; I have never appeared before the governors' release committee; a woman of my acquaintance once shared the same surname as the physician; I have never been insane, although I had one short period of forgetfulness, and I have come to believe that this was the result of my being deliberately poisoned.'

'Ah, you speak like a common lunatic.'

'Do not joke with me, sir. As I have frequently said, the fact that the King was mad does not alter the truth that several people *did* want to kill him.'

Mr Wakefield smiles. 'Let us talk about this female acquaintance then.'

'If you like.'

'Was she an intimate acquaintance?'

'Intimate enough.'

'In what sense was the relationship intimate?'

'I doubt you've got time to listen. It's rather a long story.'

'I have at least another hour at my disposal. I am not required anywhere before dinner time.'

'I will begin then. Whether or not I conclude is of no importance. Perhaps the story alone will keep you coming back.'

'I had no intention of abandoning you.'

'That's very reassuring. But you can never be certain of such a thing. Circumstances often require us to abandon those we would never voluntarily give up. Still, where to begin? I think I said the woman was a former actress. When I met her she had long given up that path in life for the more certain comforts and constraints of marriage. I was married also.'

'It's a story of intended adultery?' Mr Wakefield raises his eyebrows.

'It's a story of the heart.'

'Stories of the heart can still be adulterous.'

'After marriage they always are.'

'What an opinion!'

'When I first saw this woman – let us call her Juliet – she was standing by an ornamental pool in someone's garden. It was summer, strawberries and cream time. Indeed, such dishes, together with champagne, were being served by young men in unnecessarily stiff white jackets and ridiculous gloves. I'm not sure what the occasion was. Perhaps the engagement of another spotty daughter. I was annoyed at having to be there, but my wife had insisted upon it. "William," she often chided me, "how can we expect a decent turnout at the parties of our own daughters if we do not go to those of others?" So I went and I was bored, hot and disgruntled.'

'Ah yes – I can picture that exactly.'

'Anyway, when I first really *looked* at Juliet – not the first minute I saw her you understand – she wasn't young and beautiful in the banal way that instantly rivets all men's eyes – something about her caught my undivided attention.'

'What was it?'

'I've no idea.'

Mr Wakefield looks extremely dissatisfied.

'Rather, I understand *now* what this attribute was, having known her well for some time. But I didn't know then. Or, and I leave you to ponder this at your leisure, perhaps I only know this attribute now because I sought to dig it out, having sensed it shining like a hidden golden nugget right there at the beginning.'

'Can a hidden nugget shine?'

'Let's say a hidden magnet can still attract.'

'Fair enough. Go on.'

'Right away, I wanted her to notice *me*. I'm as vain as the next man. Well, that's one way of looking at it. Another way is that I wanted somehow to detain this mysterious quality. Look at it, know it, keep it. And how could I do that if, for her, I scarcely existed? She would walk away from that garden party into a completely separate future.'

'Yes, I recall from my younger days the particular difficulty of meeting again the women one was interested in,' Mr Wakefield agrees.

'When there are marriageable daughters, and you are yourself an eligible bachelor, the older women usually manage to provide suitable occasions. But in my age group, when everyone is married, the social forces are quite against you.'

'And so what did you do?'

'That very afternoon I decided to dispense with the usual niceties. I decided I would buy her attention. I walked straight up to her and introduced myself, stressing the "William" while allowing the "Lonsdale" to be swallowed up so that she might not immediately connect me to any of the women there; and then I initiated a conversation about money. It was as I thought – her attitude to it was the same as most. It can best be summed up by the maxim: the more, the better. Then I proceeded with the rest of my purchase.'

'How do you mean?'

'I offered her money in return for an unspecified favour at a later date. And I told her that if she later decided not to grant me this favour, she could still keep the money. What greedy woman could refuse such an offer? I can assure you, I had her complete and undivided attention.'

'A fascinating solution to the problem. But attention isn't intimacy, surely?'

'Not at all. But there is no intimacy where there is no

opportunity. A reason, I believe, why the unchristian hordes keep their women in veils.'

'An excellent idea. Perhaps we should do likewise.'

'I have no interest in prisoners.'

'Unlike myself.'

We stare at each other for a moment.

'You do not believe in altruism?' Mr Wakefield murmurs.

'I believe in my own – but not that of others.'

Mr Wakefield smiles. 'It's a common solipsism.'

'May I return to the story? Juliet's attention was only a beginning. But an important part, because without it there is no middle, no end. As I said, there was something about her that I wished to keep, and I could keep it only if she gave it to me.'

'Keeping a quality of another person sounds complicated.'

'Indeed it is. Usually when we get too close to a particular quality it goes out of focus for us. Too long up close to it, and we forget about it. Can you remember the most attractive quality of your wife when she was a girl?'

'No, I can't.'

'Quite so. And so I wished to keep this quality at the correct distance for appreciation without allowing her to snatch it completely away. In short, I had to make her want to be near me – but not too near. And as I couldn't go on paying her for ever – it was a large sum that I was forking out – I had to make her want to remain in this exacting position voluntarily.'

'You are a very complicated man. The marriage bed and the brothel seem wonders of convenience in comparison.'

'You should think twice before regarding convenience as a good way to live your life. It's very convenient here. Everything done, everything provided. And a man who thinks he's your superior even carries away your steaming turds.'

'I stand corrected.'

'Now I will ask you a question – and there is a penalty for not being able to answer it correctly.'

'What is the penalty?'

'No more story.'

'Ah. And what is the question?'

'What was the one way – the only way, mind you – of securing my goal?'

Mr Wakefield looks at me blankly.

'Go on. Think about it.'

'I'm afraid I have no idea.'

'I'll give you a clue. The money had to stop. What else is there as persuasive as money?'

'Force?'

'Force isn't persuasive, Mr Wakefield. Force is the failure of persuasion.'

'Sex, then.'

'Oh dear, oh dear. I think you are not a very sexually experienced man. Sex is not a persuasion that men have over women. Where are the brothels that women patronise?'

'This is my last try then. I'm struggling even to think. How about fear?'

'Fear is a part of it. What are we most afraid to lose?'

'Looking at you I think it's my freedom.'

'Not your mind?'

'Very amusing.'

'Anyway, I had my freedom then. It never entered my head that I would lose it. So I ask you again: what are we most afraid to lose?'

'The end of the story?'

'You are giving up without trying.'

'On the contrary. I know the answer.'

'Why don't you tell me then?'

'You bought something long considered unpurchaseable.'

'I also had to work for it.'

'And how did you do that work?'

'I made myself more gratifying.'

'It's a strange notion. We are as we are.'

'At what point are we as we are? At birth, or five, or perhaps twenty? It is my contention that we are always becoming what we are, and an insightful man can, *should*, attempt to influence that development. For as long as he can, anyway.'

'Many lack that sort of insight,' Mr Wakefield says.

I am about to reply when the apothecary appears in the doorway.

'Good afternoon, sir,' he says politely to Mr Wakefield, but his eyebrows have gathered on his brow like storm clouds. 'I was informed that you were in here. Would you be so kind as to accompany me to the physician's office?'

'Why? What do you want with me there?' Mr Wakefield asks abruptly.

'The physician has some pressing concerns. I am not apprised of them.'

'I see you like to take every opportunity available to imply there is a space between the physician's mind and your own,' Mr Wakefield admonishes him.

Mr Haslam does not change his facial expression and makes no reply, but indicates by holding out his arm that the visitor should proceed directly out the door.

'Do not worry,' I call to Mr Wakefield as he leaves. 'I believe that you have guessed the name of the persuasive force, the thing we are most afraid to lose. When you return I will tell you the end of the story.'

∿

It is morning. I have watched the sky go from pitch black to pale grey. It begins to rain. I am about to succumb to my usual pluvial melancholy when Strappado and Thumbscrew step into the cell.

'Who allowed you two to get together?' I ask suspiciously.

'We're helping each other today,' Strappado replies. 'Everyone important is away.'

'Or drunk.'

'Or sick.'

'Or drunk and sick.'

'Well, what do you want in here? Another keeper has already done the breakfast.'

'We've come to entertain you,' Thumbscrew says. 'A lunatic who misses Porlock needs entertaining.'

'And must be very easy to entertain too,' Strappado adds.

They throw themselves down on the derelict straw bale near the door. I feel a wave of fear, as if two real torturers have flung themselves down before me.

'And how are you going to entertain me?' I ask.

'You've heard of the game Tiddlywinks?'

'This is similar.'

'Called Pillywinks.'

'That's not similar at all.'

'And a bit of Bastinado too,' Thumbscrew adds.

I look at them, and wait for them to pull out their instruments.

'Are you going to torture me with words?' I ask when nothing happens.

'Like you torture everyone else?'

'Why don't you just go away? There's good boys.'

'Oh, don't worry, we'll be going. Tonight when we walk out the door you won't see us again.'

'Oh? Why not?'

'We're not working in the middle of all this finger-pointing. You never know where you are. One minute the physician's in boiling water; the next minute you're in it yourself.'

'Well, that's the way the world works,' I reply. 'Always has done, always will.'

I watch them. They are now elbowing each other in the ribs as if exhorting each other to speak. Eventually Strappado clears his throat and says, 'Before we leave, we thought there might be something you'd like us to do for you. For a consideration, of course.'

They both look at me expectantly. I now understand their intentions.

'First, I have nothing to give you. You would have to wait until I'm freed. Second, there's a man already helping me for nothing, so you're too late. And third, I wouldn't trust either of you as far as I could spit.'

'That's not what Porlock told us,' Thumbscrew contradicts. 'He said you wanted *him* to get you out of here and you'd give him a lot of money . . .'

'That was years ago,' I interrupt. 'There was a document of mine in the office here which could have been sold. That has gone now.'

'Porlock told us recently. Right before he left,' Thumbscrew objects.

'Porlock is a drunk. He forgets the order of events; and then he fabricates to cover for his loss of memory.'

The keepers look disgruntled.

'I can't see why you'd trust him and not us,' Thumbscrew whines.

'I didn't trust him actually. But I had no options. Now I do.'

'Come on,' Strappado says. 'We're wasting our time. Let's try that foreign pissabed down the hall. They say *he's* as rich as Croesus.'

'And mad as a snake,' I shout after them.

Nil desperandum

'WHO IS MAD as a snake?' Mr Wakefield asks, stepping into the cell.

'Oh, it's you again. Sometimes you give me quite a fright.'

'Would you like me to be announced?'

'If I said yes, would you do it?'

'No.'

'As I thought. Have you come for the conclusion of my story?'

'I'm afraid that will have to wait. I'm due at the inquiry shortly. In fact, I'm on my way there now. I made a detour to report on progress.'

'Well, what's been happening?'

Mr Wakefield assumes a very pleased expression. 'Things are looking up,' he begins. 'For ourselves, I mean. The ghost of James Tilly Matthews has risen to haunt the apothecary.'

'And who is James Tilly Matthews?'

'Another man like yourself. He was admitted in 1797, about three or four years before you, I think. Mr Haslam took a strong dislike to him almost at once. Well, that's what the keepers say. For nearly everyone else he was extremely likeable.' Mr Wakefield pauses and appears to be deep in thought. 'It's so difficult to untangle these things. There seems to be no doubt that he was indeed a raving lunatic at the beginning. But later, nobody knows when, his lunacy abated.'

'Excuse me, I was never a raving lunatic.'

'Of course not,' Mr Wakefield hastens to reassure me. He begins again to walk about the room, high-stepping over the ground which Horatio once occupied.

'And what was the nature of this doubtless lunacy?' I ask, though I am fascinated by Mr Wakefield's avoidance of Horatio's abandoned space. As if he fears standing on something left behind, perhaps the memory of Horatio's unsatisfactory life.

'Mr Matthews alleged he was being persecuted by a device he called the Air Loom. It was an apparatus which controlled his thoughts and which was fuelled by – in his own picturesque words – the effluvia of dogs, stinking human breath, stench of the cesspool, human gas, and gas from the anus of a horse.'

'And what's so lunatic about that? It's a metaphor for Bedlam itself. Are the cells not dog kennels and isn't this institution built straight upon the city cesspits of the past? And what was Porlock beyond stinking breath and human gas? As for equine anal pollution, it's as good a description as any for the medical science here.'

Mr Wakefield smiles. 'That might be so. But only a madman would believe that this apparatus was designed to stop him from revealing a foul plot.'

'What foul plot?'

'The plot of French revolutionaries to republicanise Great Britain and ruin the British Navy.'

'That's not madness, that's Napoleon.'

'I see you're not in the mood to agree with anything I say. But that's good – I would hate to think you were becoming agreeable. It would make me worry what they were doing to you. In fact, Mr Matthews' family agreed he was mad, but only for a very short time. They then tried repeatedly to secure his release. This is where it all gets rather interesting. Apparently, Matthews had tried to implicate Lord Liverpool in the heinous plot of the French; and as it turns out, in 1809 Lord Liverpool himself was instrumental in securing Matthews' continued confinement. Then in 1813 and 1814 the Home Secretary did likewise. All this government intervention over a man generally deemed not only sane but talented and accomplished, a favourite among the staff and patients! Mr Haslam has been getting rather a lot of stick about it.'

'And what was Mr Haslam's role in the matter?'

Mr Wakefield shakes his head as if he finds what he tells me quite incredible. 'As I said, Mr Haslam took a violent dislike to him right from the start. He published a whole book devoted to his case, ridiculing the man and his supporters. Mr Matthews also kept a book in which he detailed his treatment and other upsetting scenes he observed. He often threatened to make the manuscript public and would frequently read from it to Haslam himself.'

'Oh what a man! I wish I had met him.'

'At the inquiry, Mr Haslam said – here, look I've written it all down for you: "I conceived that the manuscript's circulation ought not to be prevented on the presumption that there existed in the judgement of those who passed for persons of sound mind, a sufficient disrelish for absurdity, to enable them to discriminate the transactions of daylight from the materials of a dream."'

'That's rich from the man who once said to me he never *saw* a human being who was of sound mind.'

'Yes,' Mr Wakefield replies with disapproval. 'At the trial Haslam went as far as to allege that even the surgeon had spent much of the last decade generally insane and mostly drunk. In fact, he said he was so insane as to require a straitjacket.' Mr Wakefield laughs. 'It's quite a sight to see each of them blaming the man on the next rung down. The physician is trying to blame the apothecary for the treatment of that other poor fellow Norris – unfortunately, it's on record that the apothecary objected to the extent of his restraints. As for cruelty generally, both the physician and the apothecary have blamed the keepers. They both denied ever having control of the servants; they said this was the job of the steward.

'Still, at least the physician has admitted responsibility for the medical treatments. He said the methods were handed down to him by his father and he did not know any better practice. The apothecary, however, made it plain he didn't agree with the medical treatments; and unfortunately for the physician, uniformity of medical treatment is now seen badly.

'The whole point of the insane being sent to institutions is that they might benefit from individual treatment: if mad-doctoring is a science – a special branch of expertise, as the mad-doctors would have it – then blanket treatments are in contradiction to the notion. After this, the flustered physician contradicted himself and said it's more by management that lunatics are cured than by medicine.'

'And is it supposed that Haslam was doing the dirty work of the government?' I ask. 'That there really was a foul plot and this man Matthews, once sane, *was* actually dangerous?'

Mr Wakefield sighs and assumes an exasperated expression. Clearly he has had enough of our apothecary and his arrogance. 'I don't think so. Haslam's hatred blinded him to the returned sanity of Mr Matthews. Probably it was Haslam himself who convinced both the physician and the Home Secretary that the man was still mad. I'm not sure. As for Lord Liverpool's original intervention, no doubt having one's name continuously and publicly mentioned in the ravings of a lunatic is an affront to one's vanity. This is the way it has all been explained. But it still remains that Haslam looks as though he can't tell a lunatic from a sage.'

'Probably that's not surprising,' I remark. 'What is more worrisome is that he can't tell a lunatic from an averagely defective, perfectly ordinary, pleasant chap.'

'In my opinion it behoves Mr Haslam to spend more time amongst the sane – his ideas about normality would become less rigid.'

'On the other hand, it's possible he would endeavour to put a high wall around the entire world.'

Mr Wakefield laughs.

'Not that he'd have the sense to stay outside,' I add.

~

It is too hot. For once the outside heat has penetrated our refugium and unpleasantly combined itself with the heat we now get from the indoor fires, fires which are now lit with the same therapeutic fervour with which they remained unlit in the recent and less recent past. A bead of sweat trickles down my forehead and drips into my eye. It infuriates me to be unable to wipe my brow. I start to fling my head vigorously from side to side. I am still doing this when a line of sombre-suited gentlemen file into my cell behind the apothecary. I freeze.

'This is an especial lunatic,' I hear Mr Haslam saying.

'Oh?' A gorbellied man of great height and florid colouring steps towards me. 'What is your name?' he asks, staring straight into my face.

'Let me see. William Norris, I think. Or perhaps James Tilly Matthews.'

'Very amusing,' the fat, tall, rubicund gentleman says.

'His name is William Lonsdale,' the apothecary informs him dryly.

'Please allow the lunatic to speak for himself sir,' the big man replies.

'Who are *you*?' I ask him.

'I am part of an inspection committee sent by the parliamentary inquiry,' he answers.

'Don't you have a name?'

Mr Haslam sighs audibly and rolls his eyes.

'You can call me Mr Pangloss.'

'Are you an absurdly optimistic person then?'

'You are familiar with Voltaire?'

'Of course. Everyone here knows Voltaire. He's in the incurables' wing with the rest of us.'

Mr Haslam coughs loudly and Mr Pangloss regards me with a long, cool, analytical stare.

'Tell me about yourself,' he finally says. 'Do you know how you got here?'

'Frogmarched by the constables, I believe.'

'Do you know *why* you are here?'

'No. Do you?'

'You have no idea at all?'

'To be poisoned? Because of a plot?'

There is a ripple of laughter along the line of gentlemen. Mr Pangloss spins on his heels, very elegantly for so large a man, and glares at the apothecary. 'Who signed the admission certificate for this man?'

'I'll have to find out,' the apothecary replies haughtily.

'Well, do so at once,' Mr Pangloss returns angrily. Mr Haslam makes a vague, insolent bow with his head and slides out the door. The other gentlemen look towards their leader expectantly.

'I am interested in assessing your sanity,' the big man says with a perplexed look on his face. 'Tell me plainly, do you know the difference between delusion and reality?'

'I certainly do,' I reply.

'Well, come on then. Tell the committee.'

'Reality is what we are deluded about.'

The line of gentlemen burst out laughing.

'And what we are deluded about isn't real.'

Their laughter skids to an abrupt stop.

'Tell me one sane thing,' the fat man persists, wiping his glistening red brow with a large handkerchief.

'One sane thing? Very well. Let me see. How about lunatics are not to be trusted? Will that do?'

Mr Pangloss stares at me again as if seeking sanity in my eyes. I try to look as focused as possible. Then he turns his back and motions the inspection committee into a huddle. For a minute or two they all whisper furiously together. They break up, and Mr Pangloss steps forward and clears his throat. 'Thank you for your time, Mr Lonsdale. We won't trouble you any further.'

'My time? I have plenty of it. An excess. You take nothing from me when you use it. On the contrary, it's I who should thank you. You have all been very . . . time consuming.'

Mr Pangloss smiles a little and heads for the door without replying. The other gentlemen laugh a little uncertainly, each eyeing the others slyly to see whether laughter is indicated, and then follow their leader out.

∾

On Saturday, Mr Wakefield comes to visit me in the afternoon. I have been dozing in the unaccustomed warmth.

'Good afternoon, your Highness.'

'Good afternoon.'

'Look what I have here.'

'A key.'

'*The* key. I can undo your chains and then you would be able to walk about the cell. However . . .'

'However?'

Mr Wakefield laughs. 'I must first hear the end of the story.'

'You won't free me to tell it?'

'The ending might change if you were free.'

'You are a perceptive man, Mr Wakefield. But I promise not to let the lack of chains go to my head.'

'Hah, I don't believe you would be able to help it. Tell me the end of the story as you must have envisaged it told: chained to the wall.'

I laugh. Freedom is a heady perfume in the air.

'You had guessed the most persuasive force last time we spoke. I could tell by the special light that lit up your eye. To Horatio, I always referred to this persuasive force as the ace of hearts. I told him that all my scheming had been to force my Juliet to play the ace of hearts which, through a series of tricks, I had smuggled into her hand. And what was my goal? Let me refresh you: to keep a certain quality of hers always within my reach, but not within my relentless grasp, and to get her to do this willingly rather than for money.

'I'll set the scene: it is autumn; we are walking in a downpour through marcescent trees. Under our umbrellas, of course. We are walking in a fashionable district and, as is our habit since the previous spring, we make sure to pass the Italian cake shop. We are talking and laughing – I have forgotten what our topic is. A few steps past the shop this particular topic is finished with and I ask her if she would like a cake. "No," she says. "I would like to do what we have just been referring to."

'As I said, I have forgotten what this was, but I remark that she can have a cake in the meantime. Being in a playful mood, I describe the cake in question, using a number of lascivious words to stimulate her appetite. I finish up with an Italian word that leaps into my mind for no reason at all other than it is a word that, for me, sums up all the delight in the world.

'She looks at me, "Why did you say that?"

'I shrug. I watch water drip off her lemon and pink umbrella.

'"It is too difficult for me . . ." she begins.

'"What is difficult for you?"

'"The levity."

'"Do we levitate?"

'"You do. On that word you just used. And others like it."

'"And you don't?"

'She struggles. "I levitate . . . on horses."

'Then we both burst out laughing at the absurdity.

'I take her hand and pat it, and then we begin walking again. Cakeless, but with other morsels on our minds. She is quiet. The rain stops. We put our umbrellas down. We come to a seat and she proposes that we sit down on it. I notice it is still wet, and point this out to her. She is impatient with my caution. We sit down.

'"I don't know what that word you used means," she says.

'"Actually, neither do I. It just sounds . . ."

'She puts her finger to her lips to hush me.

'"Why should such levity be difficult for me, William?"

'She is looking at me solemnly and my heart is beating hard. Not, you understand, because we will shortly go home and have our usual non-adulterous physical interlude; rather, because I know she is about to play the ace of hearts. I brace myself.'

'You had non-adulterous physical interludes?' Mr Wakefield interrupts. 'What pray might that refer to?'

'Ah, you are more interested in *that* than the ace of hearts.'

'I can't imagine what a non-adulterous physical interludes could possibly refer to.'

'Is touching a married woman's hand adultery?'

'I hope not. I have done it many times.'

'What about her face?'

'Well, I think that could certainly be misconstrued. Although it could still be innocent.'

'And her leg?'

'Not innocent at all.'

'Is a lack of innocence, a certain level of sexual *intention*, shall we say, adultery then?'

'Well, no.' Mr Wakefield looks uncertain. 'Otherwise the man who had an intention, yet resisted it, would be as guilty as the man who had it and went all the way.'

'Under which circumstances you might as well go all the way. My view exactly. And quite in line with biblical teachings, I might add. A man who has committed adultery in his heart, etcetera. I certainly intended to commit adultery, and I intend to again, the first chance I get; but at the point in time, under the lemon and pink umbrella, or rather just after this, we had not got quite as far as that.'

'I see that you are very wicked. But, in the interests of a good story, how far had you got?'

I laugh. I'm sure I would be able to hear the sublime Mr Wakefield panting if only I could increase either his volume or my own acuity. 'Sir, it's not done to discuss such things. Let's just say that if you were looking at us fully clothed from a bird's eye-view, the delightful creature would appear to have four legs but only one head.'

Mr Wakefield appears confused for several moments as his imagination runs through all the permutations that might fit such a description. The look of shock on his face is enough to reassure me that he has finally arrived at the right conclusion. Before he can answer I add, 'And in another variation, again looking at us clothed from above, she has only two legs – but now there are two heads. And one of them is not hers.'

Mr Wakefield takes considerably less time to picture this variation. He blushes. 'I have never been able to induce a lady to do such a thing.'

'She wasn't really a lady. Only playing.'

'I've heard it said a man would pay a large sum for such a sport.'

'Have you? That's where we differ. What you have previously got for free you don't like paying for later.'

'You'd had this experience before?'

'Often. But before you get carried away and make off with the end of my story, wouldn't you like to hear what I *was* willing to pay for? Or rather, what I sought to be given after paying out such a large sum?'

Mr Wakefield looks reluctant to abandon the topic of reciprocal oral sex and I can understand his point.

'So there we are on the seat. My heart is beating hard. She is looking into my eyes. I am thinking, How beautiful you are, how daring, how duplicitous. And the hidden quality that I perceived from the beginning seems revealed to me in all its glory. Now, imagine that while sitting there on the seat the two of us have frozen; that time has stopped. We are rigid in our postures, just about to speak.

Leave us there for a short time while I capture this quality.

'I'm rather scared of horses. Aren't you? When I was a small boy, my mother always warned me not to stand immediately behind them. "They can give you a nasty kick, William," she said. "They can kick you into tomorrow." Consequently, whenever I found myself surrounded by horses' arses – and it happened more often than you'd expect – I was utterly terrified. I'd break out in a sweat and startle the horse with my little scurries as I tried to escape. They'd all start seething and moving around me and I'd begin to scream. Untethered horses would bolt off in every direction. Tethered ones would start a few experimental cavorts. Mother would come to rescue me. I'd bury my face in her skirt and she would carry me off for placating syrupy treats. In such a way are our characters made.

'I soon realised that I was able to manufacture such a supremely satisfying outcome – Mother and sweets – just by getting behind a horse and screaming. I had learned the fine art of manipulation – a truly exquisite weapon, in my opinion. To make a short story long, I simultaneously realised that in order to manipulate others, you also have to learn to control *yourself*. The truth is, I didn't want to be anywhere near those humungous glistening rumps and unpredictable hoofs. I had to force myself. And I never got over my apprehension about horses – my original, true fear still screams out from beneath the muffle of calculation.

'Anyway, when Juliet spoke to me of her passion for horse-riding, as she did that day by the pool, I knew immediately that the quality I perceived in her was connected to this sport. And I was right. When I first saw her riding a horse, galloping away from me over her estate, I understood that this apparent marvellous effortlessness had cost her dearly. In controlling this large, sweating, wild-eyed creature, she'd also had to learn to control her own fear. Fear of falling, of failure, of any number of accidents and disasters that could arise on or off the slippery back of such a monster. It was this quality that I most wanted to keep: this controlled yet ardent desire, this determination to manipulate the thing – horses, people, life – that always wants to unseat us, throw us off, kick us into tomorrow.

'Now, unfreeze the two of us and watch her lips.

'"I love you," she says.

'And what do I reply, serenely, although my heart is beating hard and my palms are perspiring?

'"Thank you. You have now done me my favour."'

~

I wake up. Mr Wakefield has arrived. He is flushed and his keen blue eyes are shining brightly. He is obviously very excited.

'Ah, you've come to unshackle me now that I've told you the end of my story,' I exclaim before he can speak.

'No. The governors have demanded I give the key back. But I've come to tell you about the conclusions of the parliamentary inquiry into madhouses,' he announces.

'Oh? They have finally concluded? After all this time I began to think that getting evidence had become a bad habit.'

'There was a lot to cover. You'd want it done properly, wouldn't you?'

'Actually, I'd prefer it to be done fast. But nobody consults me.'

'You can be quite a frustrating man, Mr Lonsdale.'

'Would you find me more entertaining if I was polite and compliant?'

'Not at all. But I don't come here to be entertained.'

'Don't you? I always find a little entertainment goes a long way in human relations.'

'Would you like me to tell you the conclusions of the inquiry or shall we carry on discussing the best way to conduct oneself socially?'

I laugh. 'Yes let's get on with the conclusion. What are you waiting for?'

Mr Wakefield starts to walk around the cell. 'Excuse me,' he says, 'this aids my memory.' He puts the palms of his hands together and brings his fingertips up to his mouth. Then he takes them away and shakes them. 'The inquiry came to the general conclusion that there is not, in the entire country, a set of beings more *immediately* requiring protection of the legislature than people such as yourself. What do you think of that?'

'I think their notion of immediacy is eccentric.'

Mr Wakefield ignores me. 'And they made a number of additional statements which I think you will find interesting. I have made a note of those most relevant to yourself.' Mr Wakefield stops circling and gets out his notebook. 'They listed their most important concerns, the first six of which involved conditions and treatments. Then they said: "*Seventhly*, detention of persons, the state of whose minds did not require confinement; *eighthly*, insufficiency of certificates on which patients are received into the madhouses; *ninethly*, the defective visitation of mad-houses."'

'Oh, are you a defective visitation? I always suspected it.'

'Try to be serious, Mr Lonsdale.'

'Sorry. Carry on.'

'The bookkeeping here caused an uproar. There turned out to be two sets of books – one kept by the apothecary and one by the steward. Both of these turned out to contain false information. The apothecary's books were meant to be admission, discharge and treatment accounts, but were in fact nothing more than debit and credit ledgers. Upon detailed investigation, they uncovered the concealment of one hundred and forty-four deaths. Mr Haslam is to be dismissed. As is Thomas Munro, I believe.'

'That's somewhat radical, isn't it?'

'You don't approve?'

'I approve thoroughly. But I never thought they would do such a thing.'

'The charges are very serious.'

'Criminal charges will be brought?'

'Oh no, I don't think so,' Mr Wakefield replies hastily. 'I suspect they will not be able to work with lunatics in the public asylums any more.'

'Suspect? You mean they have not been forbidden from working with lunatics for ever?'

'No. Mr Haslam's writings on the subject of lunacy are widely respected. It is his praxis that is not perfect. And Mr Monro has his own private establishment. I think they will be sent packing to satisfy the public, but that will be the end of it.'

'And what about the lucid among us? Has the inquiry determined our fate?'

'Certainly. You are all to be reassessed at the earliest convenience. But for you it will be a mere formality.'

~

I wake up in pitch darkness. A wind is howling. The remnants of a dream are slipping away. In the dream I am running. That is all. Anything that could be described as context is a blur. There is nothing in the dream but free movement. I have had many similar dreams; and many dreams of tables spread with food, and wardrobes crammed with fur, and women arching back on chatoyant sheets.

But my waking dreams are of a sailing ship cleaving velvet water as it slips into a cove in Queen Charlotte Sound. I come up on deck for lunch and the sun warms me as I listen to the plash of the water. In the afternoon, I go ashore and sit on a half-moon of sand with the thick green bush at my back and catch a fish, as I now will for every meal. I cook it on an open fire and drink water from a stream that springs up somewhere in the mountains. Apart from the sea's music, the silence is total. My tailored clothes quickly rot and I become encrusted with strangeness. If I do not draw the map, draw attention, I will be alone here with my language; no one here can understand me, nor ever will.

Mr Wakefield enters the cell and startles me out of my lapse into romantic hermitism. He looks pleased with himself.

'This is the last time that we will be together in this way,' he announces.

'Oh? Are you going somewhere?'

'Not at all. You are.'

'And where am I going?'

His keen eyes twinkle. 'You are going back to the world.'

'As long as I don't turn around?'

'Why are you never pleased with anything?' he grumbles.

'Oh, I am pleased. If it turns out to be true. But many things are too good to be true. I've learnt never to count my chickens, etcetera.'

'Well, this chicken is hatched. The governors are to reassess everyone at the first opportunity. They are right this minute arguing about the date.'

'And what if they argue for ever? Perhaps I will die here while they are arguing.'

'You are in no danger of dying,' Mr Wakefield observes dryly. 'You look positively fat. I suspect they are now overfeeding you. And it is most uncommonly warm in here. How can you stay awake?'

'To tell you the truth, I hardly can.'

'Next time I come, I will come with the keys to the wing. I will conduct you to the governors . . .' Mr Wakefield shuts his eyes as if it's his own ecstasy he's anticipating.

'I want you to do something for me,' I interrupt.

'You don't think I've done enough?' Mr Wakefield replies, coming back to reality.

'I want you to go to my townhouse and fetch something.'

'Naturally I don't object. But why can't you go yourself when you're free? It's only a matter of time.'

'No, I shall require these documents as soon as I step outside. I will need money immediately. I need clothes, a solicitor. I have it in mind to make a sale as soon as I walk out of the gate.'

'It wouldn't be safe to keep such things here.'

'I will ask you to keep them then. You have always assured me you will be present on the day I'm released.'

'Very well. If that's what you want, I will do it.'

'I'll give you the address presently. First, I will tell you what it is I want and where to find it.'

Mr Wakefield takes out his notebook and writes down the details as I give them to him.

'Is that it?' he asks when I have concluded.

'Yes, that's all.'

'I will go tomorrow morning.'

I nod vigorously. 'Yes, the sooner the better.'

～

Each afternoon I expect the arrival of Mr Wakefield. By the fourth day, I am afraid that something has gone wrong. On the fifth afternoon he appears. I see at once that he is agitated. He does not greet me, but commences to walk round and round the cell until I am obliged to ask him to stop. He does so abruptly and looks me in the eye.

'I have some unpleasant news,' he says.

'I'm not going back to the world? I'm to be turned into a pillar of salt?'

Mr Wakefield ignores me. In fact, his agitation is so great I do not think he even hears me.

'This is nothing to do with your release,' he says. 'It's Wednesday, and this Saturday the governors will gather to review every patient. No, the bad news concerns the little job you asked me to do. I went to your townhouse as you requested. I found the key where you said it would be hidden. After all these years, it was still there.'

'That's because I was the only one who knew where it was.'

'I let myself in. The house is still in obvious use.'

'Is it? Well, in a way I expected that. I'm sure my family would have delved quite deeply into my affairs.' I laugh at my joke. Mr Wakefield, however, continues to look severe.

'You should have warned me. It gave me quite a shock.'

'Would you have gone there if I'd told you that?'

'Certainly not!'

'As I thought. But I'm sure it's not in use very often. Were there servants there? Food in the pantry?'

'No. But it was tidy and clean and the courtyards well kept.'

'My wife probably sends the servants over to spring-clean, and orders the gardener there every once in a while. She would never live there. It's not her kind of place.'

'I am surprised she did not rid herself of it.'

'You wouldn't be so surprised if you knew her. She doesn't have that turn of mind. I am more surprised that my eldest son hasn't sold it or put it out to rent. Probably he's preoccupied with other investments.'

'Your eldest son was killed in a duel several years ago.'

I feel as if I have been winded.

'I'm sorry to be the one to have to tell you.'

'But what has become of everything?' I cry. 'Who has been managing things?'

'I have made some discreet inquiries. Your second son, Henry, is in charge of all the finances now.'

'Ah, Henry.' I relax a little.

'Henry drinks.'

'Does he?'

'You didn't know?'

'He didn't used to.'

'I don't think he has drunk the entire estate. Yet. Perhaps your wife has kept the knowledge of the townhouse from him.'

'Is that possible?'

'Legally, no. Actually – well, do drunks go carefully through all their documents and accounts? Do they listen to their financial advisers?'

'And what of my other children?'

'Katherine and Elizabeth are safely married to good incomes.'

'And the other two? Thomas and Artemis?'

'They have gone out to the Antipodes.'

'Well at least they won't get lost, the little traitors.'

Mr Wakefield looks uncomfortable.

'I have more bad news.'

'Can there be more?'

'I went to the box you directed me to. It was indeed hidden where you said it would be. The keys were also where you indicated. I opened it and . . .'

'And?'

'It was empty.'

'There was no Molière in my box?'

'Not a scrap.'

'But there was only one other person who knew where the key was.'

Mr Wakefield looks as if he will explode. 'That lady you have been telling me about, the former actress – well, when you told me her real name, I made some further investigations.'

'You did? You have been most assiduous.'

'That particular lady – if you can call her a lady,' Mr Wakefield cries, beginning to wave his arms about, 'has long since left the town. She absconded with a Frenchman many years ago. It caused an enormous scandal. Everybody who would talk about it with me – and there weren't many – put the date at 1801 or thereabouts. In the beginning, it was believed that her paramour was an aristocrat, but he soon showed himself to be just another thorough rascal. It is said he only wanted her for her money – your money, as it turns out. At the time, nobody could understand how she had amassed such a large sum.'

Mr Wakefield attempts to recover himself from his arm-waving agitation.

'Through her husband's investigations, it was easy enough to trace the money back to yourself. And he was more than happy to testify against you at your trial. He believed you had paid his wife for sex, and your own wife believed it too. He also believed you had enabled his wife to leave him. And so you had. He discovered letters from the rogue that predated your own first payment. But nobody could understand how you turned up at the docks incoherent and raving.'

We both consider this in total silence. I remember the tall, magnificent, French-accented manservant with his basket of delights sent by Juliet.

'*She* must have poisoned me,' I finally say, although it hardly needs saying.

'I'm afraid that is all we can conclude.'

The silence in the cell is huge, solid.

'I am now mad,' I declare at last.

~

I wake up. It is Saturday. The governors will be arriving soon. I will hear the crunch of the carriage wheels on the driveway. As I proceed along the corridors to meet them, I will see their hats piled one on top of the other on the hall tables. I will see the floor littered with the butts of cigars. They will anoint me with freedom, and I will go back to the world to be happy.

The keeper comes in with the bucket and hose. I relieve myself and then he soaks me from head to foot. He goes out with the bucket and returns with a small pile of worn, clean clothes. He puts them carefully on the floor, away from the puddles. Then he goes off again to fetch the pabulum – or rather, the thick, wholesome and satisfying porridge that is now our regular fare at breakfast.

'I think I could be satisfied with a narrative of this consistency,' I say to him as he feeds me.

'What? If you carry on like that, you'll be staying. Mark my words.'

Mr Wakefield appears in the doorway.

'He won't be staying. They'll now love the way he talks. Even the crusty old buggers with permanent doses of ill-humour.'

'Yes, the way I talk will now be viewed as the ultimate panchymagogue.'

'Which means?' Mr Wakefield asks, playing the game.

'Panchymagogue? Why, it's a purgative effective against all kinds of humours.'

'Thank you for that little lesson. Now shall we get on and unshackle you?'

'Of course. What are you waiting for?'

Mr Wakefield comes over and unlocks the chains around my wrists. He bends down and unlocks the chains around my ankles.

'There you are, your Highness,' he says.

He stands back and smiles at me. The keeper looks uncertain and takes a step backwards as if a wild animal has just been uncaged. Mr Wakefield gestures towards the clothes. Clumsy, simian, I move over and attempt to put them on. But my arms are logs and my fingers gnarled. Mr Wakefield completes the task for me, tenderly doing up the buttons with all the humility of a courtier. Then he gestures to the door which is standing open. I hang back, rubbing my arms.

'Go on,' he urges. 'What are you waiting for? Your freedom is beyond the door.'

'Is it?'

'Well, your old comfortable, comforting, pleasurable prison if you prefer. Remember, even a king can't have absolute freedom. You said so yourself.'

'That's true. He rules from above but is toppled from below. However . . .'

'Yes?'

'I'm not waiting for absolute freedom. Remember that word I told you about? I haven't got it yet.'

'You are waiting to remember a word? I thought you'd given that up!'

'Only briefly. It's a very important word.'

'It must be. It's forcing you to act as if you're insane.'

'But it's coming to me. Each time I take a step – note that I have now taken four clumsy steps towards the door – it's becoming clearer. But I won't go out the door without it.'

'Listen to him – he won't go out the door without it! Perhaps the word is coat.'

'If I don't take it, I will go out of here with nothing. All my time will have been wasted.'

'I think you're pulling my leg. Words *are* a waste of time in these circumstances.'

'In these circumstances, they are all I had. And this one's a beauty, the only one you'll ever need. I can now feel it playing on the tip of my tongue. I can taste the lack of dogma in it. Dogma always tastes of metal, of the stake, don't you find? And the flavour of philosophy, how would you describe that – sort of like a soda cracker or a ship's biscuit – that's absent too.'

'Are there any other notable absences?'

'Only one. It doesn't taste of blood.'

'What does it taste of then?'

I lick my lips while Mr Wakefield looks on in astonishment.

'Hmm. I'm not entirely sure. Perhaps it has none. Could be anything. Anything you want.'

'I thought you said it was a word that would explain life? Can life be anything you want?'

'No, clearly life can't be anything you want. Events overtake us. And we overtake ourselves. Our homunculi lead us by the nose. But forget about wanting, and think about appreciating. Not in the financial sense, of course. Think about appreciating life for what it is.'

'Well, what is it?'

'It's only this, here, now.'

'You fill me with despair, Mr Lonsdale.'

'That's why you need this word, Mr Wakefield. It's the

polysyllabic, Latinate version of the same thing. And now, like magic, it's coming to me. English has a word that comes from the Latin word for *this*, a word that defines *thisness*. And that word is?'

Mr Wakefield looks bewildered.

'Haecceity.'

Then I move to the door. Walking is difficult. I feel an odd sense of vertigo, as if I am always about to lose my balance. At the door I turn and make a stiff little bow. Anything more would send me sprawling. 'Thank you for all your help, Mr Wakefield. When I have re-established myself, I hope we can continue our acquaintance. Until I find my ship, that is.'

'Of course,' he murmurs. 'Here is my card.'

I take the proffered card. 'Come along then.'

I blunder through the door into the hallway, with Mr Wakefield following close behind. Every few yards, doors open for me and keepers look as obsequious and apologetic as if I were a king. I lumber through and on to the governors' office. I stand before the governors who are seated at a long table. They consult their written material and whisper amongst themselves while I fix my gaze on a large stain on the wall above their heads. I expect them to hurl questions at me but nothing happens. Instead, they continue to whisper furiously until one of them nods vigorously and then emphatically stamps the cover of a thick wad of paper on the table in front of him. Then he makes a gesture with his hand, and before I have time to speak I am pulled backwards out of the room by a keeper.

Outside, Mr Wakefield is waiting for me. He leads me through the foetid, labyrinthine corridors to the outer door. We step out into sunshine so bright I immediately have to cover my eyes with my arm. Little by little I let the light in until, looking down, I can tolerate the brightness. Mr Wakefield then accompanies me to the outer gate. The claviger unlocks it. I find my heart beating unexpectedly fast. I feel a little hot, a little excitable. I look up. The gate stands open.

'I'll go alone, if you don't mind,' I say to Mr Wakefield. He nods and embraces me. I step cautiously out onto the street. I look up and down it, marvelling at its spaciousness. Then I begin to walk slowly away. As I do I say the word: the word that wants nothing, the word that does not berate me, bully me, does not force me to be free, or happy, the word that demands nothing be anything other than what it is.

My leg muscles unlock. I speed up. Now I'm walking quickly away down the street, and I'm at once as light as air and as heavy as the scars on my wrists. I stop to look at them. They are past healing, of course. The skin will always remember the chains. I walk on, swinging my arms high. It is summer. The sky is blue. The trees are full. And gradually the word itself fades away as I walk on into the warmth, the perfume, this special light.